HUNTRESS

ALEXANDRA CHRISTIAN

Prologue

The young king could feel her close by, even before he could see her. Something in the air changed, and he had no choice but to follow her scent toward its inevitable conclusion. She was an alluring tonic from which he could not escape. If she called to him, he would always come. So it had been since first he saw Mab, sunning herself at the edge of the stream. He urged his stallion faster, eager to once again be in her arms. He longed to touch that silken hair that ran through his fingertips like water. Hold her lithe, ethereal body against his own. Already his manhood was swollen and uncomfortable against his saddle, just thinking of her touch like cool mist. The horse whinnied and reared, feeling the darkness creeping in from all sides. Crossing into Faerie was not without risk, but Christophe knew that the power of his love would protect him. She would protect him. And this time he had no choice. He had a favor to ask of the Fae Queen.

"The human king approaches, Belladonna," Mab whispered to the handmaiden at her side. "His hunger for me is pungent this night. Can you smell it? That sweet honeysuckle sage?"

"Indubitably, my queen. Positively rank with desire." The forest nymphs lay in the low hanging bough of a tree, their nude bodies bathed in the blue light of the full moon overhead.

"He comes to ask my favor. Shall I give it to him?" Mab said, pressing her lips to the consort's temple.

"I suppose it depends on what he is willing to offer in return." Belladonna turned her head, capturing the queen's mouth in a lingering kiss. Christophe slid down from his steed, unable to stop himself from staring as their mouths moved against one another.

"My queen," he said, dropping to his knees before them. "I come in peace, begging your indulgence." He bowed his head, offering his tribute. A single pearl was poised between his fingertips. "The rarest of our jewels is only appropriate for one so rare as Her Majesty." It was rare indeed with streaks of gold like fire cutting through the shining white orb. It was said that the pearl would give its owner the power of second sight, though Christophe knew that Mab was already all seeing.

Mab tore herself away from Belladonna to stare down at the king. "A seeing stone," she said, sounding almost impressed. "Surely your favor must be of some importance. One must face the Leviathan for such a treasure. Come closer, my king, so I might look upon your face."

Christophe stepped out of the shadows and closer to Mab. Immediately, he was taken in by her celestial beauty. Her silver hair fell over pale skin, hiding the generous swell of her breast. Her eyes, changeable and glistening, searched his face for signs of intent. He longed to kiss her rose-petal lips that looked almost black in the darkness. Before he could stop himself, he reached for her, winding his arm around her waist and pulling her elven frame against the rugged hulk of his own. Such a delicate creature, yet so powerful. His lust was overwhelming, and asking no permission, he kissed her lips with a moan of desperation. It had been so long. Too long since last they met. Their tongues played, rolling over and over in time with his heartbeat until he was breathless. His lips burned with the taste of Belladonna, the poison fairy consort, that still lingered on Mab's tongue. Finally, she pulled away with a devious smile, leading him into the trees with her.

She had been waiting for him. Their secret marriage bed had already been laid upon the ground, surrounded with will o' the wisp and starshine. Their lips met once more, her mouth open to receive him. Her breath was cold as ice as it entered his lungs, filling him up and making him feel alive. The other nymph was behind him, peeling away his belt and surcoat. Though it was Midwinter, he did not feel the cold. He existed in the membrane between his world and the Fae. A paradise of sorts, glistening with dark magic. Soon he stood before Mab, his pale skin prickling with the delicate touch of Belladonna, naked and eager. Mab's lips turned up slightly as she took in his form, so changed with his age and worry. "See his eyes, Belladonna. They burn like a blue flame in the darkness. It is this fire that makes him so inviting."

"Is he not Fae, my lady?" Belladonna whispered, brushing her lips across his shoulders. Her fingertips splayed across his back, and they moved slowly as if fascinated by the warmth of his flesh.

"He is but a man, pretty Bella. His life, like the dragon's flame, burns hot and fast but, alas, is only temporary. Already his body begins to decay." Mab touched his cheek, tracing the lines of age at his temple. "What was once so fresh slowly becomes a moldering shell. Their spirit becomes desperate to separate itself from the stench of their own rot." Mab's eyes downturned, and Christophe could see the sparkle of a tear clinging to the edge of her lashes. "Such sadness... such waste. Our time together comes to a close in the blink of an eye, Christophe. Though, there is beauty in this waning. His urgency..." As if to accent her point, her fingertips drifted lower, brushing the root of his manhood before grasping it tightly. He gasped, already pushing into her hand, his desire getting the better of him. She smiled. "Do you see?"

"His lust, I can taste it on his skin," Belladonna sighed, kissing the arc of his neck. He turned to look at the handmaiden, and she devoured his mouth. She was young and aggressive. Christophe could not deny his desire. The servant fairy's mouth was the color of blood and her hair of fire. Mab had brought this one to tempt him. He knew that the queen had long desired to steal him away to her realm, keeping him forever young but forever trapped in her court. While the thought of immortality was very seductive, the thought of submitting to another, a woman at that, left a foul taste in his mouth. Christophe lapped at the young fairy's mouth then turned, only to be taken by the queen herself.

She kissed his mouth with a terrible fury. Their tongues danced as she pulled him to the earthen bed. Belladonna whined, pushing Christophe aside and reaching for her queen. He lay on his back beneath them, watching as they kissed hungrily. Mab's fingertips glided along Belladonna's body, straying to her breasts. Her palm cupped the swells gently, her thumbs flickering over their centers. Christophe found that he could not look away from them, following their hands and tongues with his eyes as they fondled and caressed. His cock throbbed uncomfortably, and he idly stroked his fingertips along the length. Mab's nipples were like the tips of ripe strawberries, and his mouth watered to taste them. No longer content to observe, he sat up quickly, turning her body toward him with a rough movement. He took the stiffening bud into his mouth, worrying it to a petrified pebble between his teeth. He drew a low moan from the queen, and she climbed atop him, seating herself over his member. With a devious smile, she rolled her hips gently in a teasing dance. He growled and reached down, grasping his cock and nudging it against her opening. Mab laughed. Her smug demeanor filled him with a momentary rush of rage, and he pushed himself forcefully inside. "Such an arrogant and impatient king," she chuckled.

"Perhaps one day I shall tame you, my lady."

Once they were sated, they lay in the moonlight, watching as the stars twinkled over their heads just above the tips of the trees that hid them in a protective canopy. Christophe felt lazy, almost drugged, as he always had after coupling with Mab. He knew that this was no accident, and that one day, she intended to trap him in her world forever. She was a trickster, and her dual nature was part of what he loved so deeply about her. But he would not let her take him tonight. Tonight, he needed her help. Her magic. He could only hope that it would not backfire.

"My queen," he whispered, feathering light kisses over her temple and cheek. "Most beautiful and terrible queen..."

"Oh, Christophe. You needn't come to me with false flattery. We've known one another too long for such tricks." Mab smiled at him a bit too broadly to show the benevolence underneath. Her true self that was not the stuff of pretty stories and fantasy. "Ask what you will, my king," she sighed, rolling over on her belly and drinking from the cup of flower petals Belladonna offered to her lips. "I suppose it is a favor to ask for your human whore."

"You mustn't speak of the queen that way, Mab," he whispered.

"She isn't my queen."

Christophe chuckled. "You're jealous of her, then?"

"I envy no one!" Mab snapped, crushing the flower in her palm to dust. "If I wanted to be in your bed, I would be, and no mortal could stop it. I just fail to see how one such as you, one favored among Queen Mab's court, could be satisfied with such mediocre company." Christophe grinned, still fascinated by Mab's jealousy and aloof compliments. He couldn't hold her contempt against her. Christophe himself often wondered how he could have abandoned his Fae lover for the pious and pristine Princess Katrin. Her people across the sea were enlightened. They had forsaken all of the old ways, preferring a strange brew of science and salvation. In their world there was no such thing as Faerie, and anyone who claimed to wield such magic was condemned to die upon a burning pyre of truth. Mab yawned and stretched, feigning laziness, but Christophe was wise to her many faces. Though she might look bored, she was taking in each and every word spoken. "Well, go ahead then. Ask what you will of me."

"My kingdom is in danger, my lady. Katrin is barren, and I fear that she will not produce an heir. As I'm sure you've noticed, she is no longer the young woman she once was, and soon her age will catch up to her."

"There have been numerous still births, have there not?"

"Yes. For many years, I've thought that perhaps we've been cursed..."

"Don't be ridiculous, Christophe! Katrin's womb is dead. New life will fester and rot. Perhaps you should not be coming to ask me for some spell, but some potion to put her out of her misery." She smiled toward Belladonna, stroking the young fairy's cheek.

"You think I should murder my queen to marry another?"

"It would not be uncommon. Or perhaps use your power to have someone else kill her in the name of the law. Accuse her of witchcraft. Isn't that what her people call it?"

Christophe stood up, anger bubbling up in the pit of his belly. He began pulling his leggings on. "Perhaps it was a mistake coming to you, Mab. I always thought we were friends."

She laughed. "We are, Christophe," she said, rising to meet him and brushing a hand across his chest. "I am sorry I've offended you. I was merely jesting. But you can't expect me to be over the moon about your little hypocrite. Come back to the bed."

He gave her a sideways glare but allowed her to lead him back. He should be used to Mab and her aloofness by now, but he could not help his anger. Christophe feared for the fate of his people should a fight for control break out. Already, neighboring kingdoms, thirsty for power, were conspiring against him. He was getting too old to fight them off for much longer. He must have a good, strong son to succeed him and soon. He wasn't sure what time they had left. It might already be too late.

"It is often said that the Fae have the gift of fertility," he began.

"They have been known to give nature a push, yes," Mab replied. "Is that what you wish of me? To help your queen conceive a son?"

"Please, Mab. I am not asking as your lover or with arrogance. Only humility and desperation. As your friend. We've known each other since I was just a boy."

"Friends? At long last you've returned after forsaking me for your human wife, and I'm supposed to forgive you? Even help you? Surely you've overestimated my benevolence."

"You don't understand, my queen... my love," he said, taking her hand and pressing his lips to her delicate wrist.

"Spare me," she spat, jerking her hand away.

"It's true! I've done what I must to protect the people of Osghast. Including marriage to a woman I could never truly love."

"Ah! But you do care for her," Mab said. "Otherwise you wouldn't be here, throwing yourself foolishly at my feet."

"I cannot put my people at risk," Christophe said. "What you said before—about my youth waning. It's true. I can feel the weight of my age a little more with each passing year. My enemies align against me, and in the years to come..."

"You fear that the kingdom will fall if your line dies with you."

He nodded sadly. "Yes, my queen."

Mab seemed to think about this for a bit, weighing each option. The Fae were not known for their charity, and to bargain with them was treacherous. He knew that she was trying to figure how to manipulate this to her advantage. "All right, Christophe. I can do what you ask. I must admit, your desperation is endearing."

"I give you my word."

She nodded and clasped her hands together, bringing them to her lips. She whispered a strange incantation that Christophe could not understand. The language was languorous and slow, whispering like the hiss of a serpent. When she opened her hands, he could see that she held a small white onion. He looked pointedly at the Fae Queen. "What sort of trick is this, Mab?"

"Do you not trust me, my king?" she asked. She offered the onion to him, and after a pause, he took it. He wrinkled his nose in disgust at the root's overpowering stench. "Take the onion to your queen. Peel away the outer skin and then cut it in half—exactly in half—and share with her. Both of you must eat every morsel, though the taste may turn your stomachs. Once you've devoured every bit, lie down with your queen and plant your seed deep within her. She will conceive a son worthy of your kingdom."

"Thank you!" he exclaimed, taking her in his arms once more.

Mab pushed him away. She allowed Belladonna to help her to her feet and drape a robe of cobwebs around her shoulders. "Don't thank me too quickly, old friend. Even one misstep and the spell will turn."

Christophe rushed home to his queen. Remembering Mab's words, he took the onion from his cloak and stared at it with disgust. He almost threw it away and called himself a fool for believing in such ridiculous magic. How could eating an onion help him impregnate his queen after all these years of false hopes? Then he remembered Katrin's tears the last time she'd delivered a poor, dead child. She had cried for many days, refusing to eat or see anyone. She had even begged the physician for a tonic that would poison her quickly and relieve her suffering, relieve him of the burden of having her as his barren wife. Mab hadn't known how close to the bone her words had cut.

Christophe went to the queen, offering the magical gift. He assured her that the Fae had long been friends of Osghast, but she would not hear of it. "Your stupidity and weakness offends me, Christophe! I would no sooner accept the gift of this demon than rend the beating heart from my own chest!"

"Katrin, please! We've tried everything else. My physician says that you will never conceive. The kingdom will fall if there is no one to take up the mantle as king."

"So I'm to be poisoned by your Fae witch whore?"

All night and for several nights thereafter, he pleaded with Katrin to see reason, but her resolve was ironclad. He supposed as king he might force her to do as he commanded, but despite everything, Christophe did care for her. And he feared Mab's sorcery. For a fortnight, he kept the onion hidden in his study. Every night he laid it on his desk, staring at it as it began to wither and spoil along with his hopes of an heir. Though he said nothing, Christophe knew that his situation was becoming more precarious with each passing day as weaker kingdoms fell to invaders. Soon they would be at his doorstep, and with no king to rule the people of Osghast, nothing would keep them at bay.

Perhaps there was hope, he thought as he stared at the onion. What if he ate the whole thing himself? Would the magic not still take effect and allow him to impregnate Katrin? It certainly wasn't doing him any good now as it sat here expiring in the gloom of the cabinet. And if there was even the slightest chance that it might work, Christophe knew he had to try.

He held the onion between his fingertips, examining the withered skin. It had begun to peel and blacken around the edges, and the flesh underneath looked almost swollen. As he rubbed his thumb over it, the skin split, and a thick juice oozed from the wound. He gagged from the stench of it and almost threw the damned thing out of the window. "No, this is the only way," he whispered. Without another thought, he bit it like an apple, shoveling it into his mouth and chewing quickly. The taste was horrible, and he thought surely he was going to throw it all up, but somehow he managed to keep it down. He ate it skin and all, practically swallowing it whole. When he finished the onion, his belly felt twisted and full. But there was something else. A feeling of lust like he'd never felt before, even in the wild fervor of his youth. Suddenly, finding Katrin to quell this hunger was of utmost importance.

Just as Mab had promised, the queen conceived. Months passed, and as the child grew within her, so did her suspicions of how it had happened. She constantly questioned him and seemed to be searching for any sign of his deceit. He tried to tell her that when she'd refused to eat Mab's onion that he'd done away with it and that their luck had just taken a turn for the better, but it was obvious she didn't believe him.

"It is a strange and wonderful magic, my dear, that brings this blessing upon us," Christophe said as they lay together in the dark one night.

"Do you believe that, Christophe?"

"I believe that we have waited so long and been so patient that the gods have finally smiled upon us. He knows that we are pure of heart, and that our hearts are swollen with love to give." He kissed her temple then. "It is all you ever need know."

A strange and wonderful magic. Words that seemed so innocent would eventually wyrm their way into her heart, poisoning her love for him. Already he could feel it. She became obsessed with knowing just how their luck had turned so abruptly. She confided her fears that the little life growing inside of her was something more. Something sinister. She was convinced there were two of them, two boys, though the court physicians and midwifes agreed she could not truly be so certain. Each night she would walk the corridors of the castle and into the gardens, not awake but not sleeping. As if she were being drawn toward something. She began to doubt everyone and everything. Her doubt and fear were poisoning the queen's mind, twisting her into some cruel stranger. The midwife said it was to be expected, but general unease was rampant throughout the kingdom as all awaited the birth of the heir. Even the common folk now thought of them as the little princes, believing in their hearts that the queen was right that there would be twins, fearing that she was right to be afraid.

Chapter One

Thalia woke with a start. She stared around the dark room to find she was alone. It was a relief and a disappointment. Just like always. Always the dreams came. Sometimes they scared her; other times she wished to never wake from them. Thalia had dreamt of him since she was a child. At first, they were just childish dreams, spurred by her mother's stories of a dragon prince. They were two children playing chase through the paths in the wood. "Come and play!" he would call to her, darting in and out between the trees. She could never catch up to him, only catching glimpses of sooty black curls that tumbled over his back and the embroidery of his cloak. She could hear his laughter, teasing and warm, echoing in her head long after she woke. In those early dreams, she never saw his face; it was only the memory of his laughter that lingered.

As she grew, her playmate did, too. His body lengthened and grew strong. The landscape of his body drew her eyes, and always she would reach out to touch it. Soon their games grew dark: sinister and sexy. He would sneak up from behind, growling low in her ear until she squealed with the thrill of her own fear. His face was still hidden in the shadows, save for the generous bow of his lips as he whispered in the dark. "Come and play with me, little Thalia," he would purr against the shell of her ear. His breath was hot and moist, like liquid fire. She would wake from these dreams all gamey and moist between her legs. At first, she feared these feelings even more than the dark forests of her dreams. These stirrings deep within her belly that drew her hands over the curves of her blossoming breasts and hips. Something was happening inside her. As she grew closer to womanhood, the fear began to disappear like the morning mist that hung over the meadow near the old midwife, Esa's cottage where she had grown up to be replaced by wanting and need of her strange companion.

Thalia wrapped her meager blanket around her shoulders and stood up, making her way to where the fire had died to embers in the hearth. She rubbed her eyes, still trying to shake the sleep from them. Whenever she dreamed of the dark prince, she awoke feeling drained. Almost as if she'd spent the whole night chasing him. Though she could still feel his body burning against hers, the reality of his absence left her cold. Grabbing the poker that stood in the corner, she used it to stir the ashes, sending sparks popping toward her. She shuddered, catching just a whiff of the sulfur from the cinders.

She knelt by the fire, staring into the flames, warming herself. Even as a child, the fire had fascinated her. So many times Esa had pulled her away, insisting that she was too close. But she couldn't help it, even now. She had respect for it but did not fear it. Fire was an entity that was neither living nor dead. It fed, breathed, and consumed. Perhaps that was why she had been chosen, this kinship she felt with fire. It was in her blood.

Thalia ran her fingertips over the dark mark that stained her wrist. The mark of the slayer. Legend said that the ancient slayers from her homeland of Tarkin bore this mark. Three dark slashes that surrounded her wrist. The skin there was rough and raised slightly. She was born to slay dragons, and so she had done, killing dozens of the mindless wyrms that plagued the outer reaches of the continent, devouring the countryside in clouds of ash and despair. They fed on the death and decay they wreaked.

Some called her Huntress, others simply Slayer. Tarkin was a realm known for its slayers, and Thalia was the best of her kind. Small and graceful, she had almost a supernatural ability for hunting these beasts.

There were some that called her a snake charmer. The dragons seemed to come to her with an almost docile manner. One legend claimed that a dragon had literally bowed down to her and given its head willingly. A ridiculous legend, but there was no doubt—the small Tarkinian Huntress was good.

Some said that she could speak to them, but no dragon had ever uttered a word. Only a scream as she slashed at their hearts. They were animals like any other, and like any animal, they depended on a heart, lungs, and a brain to survive. If one of those were taken, the beast would fall. There was nothing magical about them, despite the tales of the Ancient Ones that could speak and cast spells. Those friends of the Fae. If they had ever existed, Thalia and her kind had long ago annihilated them.

"Thalia! It's moving!" The shout of the boy outside her tent dragged her from her reverie. She could hear the rustling of fabric as Markus barged inside. "You have to come now, Thalia!"

"What are you talking about?" she yawned, throwing down the poker casually.

"The dragon! It's moving! It'll be here in a few minutes. We have to be ready!"

She raced to the door, throwing back the blanket and peering up at the sky. Markus was right. Just over the horizon, the sky had gone all purple with the impending dawn, but there was something more. Orange flame lit up the western sky. A soft glow that left no doubt to what was coming. First would come the flame, then the heat, and the last thing anyone still foolish enough to be close would hear was the leathery rustling of its wings.

"Thalia!" Markus shouted, snapping her out of her reverie. She immediately sprang into action. She rushed around the room, pulling on body armor and trying to find her boots. She grabbed her crossbow just as the dragon screamed, bringing them to their knees as they held their ears. "I hate when they do that," Markus exclaimed, grabbing his own sword and shield as they rushed out of the tent.

She could smell it before they could see it. The stench of ash and sulfur like the pits of Hell overwhelmed them. "Gods, how do they sneak up on anyone? They smell like a pile of burning shit," Markus complained, pulling his tunic over his nose. Thalia wasn't listening. She was too busy watching the sky. She wanted to see it when it burst through the trees.

Dragons both frightened and fascinated her. Everything about them was built for the hunt. Their massive bodies were covered in impenetrable scales, but they could move with an almost feline precision. Their talons were razor sharp and grooved so that once the prey was caught, escape would be impossible. They could lock around even the smallest wriggling creature and hold on. The beating of their wings could create a gale that would level whole villages. Then there was the fire. Dragons were made of it. It flowed through their veins like blood, making their flesh steam. Just touching the hide would scald one's hand, peeling the blackened skin from the bones. A deep breath was all it took, and the flames would spew forth from the beast, burning everything it its path.

"We must draw it away from the villagers, Markus. Hurry and get everyone inside! Out of sight and quiet." He ran off into the streams of screaming villagers, running to and fro. The stench of brimstone and sweat was so overwhelming, it burned Thalia's eyes. The thick odor of terror was nothing new. It was everywhere she went and fueled her fury. She ran toward the western gate. Her arms ached with the weight of the heavy crossbow. Many were surprised that she could wield the rustic weapon with any accuracy, but it was the weapon of her father and his father before him. The only real problem was that to deliver a kill shot, one had to be standing in the furnace. A dragon was only vulnerable when he breathed fire. For a fragment of a second, he would expose his chest, and if one were clever and cunning, one might be able to deliver an arrow between the soft spaces in the scales and pierce his heart. Otherwise, there was nothing for it but a lucky blow that distracted the wyrm long enough to let you get away. Despite the rumors of her might, Thalia had never taken the head of a dragon. It would take one much stronger than herself to slice through the iron ropes of sinew and tissue, much less penetrate the scales.

Emerging from the gates, she ran into the clearing that surrounded the village just as the dragon crested the tree line. It hadn't seen her yet and soared in and out of the clouds, patrolling the area for any movement. Thalia was still. She wasn't quite ready to show herself. A dragon's vision was sharp when the target was moving, but if one could be still, really still, it couldn't focus. Thalia watched as it plummeted toward the earth then pulled up fast into the mist once more.

"Hurry, Markus!" He rushed behind her, his pack full of odds and ends rattling behind him. The dragon screamed once more, and though they could not see it, the pounding of its wings against the wind made the ground tremble. "It's close." Again, Thalia hoisted her crossbow from behind her back. Markus dropped his bag, going to her, a flint and steel clutched in his hands.

"Does it know we're here?" Markus shouted over the din. He fiddled with the flint, trying to ignite the bit of oiled cloth tied around the end of Thalia's arrow. After several attempts, it lit suddenly, making both of them jump with the whiff of sulfur.

"No, but it will momentarily. When I say run, run as fast as you can toward the trees!"

"Thalia! This is a large bull; let me take it down," he said, trying to pull the crossbow from her hands. "I can do it." She smiled, a thousand unsaid apologies flashing in her eyes. Ambitious fool. Markus was only a boy. His parents had been killed five years previous by a pair of particularly nasty green dragons, and he had begged to be taught to slay. Thalia had tried to resist, but the boy had followed her around until finally it was inevitable that she let him help. He was good. She had taught him well, but he had the recklessness of a child. Thalia feared that one day she would be scattering his ashes to the wind like so many of the slayers before him.

"Markus, you're not ready," she started.

"Please, Thalia! I'll never be ready if you don't trust me." Her resolve wavered for one second, just long enough for him to take the crossbow and run toward the center of the clearing. "I've got it!" he shouted. Going down on one knee, he aimed for the sky. The first shot, just a single bolt of fire into the clouds, would draw the beast toward them and away from the village. Thalia watched as the burning missile streaked into the sky, lighting up the clouds for a moment before disappearing. Then silence. For several moments, nothing moved. Even the birds seemed to flee the sky, and the air grew still. Markus looked back over his shoulder at Thalia. "Where did it go?" he shouted. "Do you think we scared it away?"

Before she could answer, the beast appeared from nowhere. It dove toward Markus, skidding over his head so close that the boy fell to the ground, rolling over and over. His shield and the crossbow flew in opposite directions, leaving him exposed and unarmed. "Markus! Get up!" Thalia screamed. She ran toward him, pulling her own sword from the baldric at her back. The boy struggled to his feet, grabbing at his shield and scrambling toward her. The ground beneath their feet shook as the dragon landed behind them, and Markus slipped once more, falling in the mucky grass. The dragon roared, deafening Thalia and drawing a scream from the boy. With an inhale that seemed to suck in all of the available air, the dragon breathed a magnificent plume of flame toward Markus. Only the boy's superior dexterity saved him, and he rolled to the side, dodging the brunt of the fire. "Markus! Stay still!" Thalia screamed. But it was of little use. The dragon had already locked on to the boy, snarling and stalking around him. The dragon reared back, inhaling once more to burn the boy to ash. With a savage bellow, Markus struck out, pulling his own sword from the scabbard at his side and plunging it as hard as he could into the dragon's chest.

"Yes!" Thalia shrieked, almost laughing as she watched. The beast stumbled backward, flapping its wings wildly, trying to get away from the boy and his stabbing sword. It took wing sloppily, thrashing against the wind, trying to dislodge the sword that was caught between the scales on his chest. With a frustrated roar, it succeeded, throwing the weapon at the ground hard enough to drive it into the dirt to the hilt. "Run, Markus!" Thalia shouted, taking up the crossbow. She dropped to her knees in the grass and began loading another bolt into the groove. Dragon bolts were heavier than ordinary hunter's bolts with a sharper tip fashioned of deep mountain stone. They required a tighter, heavier crossbow that was not easy for a woman to wield, but Thalia was no ordinary woman.

The dragon grazed them overhead as if taunting the slayers that their splinter of a sword would not defeat him. Thalia looked up, and Markus was nearly within her reach. She got up and raised the crossbow, using one arm to steady the weapon as she tracked it across the sky. Then suddenly it dropped, hiding in the mist. "Where...?" she stammered. "Markus!" she shouted, her voice an echo in the fog. And then, with a burst of flame and a rush of wind, the beast rose up, grabbing Markus in its talons and streaking into the sky with him. Higher and higher it flew, and Thalia could only watch it as it climbed. Markus was screaming in its grasp, the jagged claws tearing into his skin. His voice faded as they rose until it was gone, swallowed up by the clouds above.

Thalia dropped the crossbow, her heart sinking as she realized that the dragon was gone. And with it, Markus. "Stupid...," she snarled. "It should have been me!" she shouted into the nothingness. Then suddenly, a distant whistling sound caught her attention. She looked up just in time to see what was left of her friend and protégé plummeting toward the earth. His broken body bounced on the ground when it hit, his blood splattering over the grass and staining it red. Thalia ran toward him, closing the distance quickly. The dragon appeared out of nowhere, landing between Thalia and Markus's body. It roared as if in warning, but she stood her ground. "Come on, you bastard," she growled. "Come and get me." She raised her shield, dodging the first spit of fire. "You'll have to do better than that," she murmured, taking another step. It growled and hissed again as she raised the crossbow. Her heartbeats marked the seconds as the dragon reared back. "Now or never..." she whispered, closing her eyes. It opened its mouth, sucking in the precious air that would ignite its venom. Just before the spark, Thalia let her bolt fly, true and swift, straight into the gullet of the serpent. Its scream pierced the air, and she knew her ears would be ringing later. It hissed and spit, the point of the bolt burrowing farther into its flesh as it struggled. Thalia loaded another bolt into the crossbow and leapt onto the back of the injured dragon. She was so small, so light and dexterous, that the beast never felt her weight as she climbed atop its head and fired the final bolt into its brain. With a weak snarl and a shudder, it died under her feet.

Thalia reached down and pulled hard on the bolt sticking out of the dragon's scales. It gave way finally with a sickening sucking sound. She brushed her fingers over the tip, gathering a bit of the serpent's blood and bringing it to her lips. The bitter taste of copper and ash was satisfying, and she savored it. In the distance, she could hear the townspeople emerging from their homes and running to the clearing to see the slain beast. Thalia leapt down, pulling a single scale from the breastplate and depositing it in her bag that lay discarded at the edge of the forest.

"Hurrah! Bless you, child!" A round parish priest ambled toward her, holding a leather pouch. "You've saved us."

Thalia did not respond but slung Markus's pack over her shoulder. "Let the body rot in the field. It will turn rancid, and the stench will be nearly unbearable, but it will fend off any others." He followed as she sprinted over to where the boy lay dead. Kneeling down, she kissed Markus's forehead and pulled the chain from around his neck. The charm was a dragon's tooth that she had pulled for him at his first hunt. "I will burn the boy at dawn. Have your men bring him to the pyre at the square," she said, biting the inside of her cheek to fend off her tears.

"Of course, Mistress," the priest answered, beckoning to a group of men. "Here is your payment. I pray it is enough."

Thalia took the purse, her stomach rolling over as she heard the gold coins clattering inside. "For one boy's life? It is never enough."

Chapter Two

Katrin's screams echoed throughout the great halls within the castle. Surely the labor must be killing her. Those were the whispers among the servants as they slinked silently through the halls to the secret place where the queens of old had borne the monarchs of the kingdom for thousands of years. There she lay sprawled on a gilded feather bed. The linen coverlets, once bright white, ran red with the blood of the queen.

"My queen," the midwife Esa began. "They are close. You must only push when I say, or you will be in danger."

"This is evil magic," Katrin raved, pulling at the sheets as the servants tried mopping at her sweaty brow. "The Fae witch is trying to kill me."

"Hush, child. It is the pain poisoning your mind, but it will be over soon." The old midwife stirred a cup of blueberry leaf tea and held it to the queen's lips. "Drink this tea. It will help with your pain."

Katrin slapped the cup away, shattering it against the wall behind. "Get it away! Let the pain come! I hope it will kill me as punishment for what he's done!" Suddenly, Katrin lurched forward, a scream issuing forth from her throat, so shrill that the old woman's blood ran cold with fear. This birth was unnatural. The queen thrashed so violently that for a moment the midwife feared that she would launch herself out of the bed.

"You must calm down, my queen!" She threw back the sheets and gasped.

The first child was coming too fast. "It is time, Katrin! You must push hard, but stop when I say." The queen nodded, sitting up as the other servants supported her weight. "When the pain begins, bear down!" She did as she was told, her screams echoing off the walls.

"That's it, Katrin! Very good," she said, cleaning the blood from the queen's thighs and belly. "It won't be long now."

Katrin panted. "I can feel it... I can feel life slipping..." She fell back on the bed, too exhausted to continue.

"You're going to be fine, Highness," the serving girl at her side whispered. "You are strong. You will survive this." She pressed a cool cloth to her forehead. Katrin looked up into her face, and suddenly her eyes were clear. The small girl was extraordinarily beautiful with ruby lips. Her delicate features hid the mischief that clearly lurked under the surface. Katrin's mouth opened and worked as if she were trying to say something, but the words would not come. The serving girl smiled and tried to brush a lock of the queen's hair away from her forehead.

Katrin jerked away. "You... you're one of them," she whispered.

"I don't know..."

The old midwife shook her head. "It's just the pain..."

"No!" Katrin shouted with more strength than she'd had before. "Get this thing out of here! Take it into the forest and kill it! It is one of Mab's servants!" She made to strike at the serving girl who shied away just in time.

"Highness! She is just a chambermaid!"

"Then her presence here is not required!" Katrin hissed, reaching beside her and throwing the water basin toward the servant. "Get out! Now, before I have you beaten from this castle!" The girl took another look at the midwife, who nodded and waved her away. Another contraction overtook Katrin, and her body jerked forward.

"Push now, Highness!" the midwife shrieked. "Once more and the prince will be here!" The final contraction drew another scream from the queen, and she sat up, pushing down with all her strength. "Highness, he's almost here!"

"It's burning! I'm being torn apart! Lord help me!" Soon her screams were drowned out by the cries of the firstborn son.

The midwife held the boy child high, thwacking him on the back so that he might breathe the fresh air. He shivered and shook then let out a scream that could be heard throughout the castle grounds. "He is strong, my queen!" She cradled the infant to her breast and began to wipe away the blood before handing him to Katrin.

The queen held the little prince close, kissing his forehead gently as he cried. "You will be king, someday, little one. Such a good king. I shall call you Tristan. It means strength..." Her words trailed off in a scream, and she nearly dropped the baby. "Esa!" Katrin cried, clutching at the old woman. "What's happening?"

Esa took the newborn prince and lay him in his cradle. "Hush now, child. Everything's all right." She didn't quite believe it herself. Esa's eyes grew wide as she watched a gnarled, inhuman shape writhing just under Katrin's skin. Her screams were deafening. Something was wrong. Even the stillbirths had not produced such agony. Suddenly there was a terrible commotion just outside the door.

"Sire, it isn't proper! The queen..."

"Out of my way, boy, or I'll run you through myself!" The king crashed through the door to a nightmarish scene before Esa could stop him. The queen lay on her back in the middle of a blood-soaked bed. Black blood dripped from the sheets and down the walls surrounding them. The servants had fled, save for Esa and the tiny prince that wailed from his bassinette.

"Sire... sire, please... something is terribly wrong..." Esa hissed. "You must go and let me attend to her."

Christophe started to reply when Katrin began to scream once more. Her body rose from the bed, her back bent at an impossible angle as something writhed in her belly. The flesh rippled and rolled as what he could only assume was his child began to claw its way to the surface. "You!" Katrin cried. "You brought this upon us!" She was quickly silenced as a clawed hand tore through her flesh, ripping her from chest to navel. There was a terrifying hiss as the gash opened wide. Whatever it was began to crawl from inside, making its way through the trench it had forged with its talons. Esa was frozen with fear as she watched the thing. Thing was the only word she could think of to describe it. Dark crimson scales like fire and ash covered its body. A strange, misshapen head with sharp horns and a searching, open mouth full of razor-sharp fangs worked its way from inside Katrin, licking her blood from its lips. As it emerged, it flapped large, nearly transparent wings that sprang from its back. It wasn't very large, but its deathly screech filled her with fear.

"Is this my son, Mab?" the king cried to the darkness, his voice smothered by the sound of the dragon's roar. "Is this what you've wrought upon me?" The *dragon climbed atop Katrin's chest, searching out a nipple to feed from her warm corpse. "No!" Christophe bellowed, rushing toward it and pushing it away from her. The dragon turned, whipping its tail around and crouching down on its haunches. It hissed and spit a weak spark of flame at the king. He darted to one side, forcing the dragon to turn. It wasn't steady on its feet, and it was slow, unable to spring. Using the distraction, Christophe rushed forward, grabbing the dragon by its tail. It thrashed and spit, but the king would not be deterred. With a shout of anger and force, he heaved the dragon out of the tower window, watching as it fell to the forest below.*

As soon as the beast was gone, Christophe rushed to Katrin's side. "What have I done?" he cried over and over, pulling the ruined queen into his arms. Her body hung lifeless and bleeding in his embrace. "I'm so sorry, Katrin...so sorry..." Esa stood silently watching, her heart breaking for the king. Years later, she would think on this moment as the time she watched a great king die. He sat there at her bloody bedside for hours it seemed, just holding Katrin's body against his chest. The prince whined in his cradle, but even he must have sensed the sadness and kept quiet. Esa wanted to leave him be, but now that the screaming was done, the physician and servants would be rushing in to discover the queen's fate.

"Sire," Esa began, gently touching his arm. "Sire, you must leave her now. Let me clean up..."

"Don't touch her!" he screamed, jerking away from the old woman. "You stay away from her!"

"But, sire..."

"You! You were supposed to save her!" he snarled. "You let that... thing devour her!"

"I didn't know, my lord. I tried my best..."

"Get out."

"And what of your other son? He will need you, Highness..."

"Get out!" he screamed, getting to his feet, letting the queen fall back against the pillows. His figure loomed over the old midwife, and she cowered at his feet. "Leave this castle! This town! You are banished, old woman. If I ever see you again, I'll have you locked in the Screaming Tower while the vultures claw at your eyes and tear the withered old flesh from your miserable bones!"

When he lunged at her once more, Esa ran. He was crazed with heartbreak, and there wasn't a doubt in her mind that he wouldn't carry through with his threat. She blew past the guards, down the spiral staircase to the courtyard below. It was nearly dawn, and she could see the first rays of the sun peeking over the horizon as she ran down the rolling hills to the forest that surrounded the castle. As she drew further into the shadows, she began to change. The shriveled skin sloughed away, leaving her true form behind. Her tangled gray hair was once more sleek and fiery, her back straight and her skin as smooth and pale as unblemished snow. The poor human queen had driven the serving girl from her bedchamber, thinking she was Fae. But it was Esa who served Queen Mab.

Belladonna looked back over her shoulder, making certain that she hadn't been followed by the king's guard. She could hear the stream nearby and breathed a sigh of relief. None of them would venture this far, knowing that once they crossed the stream they were in Faerie and, therefore, governed by Queen Mab. She sat down on a rock by the water and breathed heavily. Carrying around that tired human form was almost more than she could stand. She'd have to remember to complain vigorously to Mab when she saw her again. After all, Bella's going to spy on Christophe and his ill-fated queen had been her idea anyway.

Bella stood and stretched her back, trying to let the horror of the day slip from her shoulders as easily as the old midwife's skin. That was when she heard the whimpering. She paused, listening for it again, but all was silent around her. She shrugged, walked over to the water's edge, and considered a swim. She'd almost decided to jump in when she heard it again. This time it was louder and sounded like more of a growl. "Who's there?" she called. She began to creep along a rough path, following the sound until she came to the stone base of the hill atop which set the castle. "Who followed me? Show yourself so I might turn you into a warty old toad!"

There among the craggy stones lay the tiny dragon hatchling that Tristan had tossed from the castle window. It was weakly crawling over the stones, trying to make its way toward the stream. The queen's blood still peppered its muzzle and chest, but all of its ferocity had evidently been spent, and it looked up at the fairy with an intelligent stare. "There now, beastie," Bella whispered.

The dragon squeaked a tiny roar, and Bella laughed in spite of herself. "No need to be afraid," she said, holding out her hand and beckoning it gently. It crept closer, its tiny limbs struggling over the rocks. Its wings kept getting in the way and finally defeated the beast, sending it tumbling over the last obstacle and rolling to a halt at the fairy's feet. Bella knelt, expecting that the pitiable crea-

ture would try to attack her in some way, but instead it whimpered again, cowering. "How did you survive that fall, little thing?" she whispered, drawing a cautious fingertip down the leathery scales between its large eyes. It heaved a tiny sigh and nudged against her hand again. "Oh, you like that, I see," she said, rubbing the bridge of its nose.

After several moments, it became apparent that this dragon was not a horrible, mindless creature that was bent on destruction and death. It was a baby that had been thrown away. Bella found her heart warming to the beast and took it in her arms. "All right, little hatchling. No need to be frightened." The dragon's skin was warm, almost too warm, even for her. A human would not be able to touch it without burning himself. How on earth had Christophe managed it, *she thought. Looking down into its face, Bella couldn't help but notice its eyes. They were not yellow or red as one might expect, but an icy blue with orange flecks like fire that glinted in the light. "Fire and ice," she whispered, tickling its belly.*

"I think I shall call you Malik," she whispered, kissing the end of its nose. The name laid heavy on her chest. The name of the ancient Dragon Lord who had called her goddess and worshipped at her feet.

The hatchling sneezed tiny sparks, setting the ends of Bella's hair on fire. "Oh!" she exclaimed, patting out the flames. "Naughty thing."

She cradled the tiny dragon in the crook of her arm as she sat by the stream. Its eyelids were heavy, and it gave a yawn that was so comical that Bella couldn't help but laugh. The beast looked up at her with an almost offended expression. "Whoever heard of a dragon yawning?"

"Who indeed?"

Bella gasped and looked up to see Mab lounging in a low-hanging branch. "My queen! You startled me." She hated it when Mab just appeared out of nowhere.

"You've been gone a long time. I was beginning to think you'd abandoned us." Mab giggled and slid down from the branch. As always, she moved with an ethereal grace over the mossy ground, making her way toward where Belladonna sat with the baby dragon. "Where did this little beastie come from?" she asked as she approached. The hatchling snarled at the fairy and curled into Bella's chest.

"Your human lover."

"Christophe?" she asked, batting at the dragon's tail that swished back and forth.

"This is the baby you promised him. Of course you knew that already." Bella turned away, not wanting to look at Mab's face. This was obviously what she'd hoped for all along.

"Oh, Bella, whatever do you mean?" she asked, barely able to contain her laughter.

"Don't play innocent, Mab. That's why you sent me to Thane isn't it? You knew something terrible was going to happen when you gave him that onion!"

"I promised that Katrin would conceive a son worthy of Osghast." She reached down and stroked the horned protrusion that highlighted the dragon's brow. "And so she did. A son as ugly as the heart of his father."

"Sons."

Mab's expression darkened. "Sons? What are you talking about?"

"There are two. A human son and… this."

At Belladonna's words, Mab began to laugh in earnest. Her voice shook the forest around them, and the birds in the trees took wing. "That fool!" she cried. "He ate both halves!"

"What…"

"The onion. He was to peel and eat exactly half, giving Katrin the other half. She must have refused him, and he ate the entire thing himself in his panic." She took the tiny hatchling from Bella and examined him closely, despite the hisses and spits. "You are a spirited one, aren't you, little beastie? A little prince encased in a prison of iron scales. I wonder if we peeled back your layers, would there be a child inside?"

"What should we do, my lady? Christophe cast him out."

Mab chuckled to herself and handed the hatchling back to Belladonna. "You must destroy it, of course."

Bella's eyes grew large, and she clutched the dragon to her chest protectively. "Destroy it? Why would we destroy it?"

"I didn't say we; I said you. But the answer is obvious, isn't it?"

"Not to me! It's… it's just a baby!"

"That will grow into an enormous, fire-breathing monster in a year's time. Dragons are not meant for the human world. That's why the Fae have allowed humankind to kill them off. And this creature is born of a woman. If it is allowed to grow to maturity, it will not be one of those mindless animals that fly

around the mountains and hide in caves. It will be a Dragon Lord, capable of speech, reason, and magic. And greed. He is Faerie Kind, Bella. Like you and I, he does not belong here. If you allow it to live, it will learn the truth and destroy this world. His very existence is an abomination that will upset the balance!"

"Then let me bring it to Faerie. There he will be safe. If what you say is true, then he has a Fae form..."

"Are you mad? Allowing such a creature in Faerie? The very idea!"

Bella stared down at the dragon. It was almost asleep in her arms. A sound somewhere between a snore and a purr thrummed as the hatchling relaxed. She knew right then and there that no matter what Mab said—she could not kill it. "I... I won't do it..." she murmured.

"What?"

"I've never defied you before, my queen, but I can't. If this dragon is to be destroyed, then you will have to do it."

Mab's eyes narrowed, and she loomed dangerously over her servant. Bella shivered with the chill of the queen's anger, but she would not give in. "You would risk my wrath? Over a... cursed creature?" Bella did not answer, but her resolve was evident in her eyes. After several moments, Mab chuckled lightly and began to pace. "What are you willing to risk for this creature, Bella?"

"What do you mean?"

"Well you must, of course, realize that if you defy me, you'll be locked out of Faerie until my wishes are fulfilled."

"You... you can't!" Bella stammered, laying the dragon aside to throw herself at Mab's feet. "Please, my lady!"

"I assure you I can. And will. You will be confined to The Veil, only able to take your true form by moonlight. But take heart, dearest Bella. A dragon will only live a few thousand years. A mere blink of an eye for a fairy."

⚬❧⚬

The heavy knell of the alarm dragged Esa from her memories and into the street in front of her meager cottage. She had lived as an old human woman for more than twenty years now. Long enough to see Mab's terrible prophecy come true.

She was nearly caught in a wave of panicking mob as they rushed down the street. They screamed and cried, pointing toward the cloudless sky. "Dragon!" They dropped their baskets from the market and scooped up their children.

Esa grabbed a small child who stood there weeping and dragged him along with her toward the armory. The attacks were coming more frequently now. The town fathers had sent word to the king for assistance, but no such help would come. Esa knew that the king would never come to save them. And she knew why. The people of Isling were on their own. Now all they could do was flee in terror and pray that this time the dragon would be satisfied.

"Hurry, child! Into the cellar!" Esa shoved the child toward the rough stone stairs. Her old, cumbersome body was slow, and once more, she cursed Mab under her breath as she was nearly trampled by the scores of people running toward the caverns beneath the castle. It was the only place that was safe anymore. As she heard the cries of the children, Esa's guilt consumed her. She was disgusted by her own weakness.

Dragons were supposed to be the stuff of legend. Their kind had been driven out of Osghast thousands of years ago. The only fire drakes that remained were in the outer regions of the continent— barren places surrounded by craggy mountain ranges and few settle-ments. But Queen Mab's treachery and her own weakness had brought down this plague upon them.

First there was the fire over the mountains. Then the lightning that streaked across the sky until it was torn and black. The beating of its wings was the rumbling of thunder that you could feel deep in your chest. Like the crushing of leaves beneath your feet only multiplied indefinitely. For weeks, it flew over the countryside, burning crops and fields and forest. Then it came to the villages, then the towns and into the square, making its way across Osghast. Anyone who couldn't run was doomed. The people in the market town of Isling fled into their homes and the tunnels beneath the street. Even into the crypts, praying that the bones of their ancestors might protect them from the fire and razor-sharp talons. The town fathers told everyone to hide and stay calm, that the dragon would tire of them and move on. Then they enlisted The Council to cast some spell of protection against it. When that didn't work, they began to offer a reward for the hide. Scores of men ventured into the deepest caverns of Gwynfir, the entrance to the mountain kingdoms. Almost none returned. Only a few of the strongest ones, laid low by the beast and babbling about hellfire and ash and gold, would return to tell their tales. And then worse than the beast itself were the dragonslayers. Wild men from the north who came to Isling in their shiny armor made of dragon scales. They broke the treasury with their deceit and still offered no relief. There was nothing left to be done. And so it had been for the last twenty years.

Esa ran, gathering as many of the children as she could and urging them into the tunnels. It was fast. The children of Isling had learned from birth about the stench of brimstone and the shriek of the dragon as it emerged above the highest peaks surrounding the tiny village. They knew what to do, falling in line behind the old woman and letting her shuffle them to the safe havens. They didn't even fear the darkness of the caverns anymore. They had learned to love it. To see it as their salvation. "Stay close together! Don't look back!" The towns-people climbed over one another, desperately trying to get as far into the tunnel as possible. Large chambers had been carved into the stone walls where more of them could pile inside to wait out the storm.

Finally, Esa heard the scraping of stone against stone as the gate was closed. Darkness fell as the room was sealed, blotting out every bit of light save for the tiny peepholes at the level of the street. From here the sentries could see what was happening. They would know when it was safe. If it would ever be safe again. And then there was silence. For endless minutes they sat, waiting and praying. Wondering if this hiding place would become their tomb.

"Nan Esa, are we going to die?" one of the children asked, her lip trembling as she clutched her kerchief close. "Is the dragon going to eat us?"

"No, child," Esa replied. "Why, you're hardly a mouthful for a beast such as that. You stay here close to me. You'll be safe." She offered the little girl a smile and gathered her to her rather considerable breast. Esa was the most trusted midwife in the village, but she did not feel so trustworthy this day. Though she promised that the child would be safe, she wasn't sure how much longer they would be able to run. She had seen up close the sort of damage that the dragon was capable of.

She had been there on the day of its birth. Esa knew that the dragon would not be satisfied until the town was razed to dust, never to be rebuilt. Either the king of Osghast would help them, or they would all perish in the fires of the beast.

The roar of the dragon broke the silence. The children screamed, putting their hands over their ears to block out the painful rumble that rattled their bones. Then a liquid hissing as it exhaled fire. Suddenly the air was too close, and Esa could feel the stones heating up. It knew they were there, could smell them. It could hear their cries. "Hush!" Esa commanded, and the room was silent save for the whimpers of the children. The ground shook as the dragon landed just above their heads. Esa could hear its breath, sniffing them out. Suddenly a single eye, golden with flecks of red flame, appeared in the peephole. The roaring was replaced by the screams of the children at seeing the eye of the dragon peering down at them through the bars.

"I see you." The dragon's voice was as clear in Esa's mind as the sound of the crying child at her feet. "I told you to stay away from the towns today." Loose cobblestone dust fell from the ceiling as the dragon trudged down the narrow lane above them, dragging the massive tail behind him. His wings scraped past the humble buildings and homes, tearing them down with a minor flinch of muscle. "Tell them to run, Mother... back to their holes. Run for their lives." The serpentine voice in her head filled it to bursting, and she closed her eyes. "Live to run again."

"We have to get out of here," Esa whispered. "Through the tunnels."

"But the dragon," the sentry hissed. "It's still there. We'll never get past him."

"It's not us it wants," Esa said. "If we stay, it will matter not to the dragon. If we move quickly, he will let us go." She locked eyes with the sentry, pleading with him to listen. She had always warned them before. The people of Isling had only survived because of the seemingly all-seeing eye of the midwife. Some said she was a witch; others said she was a servant of the Fae that could speak to the dragon. Whatever she was, her help was the only thing keeping them alive, and the sentry knew it.

"To the tunnels! Lock arms and stay together!" They obeyed the sentry, allowing Esa to lead them through the labyrinthine network of tunnels beneath the street that would eventually lead them to the forest just outside of town.

"Run," the dragon's voice hissed. "Run, little rats. Back to your hovels!" Esa screamed, covering her ears as he roared, their connection still raw. Looking back over her shoulder, the last she saw of the village was red flame leaping toward the blackened sky.

Chapter Three

"The entire village, razed to the ground, sire. Isling was not the first and will most certainly not be the last. We're running out of options." The minister from Isling looked near frantic as King Christophe paced. "Please, sire. We need help!"

"It seems to me that your problem is solved, Grafton. If the dragon has razed the city, there seems to be little reason for the dragon to return."

"Sire!" the red-faced little man exclaimed. "The dragon will return! If not to Isling, then to any of the market towns surrounding the kingdom! It seems bound and determined to destroy your kingdom around you. How long do you think it will be until he enters the gates of Thane itself?"

Christophe rounded on the minister, his anger ignited by the implication that he was impotent to do anything. "No creature of man nor beast is that bold, Grafton! And you might want to remember to whom you speak."

"I did not mean to suggest..."

"Did you not?" the king snarled, nose to nose with Grafton. Christophe had always hated this merchant who had managed to buy his way into lordship over the market district. He was not of Osghast.

A *singh*, a gypsy of the Borderlands. Filthy tinkers and circus performers, they were. When none of the surrounding rulers had been able to infiltrate Osghast, the singh had come in with a far more sinister plan: killing off the Osghastian market towns with their cheap goods. Isling had been overrun with them since Grafton came to power, and now Christophe could only hope that the dragon might cleanse his kingdom of their kind for good. "Perhaps the singh have aligned with this beast!"

"Sire! I have ever been loyal to Your Majesty, as have the people under my lordship. However, if you continue to turn a blind eye, you may have very little kingdom to rule!"

"Do you dare to tell me how to run my own kingdom, Grafton? I have executed men for lesser offenses!"

"Sire, I would not presume to tell you how to run your kingdom, but your options are dwindling. This dragon is a product of evil intent, and mark me, if you don't destroy it first, then it will surely destroy you."

The king stared at Grafton, searching for some threatening words that would quash the argument, but sadly he could find none. "I shall take your words under advisement, but for now, leave me be!"

"But, sire..."

"Get out!" Christophe shouted, taking a step toward the grimy little coward.

Grafton gasped, stumbling over the end of the rug at his feet. "Your people are losing faith, my lord. I pray you will not think on it too long." With that Grafton gave a short and obviously reluctant bow before taking his leave. Christophe watched as the man shambled from the room. How he hated him, but he was right. Something would have to be done.

The door of the study slammed behind Grafton, reverberating off the walls and then silence. Christophe sighed and held his head in his hands. Had his kingdom come down to this? Petty arguing with fools? He remembered his childhood clearly and never had his father bore such troubles. It was peaceful then as it had been for a thousand years before. As he stared out of the window looking down on the cliffs below, the rushing ocean crashing upon the rocks seemed to echo his mood.

The royal castle at Thane had stood on this spot for a thousand years, a fortress of stone and iron that served as a testament to the unfaltering strength of the Laurenz line. It was purposefully set on a high cliff at the farthest corner of the continent as a show of power to anyone coming to the great kingdom of Osghast by sea. At high tide the rough Cryspyn Sea sent sprays of foam over the rocky crags, making it appear that smoke rose all around it. The grounds of the castle were surrounded by a dark forest that many men were afraid to venture too far into for fear they might stumble through the gates of Faerie, never to return and forced into servitude at Queen Mab's court. The avenue ran parallel to the river through the forest and into the city of Thane. A healthy market thrived here with goods brought from all over the continent and across the sea. For centuries, the prosperity and peace his line had brought to Osghast had spread from the capital like a vast web over rolling hills and green fields where farmers grew everything from the finest grains to the sweetest of apples. At each corner of the realm were the other market towns of Isling and Gylbreth. The smaller, lesser kingdoms of Kronin, Tarkin, and Ezrebare bordered the country along the rushing River Kell. Osghast had been the crown jewel of the continent for as long as anyone could remember, the greatest power in the known world since his ancient ancestor had defeated the Dragon Lords. But now it seemed the Dragon Lords would have their revenge. The world was bearing down on Osghast from every side. The lesser kingdoms that had always cowered before them now boldly threatened war. Barbarian tribes from the north raided his borderlands. And the dragon... the cursed dragon. Soon the great kingdom he had inherited from his ancestors would be nothing more than a burned-out ruin. A monument to his failures. Perhaps he deserved as much.

"Father? Is everything all right?" Prince Tristan peeked into the parlor before entering, closing the doors behind him. "I heard shouting."

Christophe smiled wanly at his son. His beautiful son, so like his dead mother. Looking into his face, he could almost see Katrin's changeable green eyes staring back at him. If only he didn't see that glimmer of greed lurking there. Tristan's birth was cursed. Christophe had always felt it. From the moment Mab had given him that onion, he'd known that naught but evil could be born of such magic. In the darkest corners of his mind, Christophe knew that this was why he'd always kept Tristan at arm's length. Never loving him as a father should. "It's just Grafton."

"I know. I saw him leave. He looked upset."

"Well, that's hardly surprising. It seems that the Gypsy King always has some kind of bee in his bonnet. If only he would spend more of his energy collecting merchant taxes from his people." The king made no secret of his dislike for the Minister of Isling. Their heated debates were a common occurrence.

"Father..." Tristan began. "I couldn't help but overhear. You know that ordinarily I would never speak out against you. And I'm not now. That's why I wanted to speak to you in private, but... I'm afraid that Grafton has a point."

"Oh?" Christophe could already feel the muscles in his jaw aching as he gritted his teeth, lest he lose patience with Tristan. "And what point would that be?"

"The dragon of Gwynfir has begun to be more of a problem than we ever anticipated. We simply cannot ignore this threat. Isling is not the first of our holdings to be attacked. Over the last several months, the dragon has burned out several market towns and outposts. The people are crying out to us for help! Some have even resorted to bringing dragonslayers from the north..."

Christophe pinched the bridge of his nose, pacing back and forth before the fire. "What would you have me do, son? The days of legions are over. And that's what it would take to slay the dragon. You all seem to believe that I'm just sitting here in my study, ignorant of the world around me! Messengers from Gylbreth, Ezrebare—all over the continent have come with reports of this beast. They say he breathes walls of flame that can destroy an entire village in seconds. That his roar shakes the earth, rocking the very foundations of the strongholds. He'll carry off women and children and make swift meals of any man who might try to defy him. Not even with a hundred thousand knights could you defeat this foe!"

"So you're willing to just scuttle behind your castle walls and watch your people—*my* people—burn?"

"When last I checked, Christophe was king of Osghast. Not Tristan!" Christophe spat. "I will keep my own counsel on how to protect her!"

Tristan watched as his father stormed from the study. He did not have the strength in his gait that he once had. He was weary with age and worry. It pained his father to see his people suffering, but pretending there wasn't a problem was his only defense. He wanted to shout in frustration, but he knew it would not matter. If only his father would step aside, retire to the country, and make way for him. There was unrest all over the kingdom, not just in Isling, but in the other market towns and outposts. Traders were avoiding their country as news of the fire serpent traveled across land and sea. Ambitious kings had their eyes fixed on Osghast. Centrally located on the Cryspyn Sea, it was ideally placed for commerce and travel. The king of Osghast ruled most of the continent, not by force but by default control. It was an enormous power much desired by the lesser kings in the borderlands. The dragon would kill Osghast not by destroying its people, but by cutting out its heart. And his father was apparently going to stand by and let it happen.

"Begging your pardon, Highness." Tristan turned to see Grafton cowering in that loathsome way of the nobility. Politicians. With their serpentine smiles and loose tongues, they would lick a man's boots while they stabbed him in the back with their daggers. Tristan hated them.

"Rise, Minister."

"I did not know anyone was here. I'm afraid I left my cloak." Grafton gestured toward the chair where his gilded cloak lay draped. "Do you mind if I get it?"

"Please," Tristan replied, stepping aside. He watched as the little man pulled the fur-lined garment around his shoulders. The cold weather did not suit the gypsy king. His dark complexion was a remnant of his ancestry. The singh were a desert people, slowly driven across the continent by their treachery. "Is what you say true, Grafton?"

"About what, Highness?"

"The dragon of Gwynfir. Did it raze Isling to the ground?"

"The markets and most of the homes in town. We will rebuild, but it will be some time before the town is back on its feet. Assuming that the dragon will leave us be." He gave another short bow and started out again.

"Grafton!"

"Yes, Highness?" The old man turned. He was proud and unflinching. Grafton was very brave and very irreverent. This made him extremely dangerous. "What service might I perform for the Crown Prince?"

"You can stop kissing the back of my trousers, Grafton. I know if given half the chance you'd feed me and my father to the beast yourself."

Grafton feigned an innocent expression of shock. "But Your Highness, surely you don't think—"

"But you're also a businessman. Which we both know is why you're really here. Not some over-inflated sense of civic duty."

"I care about the people of Isling!" Grafton exclaimed. "You haven't seen the destruction that the dragon has wreaked upon my people! Homes destroyed! Women and children wandering the streets hungry! The dead and dying lying in the road! Those who fled to the shelters nearly died because they were buried underground for days! Don't tell me that I don't care about the people of Isling!"

"You care about using them to line your pockets! And who can blame you? You're their protection, Grafton! Why shouldn't you reap the benefit of their blind faith?" Tristan paced, his thumb poised gently between his teeth. "Of course, for once, we have a common goal, Minister. A common enemy, if you like."

"I assume you mean the dragon."

"Of course." He paused, peering at Grafton. Almost studying him.

He was trying to decide if he could trust him. Or rather, how *long* he might trust him. "Help me then, Grafton. Help me slay the beast. A show of strength is just what we need. Our kingdom will prosper again if we can cut out this poison."

"But how, Highness? Isling is defunct. Osghast is significantly weakened by your father's poor management of his power."

"Be careful, Grafton."

"But it is true, my prince. You know it is. We have very limited resources. Our knights are few. No allies to swoop in and protect us. We are on our own."

"Tell me how to kill it. You've seen it. Breathed its foul breath..."

"Yes, but..."

"This beast is nothing more than an animal. Like a stag or a horse. It can be killed!"

"With all due respect, Highness, a stag does not generally breathe fire."

"No, but..."

Grafton shook his head, obviously frustrated with Tristan's delusions of grandeur. His courage was bolstered by the fact that he had never seen the beast. He did not know what it could do. "You don't understand, Prince. The beast of Gwynfir does not just breathe fire. His breath is poison. His enormity is... unfathomable. He shakes the whole of the earth when he walks, and his wings set off a gale that will level anything its path."

Tristan growled in frustration, slamming his fist down on the side table with an audible crack. "I refuse to believe that some witless, evil... *wyrm* is mightier than Osghast!"

"Begging your pardon once more, Majesty. There is one who might help us, Prince. For the right price."

Tristan rounded on Grafton, his brow knitted with tense concentration. "Who? And I should warn you that I do not put much stock in wizards or soothsayers."

Grafton laughed. "You may well before our task is complete. You may even wish for it."

"Go on."

"Go into the Dark Wood just beyond the borders of Thane. Seek out the Dark Lady."

"The Dark Lady? Grafton, if this is some kind of gypsy trick…"

"There is no trick, Prince. Queen Mab, the Dark Lady of the Wood and the Queen of all Fae. She is familiar with dragons. There are some that say she gained her power when she was the lover of an ancient Dragon Lord. Go to her and beg her favor."

"And how do I do that?"

Grafton smiled wide until Tristan could see a glint of gold tooth. "Offer a gift."

Chapter Four

"Filthy tribe bitch!" Thalia was pushed down the stone steps of the tavern, coming to rest in a wet, mucky puddle below. She shook the muddy water out of her hair and looked up at the sweaty mountain of noisy flesh barreling out onto the porch. "Get out of here and never come back!" he snarled.

"You'd better hope I don't, old man!" she shouted. "The next time I see you, your painted whorebeasts will be picking your innards out of their hair!" Evidently the look in her eyes was enough to convince him of her seriousness, and he turned back to the safety of his establishment.

It wasn't easy, but Thalia stood, groaning as the stays in her ragged old bodice stabbed into her ribs. She smoothed her hair back as best she could, trying to keep some semblance of dignity as she limped down the muddy road toward the village gates. With every step, it became harder to breathe, and she pulled at the knotted strings at her middle. How most women wore these all the time was still a mystery. She wasn't used to being bound up so tightly or having to maneuver around in long skirts. Further proof that she hadn't belonged here in the first place.

Perhaps it was a blessing that her employ with Mr. Cabbagestalk had been so short-lived, though when she'd started, it had seemed a blessing. After Markus's death, she had known she was done slaying dragons. She wanted a normal life, a quiet life, a life where she didn't have to weigh life and death in her hands just to survive. She'd begun working at Cabbagestalk's tavern as a barmaid, a mindless task that she hadn't exactly enjoyed but that kept her tired and busy enough to keep her mind off Markus and dragons. But in less than a week, Cabbagestalk had become convinced by her blond curls and unblemished skin that her talents would be better utilized elsewhere. When he had tried to sell her virtue to a merchant passing through, she'd refused. Vehemently. He had been able to offer a warm place to sleep and scraps of food, that had hardly seemed adequate compensation for her honor. If that was the lot her station in life could provide her without her slaying skills, she was in dire straits indeed.

Thalia's stomach growled insistently. Since Markus's death, food had been in short supply. The gold given to her by the old friar had seemed tainted. She hadn't been able to bear the thought of carrying it with her, so she'd given it to the church in a neighboring town. It had seemed like a good idea at the time, even noble, but now as she walked away from the only other source of income she had found since, the taunting ache in her belly called her a fool. *Esa*, she thought. *Esa will take me in*. But Esa was in Isling.

When she reached the gates, the road continued into the surrounding forest. She hoped that there would be a stream or something close by where she might catch something to eat. The meager pack she had slung over her back didn't have much in the way of weapons, just a few crossbow bolts and a hunting knife. Fish would be much easier. She didn't feel much like chasing down a wild animal and killing it with her bare hands, but the hunger pangs were insistent.

Thalia walked for hours until the sun began to dip low in the sky. It was cold and dreary, and the road had become so narrow and overgrown that she could barely make it out any more. The forest was dense here, and despite the fact that a stream rushed parallel to the road, she hadn't had much luck with hunting or fishing either. Only a few berries and wild onions kept her from passing out. She dragged through the underbrush, and the weight of all that had happened grew heavier and heavier on her shoulders. Soon it began to rain, and the drops on her cheeks quickly turned to tears. Finally, she couldn't walk anymore and collapsed on the muddy ground.

"I'm so sorry, Markus," she sobbed. "I'm sorry I let you run out on your own. I'm sorry that I took you away from your home. I'm sorry I couldn't save you!" She lay down with her cheek against the cold ground, perhaps hoping that the rain would pool up around her and she'd drown, lying in a puddle of her own regret. "I've made such a mess of things."

❦

Lost and wandering. Through endless fields of blue and black, Thalia swam away from consciousness and into her dreams. She could feel it. The Veil between life and death where she floated weightless and waited for him. It was her only comfort. The scent of ash and rain permeated her senses, and when she opened her eyes, he stood in the distance, leaning against an ancient oak and staring out at the world. He wore a cloak of deep inky blue-black that almost matched his hair. For a moment, Thalia thought she might see him change into a raven that would fly away if she got too close.

"Is it you, Prince?" she asked, sitting up. Her head ached, and her cheeks were raw from angry tears. "Can you hear me? Or am I dreaming?"

"Is there any difference between dreaming and waking?" he asked. His voice was like an autumn breeze in the night.

"I'm not sure," she said, struggling to her feet. "I'm so tired. I'm not sure what's real anymore." As she approached him, he tensed and was almost startled when she touched his shoulder.

"You shouldn't have come," he said, shying away from her touch. "You cannot take refuge here, Thalia. This place isn't for you."

"But why?"

"Why doesn't matter. It's a pretty fiction, and neither of us are children anymore." He turned, and for a moment, she could see his profile silhouetted against the moon above. Thalia's heart gave a flutter, and she rushed to him again, throwing her arms around his waist and pressing her cheek against the warmth of his back. "Why must you make this so difficult?" he asked, neither turning to her nor pulling away.

"Because I don't care about the whys either. I don't care if I don't belong here. I don't want the world anymore; I only want you. Here, protecting me like you've always done."

He turned around, gripping her shoulders. His face was obscured by shadows once more, but his eyes glowed fiercely. "Never say that, Thalia!"

"But it's true. I would gladly drown myself in the Cryspyn Sea if it meant staying here with you!" She was sobbing again, burying her face in the folds of his cloak. Her heart was so heavy. She could feel it shattering in her chest, leaving a cold and empty place that was darker than the night around them. "He trusted me! And I let him die! It just doesn't seem right that I should go on living."

Finally, he pulled her into a warm embrace, holding her close as she wept. Her body shook with the force of her tears, but he held on tightly. "But you do. And you will. You didn't kill him, Thalia. Markus chose his own path just as you must choose yours." He pulled back, tipping her chin higher until their eyes met. "But your path is not here."

⚜

Thalia woke with a start. She was surprised and disgusted to find herself lying in the dirt once more. "Path indeed," she snarled, sitting up. As she got to her feet and gathered her pack, she noticed a crossroads up ahead and sighed with relief. Perhaps she wouldn't be lost in the forest forever.

Chapter Five

Esa made her way down the path toward the ruins of Ellythin. Legend had it that there had once been a great kingdom of men here, perched on the cliffs by the sea. Now all that remained was the hollow keep, done to ruin by the Dragon Lords of old. The ancient king had been driven out of this fortress into what was now Osghast, and thus the house of Laurenz had begun its reign over these lands. The hatred and vengeance that had begun with the destruction here had prompted endless wars between men and the Dragon Lords until finally it had seemed that the whole dragon race had been eradicated. The kingdom of men had grown arrogant and reckless in their illusion of victory. Esa and the rest of the Fae had watched as they raped the mountains for riches and wasted the fruit of the forest. They were like spoiled children. Greed and malice invited evil; now their destruction even threatened Faerie. Perhaps she should just let them burn. Let Malik take his revenge and obliterate any trace of them. It was only her own guilt and her need to put things right that made her journey so deep into the angry forest.

"Malik!" she called. "Do not hide yourself from me, Serpent." As she approached what had once been the entrance to the fortress, she could feel that it was noticeably warmer here. He was close. The gentle exhale of the breeze against her wrinkled cheek was his breath, and the shiny rocks she stepped over were the leathery spines that adorned his tail. A dragon was good at not being seen, but Esa was wise to him. After all, she'd known Malik since the day he was born. She could always find him. "Get up, you hoary beast!"

Esa could feel his approach long before she saw him. A tremor of fear that began in her chest reverberated down her body and morphed with the quaking beneath her feet. Though she was certain that Malik would never harm her, his presence was overwhelming, and she could not help but cower before him. She could hear the waves below crashing against the rock face, but all else was silent. The trees were still. Even the birds wouldn't sing so near his lair. As she reached the gates a roaring sound startled her, and she looked toward the falls at the base of the mountain that poured into a stream that would wind its way around the sharp rock and empty into the ocean below. Malik reared his head from beneath the spray and yawned a growling roar. His scales glistened with the drops of foam that clung to their iridescent surface. Those scales were stronger and harder than any armor could possibly be. They could withstand the iron bolts of a dragonslayer and the heat of his own breath. He rose from the stream, standing to his full height before her, stretching like a man just awakened from a long nap. Plumes of steam curled from his nostrils wrapping his enormous serpentine head like a crown. Esa tried not to concentrate on the rows of sharp fangs that flashed pearl in the sunlight as he yawned again. Instead, she preferred his eyes. They were still fire and ice—blue-green oceans with a kiss of amber fire. His eyes were a clue into the man that lurked beneath this outer shell of grotesque distortion. "It's about time!" Esa scolded.

"I've been following you for two leagues, old woman." He chuckled, a low rumble of thunder. "Your human form never ceases to amuse me, Faerie Mother. But you're safe in the grove now. Even Mab can't block out the moonshine. Shed this wrinkled pelt and show me your true face." At his command, Esa's body strained and contorted until she stood tall once more. The steel-colored tangles of hair lengthened and coiled until they shone copper in the moonlight. The lines of age vanished, and her eyes were sparkling with mischief once more.

"This is how you prefer me, then?"

"Of your two faces, this one is the truth," Malik snarled. "The arrogant poisonous fairy."

"Such harsh words for one who saved your life." Belladonna clucked her teeth and approached. She looked way up to see him. His size was immense, and she marveled each time they met. The tips of the horned protrusions over his brow would break through the high canopy of trees when he stood at his full height.

"Is that what you did?" he hissed. "If you can call living in exile as a hideous beast saving me, then thank you, my queen." He bowed his head to her level, feigning grace.

Bella's expression softened, "Destiny has a role for you yet, my serpent son."

"Why have you come?" Malik growled. "Did you come pleading for your human pets once more?"

"Would it sway you this time?" she asked, stroking her fingertips along the rough scaly bridge between his massive eyes. She knew it would calm him. It had since he was a mere hatchling, hissing and licking at her hand.

"Of course not," he snorted, snapping his head up and startling her. "What reason would I have to spare them?"

"Please Malik," she pleaded, falling to her knees as he whipped around, his spiny tail grazing over her head. "I know that you are angry. That you hate Christophe and your brother for what was done to you. But the realm of Osghast is under the protection of the Fae, and I beg you to abandon this vengeful mission. Do not make them pay for Mab's sins. Show some mercy!"

"As they were merciful to me?" he bellowed. He raised up on his hind legs and spread his black wings wide behind him. They glowed like molten lava flowing in cracks of pumice stone. "Ruled by a murdering fool who would cast out his own son and leave him to die on the rocky crags! These are the creatures whom you so passionately defend."

"He is their king." She hung her head, feeling the icy sliver of a single tear roll down her cheek. "You must understand, my son..."

"Do not call me your son," he snarled. "Would a child born of the Fae be so distorted?"

"But you are. I suckled you at my own breast, Dragon Lord. Cared for you and kept you hidden. Mab wanted me to destroy you. My defiance of her is what's kept me trapped here! That and..." Her voice trailed off as she turned away from him.

"The girl child." Malik huffed and narrowed his eyes. They had been playmates since infancy. Thalia. The abandoned orphan of Tarkin had been the daughter of the greatest of that city's dragonslayers. When her mother died, her father had rejected the child, and she had replaced Malik as Esa's nursling. He should have been jealous. He should have hated her.

But Thalia had loved him first. As the fairy Belladonna, Esa had taken the baby into The Veil, the world between worlds where the boy Malik could take a human form. The baby had smiled at him, laughed at the sound of his voice. Not even his touch had hurt her. Thalia had been born to be a slayer, but Malik could never hate her. She had been the first living creature to reach out for him, to welcome his touch. He had left his mark on her, but it was not a scar. It was a gift, a connection between them that had endured ever since. At first Esa had feared this connection, but the infant Thalia had become the only one who could quell the rage that burned so deeply within Malik. And even when the dragon had grown to his full shape and left Esa and her mothering behind, the human girl's connection to him within The Veil remained. With her Faerie sight, Bella knew that for years when the girl had assumed that she'd been dreaming, Thalia had been straying into The Veil between her world and Faerie for nighttime games with the dragon prince. In these visions, she saw his true form, the prince he ought to have been but for his father's treachery and Queen Mab's curse. But it was only a clever illusion that dissolved in ash if she gazed too long or tried to touch him. Now that they were older, their games had grown bolder, and Belladonna knew the urge to touch must have become almost too much for them to bear. Bella suspected this was the cause of the dragon's sudden ferocity, the reason he had become so intent on burning his father's kingdom to ash. "I asked that you not speak of her."

"Malik… I… you must listen to me…"

"Well, I'm here, aren't I? So spill it before you burst with all your huffing and stammering."

"Your anger has finally gotten the attention of the king…"

"Good!" Malik snarled.

"Not good," she said. "The king knows who you are. The only reason he hasn't tried to destroy you before now is because he knows. And I fear that your brother is not so patient. He will destroy you not because of the destruction you've wrought but because he fears you."

Malik heaved a bored sigh and flopped over on his side. "How do you know these things?"

"I have foreseen it. Tristan will try to use the girl to destroy you."

"Why are you telling me this, Bella?"

"Because Thalia needs your protection. I don't think that Mab is quite finished with her sinister games. She hates Christophe and will stop at nothing to destroy his world. She sees you as his ultimate weakness. She will play on that."

"So let her," Malik said. "My father deserves whatever havoc Queen Mab can dish out."

"Arrogant and witless wyrm!" Bella shrieked. "Christophe's fate is irrelevant to me! As is his brat's. You and Thalia are all I care about! Your fate and Thalia's have been entwined from the beginning…"

"And you figure if you can beat Mab at her own game that she'll yield and you can go home," he murmured.

"Tristan will try to use her abilities as a dragonslayer to destroy you," she said, ignoring his grumbling. "To him, you are nothing but a monster, but the magic he will use will mark her for sacrifice. And then I will lose you both. Tread carefully and be kind."

"How can you be so certain she will be chosen?"

"She has to be. The old magicks are clever, cleverer than Queen Mab. And everything depends on it."

Chapter Six

Tristan was uncertain. It was a most unpleasant feeling that he had rarely experienced. The ancient wood rose up around him looking like the gnarled fingers of a giant, reaching up from beneath the earth. The Dark Wood was cursed, they said. All manner of creatures made their homes in the shadows of the petrified yews. Some that were not pleasant or even of this world. Time and space seemed to drift further away as one trod the Faerie road. He had often heard it said that The Veil here between worlds was thin, and a careless traveler might find himself trapped in the realm of the Fae, forever beholden to the queen, or perhaps even her slave. Tristan had heard these warnings since childhood, but he wasn't about to let that deter him. He carried a bravery that was sometimes mistaken for foolishness, but it was obvious that he was going to have to prove his worth to his father. The dragon must be dealt with, and Queen Mab was the only one who might help.

The young prince thought over Grafton's words as he made his way down the serpentine path toward the center of the forest. "Go deep into the womb of the wood and find the sacred lake. Bathe in the cool water and be still. Mab will come to you, but stay sharp. Her pretty words will seduce you. She will fall on her knees and offer lascivious and forbidden favors. Do what you will, sire, but you must be away from the wood by the moonset. Once the moonlight disappears, you will be trapped in Faerie forever."

Over fallen branches and squishy ground and moss, he picked his way down the overgrown path in the failing light. And then he could see it. Illuminated in the moonlight was a break in the trees with a vast, silvery lake just beyond. Tristan was transfixed by the sparkles on the water that danced and winked like diamond dust on the surface. Forgetting all inhibition, he discarded his clothes in a flurry of linen and brocade, running toward the lake.

As soon as he jumped into the cool water, he could feel that something had changed. All around him, the air was electric. He felt exhilarated and lustful. He could smell the spiced scent of jasmine and honeysuckle. The Fae Queen was indeed close, and he remembered Grafton's words. His body was tense, the muscles in his belly and thighs hardening as his member dipped and bobbed below the water's surface. Tristan dunked his head under the cool water then shook it out. He needed to get hold of his senses, or she had already defeated him.

"What's this?" A whispering voice rode on the night breeze. It was so airy that for a moment Tristan thought it might be his imagination playing tricks. "A young prince wandering in the forest." He closed his eyes, almost feeling the breath on his throat.

"I can hear you," he called, feeling like an absolute fool. "Is that you, Mab? Whispering in the dark?"

Laughter that began quiet and playful suddenly thundered in his ears and the forest all around him, scattering the sparrows that nested in the canopy above. Tristan steadied himself, determined not to be afraid. He said no more and began to swim. Gracefully he stretched, pushing the heavy water aside, letting the chill soothe the primal lust that sat heavy within him. He dove down deep, seeing how long he might hold his breath. And then, he noticed, hovering just above the surface, was a ball of light. He pulled himself higher, emerging into the Faerie light.

It was blinding, the halo of light that radiated around the Faerie Queen. She was every bit as magnificent as the old tales told with her silvery hair and eyes of amethyst. How could any man, mortal or otherwise, resist her? "By the gods," he murmured.

This amused Mab, and she threw her head back, laughing at his uttered prayer. "Your gods have very little to do with it, prince. But thank you for your compliment."

She lowered herself to a branch that hung low over the water. When she reclined, the ends of her long hair made ripples along the water's surface. Try as he might, Tristan could not help being fascinated by the beauty of her naked form. He could feel himself flushing with heat, and for a moment, he wanted to dive beneath the current once more to hide the lust blossoms on his cheeks. "What brings you to the sacred lake tonight, Prince Tristan? Do you have business with the Fae?"

"How did you know my name?" he asked.

She smiled, her red lips splitting her countenance in two. "You look like your father."

"You know my father?"

"Of course. I have always known him. And when I say *know*, I mean that in every possible sense."

"So it is true what they say? That you take every human king as your lover?"

"Not every," Mab said. "Only those who amuse me. Something about the arrogance of a king of men entices me. I rather enjoy toying with them. Making them beg for my favor." Reaching down, she picked up a water lily that was floating along the surface of the lake. She brought the flower to her lips and sipped at the sweet nectar caught inside. "Is that what you wish, prince? To win my favor?"

Tristan scoffed. It was true that Mab was beautiful, but her conceit turned his stomach. A woman should be demure and submissive, bending to the will of her man in all matters. Mab was a plaything. Magical, yes, but no match for a king. He would let her think what she liked, but he would not hesitate to clip her wings if necessary. "Of course, my queen."

"And what do you bring in offering that pleases us?"

"A promise," Tristan said, swimming over to where Mab lay in the bough.

She laughed again, her voice filling up the wood. "And what is that? The promise of a man? You're very funny, prince."

"Perhaps, my queen. But one of your faithful servants assures me that this gift is of the highest value. The blood of young maidens is precious to the Fae, is it not?"

Mab smiled. "You would sacrifice children to my court? Truly this favor must be of the utmost importance if you are willing to sacrifice innocents."

"A few peasant children or the blood of my entire kingdom?" Tristan said, his jaw tight with frustration. "If you refuse, my queen, I fear that my father will let us all die in the fires of the terrible wyrm!" Tristan hid his face in his hands, angry with himself that he had let his desperation show. He believed in the truth of Grafton's words. The dragon would not be sated until all of the earth was burned to dust.

"The wyrm. You seek my help with the dragon that lives deep within Gwynfir." Mab sat up, a twist of her wrist making the bough bend and curl until she sat on a throne of gnarled wood. She pulled her knees up, resting her chin on them as she thought.

Tristan rose, standing on the floor of the lake and walking toward the throne with his head down in reverence. "I was told that you had a connection to the dragons. That you could speak with them. If this is true, my ladyyou could tell me how to defeat it." Leaning forward, he kissed the tops of her feet. He marveled at the sugary taste of her skin. Perhaps someday he might pull off her wings and put this fairy in a gilded cage by his bedside. "Once the dragon's head is mounted in my throne room, I shall bring you one hundred maidens of the kingdom to use as you will."

Mab seemed to think this over. Her lips turned up at the corners in a devious smile. The vanity of the Fae must be true. "A dragon's greatest weakness is his pride and avarice," she began. "But the dragon you fear is no ordinary dragon." Tristan nodded. "It is not an animal. It is a man cursed. Cursed by a Fae witch. His anger consumes him like the fire that he breathes."

"But why Osghast? What reason would this dragon have to raze my kingdom? Surely not some blood debt. Dragons have been driven from our realm for a thousand years!"

"Do you not know the reason, young prince?"

Suddenly Mab burst into peals of tinkling laughter that made the wind in the trees blow, chilling him to the depths of his soul. Tristan got the distinct impression that Mab was laughing at him. He felt hot blossoms of embarrassment glowing in his cheeks, and he knelt beneath the water. "And just what is it I am supposed to know?" he asked, using a façade of anger to mask his humiliation.

"Your father lost favor with someone of great power," she replied, her voice suddenly stilling the trees. "There is a curse upon his house that will plague the land until it is set right."

"The dragon has been set upon us? By whom?"

Mab chuckled once more and shook her head. "Foolish prince. A dragon is not an assassin that one can invoke like a dark spell. Especially not a dragon like Malik."

"It has a name?"

"Of course. A creature so great is not some mindless serpent. You would do well not to underestimate him, prince. That is, if you want to stay alive." Mab stroked the tip of her finger along the twisted coil of branch until the tree shifted shape once more, allowing her to slip into the water with Tristan. He watched with the lustful eyes of a lover as she swam toward him, her lean form cutting through the cool currents easily. She swirled around him like a curious fish, barely letting her body graze his. "He knows you well, my proud and foolish prince."

"The dragon? Knows me? How?"

She offered a knowing smile, ducking under the water and slithering between his legs before breaking the surface in front of him. She was so close that he could feel the warmth of her body and smell the honeysuckle perfume of her skin. "He is your brother, of course," Mab whispered, letting her lips caress the shell of his ear.

"My brother?" he gasped. He threw his head back and laughed heartily. "You... you are very funny, my queen."

"You doubt the truth?"

"Why wouldn't I?" he boomed. "I don't have a brother."

"Things are not always what they seem," Mab replied.

Tristan narrowed his eyes, unable to speak. Could she really be saying this? The Fae had always called themselves friends to the

Osghastian, but she must be in league with the dragon! His brother, indeed! "What proof do you have that this... *creature* is my brother?"

"My servant watched him tumble from your mother's womb!" Mab hissed. "His talons grabbed at her flesh and rended her from breast to sex. He tore her open and fought his way to the light in a spume of fire!"

"I don't understand." Tristan's voice stuck in his throat.

"Silly boy. Malik is your twin, a son of Christophe. And he has just as much right to the throne as you."

Tristan felt the blood drain from his face. He could not have felt more frightened confronting the dragon itself. "This... this cannot be! I don't believe you!" Suddenly he felt faint and began fighting his way back toward the shore, leaving Mab behind. He wished he'd never come. Damn that gypsy fool!

"Running away doesn't make it any less true, son of Christophe." Tristan stopped, his fists clenched at his side. If fairies weren't immortal, he'd liked to have wrung her skinny little throat. "Your father only wanted to produce an heir. But there was a terrible price, Tristan. The Fae witch..."

"Fae witch? One of you?"

"Of course. Who else would have the power to create such a thing? Christophe was careless, greedy for the gift of his Fae lover. He did not heed the witch, and it turned your brother into a terrible beast. He is a dragon, Tristan, but he lives. He is your blood and as such..." Mab paused, rising from the water. Tristan wasn't sure, but as the moonlight filtered through the gloom, he thought he saw a secret, most devious smile. "As such, he has claim to the throne."

Tristan's heart skipped a beat as he processed her words. She was right. A twin brother had just as much claim to the throne as he. Perhaps that was the beast's motivation all along. To blot out his father's line and take back Osghast as a Dragon Lord. He squeezed his eyes shut until white starbursts appeared behind the lids. He wanted to block out the evil sprite. "I do not share blood with a creature," he growled, grabbing Mab's wrist tightly. He wanted to twist it hard. He wanted to hurt her for spouting such lies! "My father was right!" he hissed. "Deceitful and cruel sprites!" He threw the fairy to the ground, kicking her aside. He reached for her once more, but when he touched her skin, it burned like fire, and she winked out in a wisp of firelight, only to reappear in the trees above him.

"Do you think that snuffing me out will save you? Or your precious Osghast?" she hissed. "Malik will strike at your heart over and over until there is nothing left but desolation and filth! He has no mercy for your kind. He wants vengeance for the life that was taken from him! All his thoughts are set upon it. An unquenchable bloodthirst that blackens his heart. A thirst that makes him dangerous. Hard to kill."

She reached down, touching the surface of the water with the tips of her fingers. An image materialized just under the surface, the image of a woman, he thought, but he couldn't make out the details from where he stood. "There is a child of Tarkin. A most accomplished drag-onslayer..."

"We've tried dragonslayers!" Tristan said.

"But not this one. The Huntress they call her. They say that she can speak to the dragons in their own tongue. Only she will be cunning enough to slay Malik." Tristan stepped forward, wanting to see the face of this magical creature that might save his kingdom, but as he approached, her image faded into speckles of moonshine on the water. "Find her."

"How?" Once more, he could feel his anger welling up, and he took a step backward. "Help me find her!"

"Destiny is not some battering ram with which you might tear down the gates. The pieces will fall into place in good time. She will come to you. I have foreseen it."

"No!" he shouted, jerking his tunic from the ground at his feet. "I will not listen to all this rubbish about magic and destiny! A man makes his own destiny!"

"The only way to save your kingdom is to destroy the dragon prince!" she shouted. "And the Huntress of Tarkin is the only one who can do it."

Tristan's stomach rolled over. A woman! How dare this fairy suggest that a woman would be more capable of slaying a dragon than himself. Tristan wanted to assure his ascension to the throne. If he could kill the dragon, then the people would immediately call for his father's retirement. "I will lure this beast to Osghast, straight into the heart of the kingdom. A maiden sacrifice like the days of old. A promised bride. But this time he will not find pleasures of the flesh or a love that will melt his black heart—there is only death for the Wyrm of Gwynfir! I will tear the beast's heart out with my bare hands and devour it while it still beats!"

"You're a child," Mab began, materializing at his side. "Strength cannot defeat him. Or your delusions of grandeur. There is magic afoot here that even you, with all your blustering and brawn can't touch. The dragon is under the protection of a powerful fairy."

"What do you know about it?" he snapped. He rounded on the Fae Queen, a frightening fury burning in his eyes so strong that she took a step back. "This fairy bitch and her beast of hell murdered my mother, the queen. Now they seek to destroy my kingdom! There is no mercy or forgiveness for the likes of them."

Chapter Seven

His form was pure shadow made of black smoke that curled and danced over her as he slowly materialized. He hovered there, letting her watch and wait, every second seeming to last longer than the one before.

"Back again so soon?"

"Always." Thalia shuddered, peering into his eyes. They were like ice and fire: the cool blue of the mountain stream with flecks of flame that burned deep within their sockets.

"Careful, little one. Retreating so far into one's dreams is dangerous. You may not find your way out again." The last time she had found him, she had been desperate, ready to leave her world behind forever, and he had tried to push her away. But now that she was more at peace, he seemed calmer as well, teasing but welcoming again.

"An eternity of sleep is not long enough to tremble in your presence, my lord."

"You find me a fearsome bedfellow, then?"

"Shouldn't I?"

He laughed, a deep rumble that moved the ground beneath them. "You have nothing to fear from me, Thalia. You have great power, perhaps far greater than my own." Suddenly he was a swirling column of smoke and shadow once more. She gasped, feeling as if ice crystals scraped at her skin as she sat up. Then he stood before her in the flesh again, draped in a black robe. The cloak cast a shadow over most of his face so that only the sharp angle of his nose and cheek were visible. His torso was bare, and the moonlight glimmered off his pale skin so brightly Thalia had to squint. Loose waves of jet black hair fell over his brow and down to his shoulders, hiding half of his face.

"I would hardly liken myself to one so great. But my lord, why do you hide your face from me? We've met so many times, but I've never really seen your face."

"I fear that my countenance would frighten you."

"Never. You've always shown me kindness, prince. Why should I fear you now?"

In a graceful movement, he dropped to one knee, taking her hand and pulling her close. The heat from his body was intense, and steam rose from his skin in thin plumes of ether. "Never fear me, Thalia. I am forever your servant." His kiss, finally fulfilled, was searing. He tasted of ash and flame. It was a flavor that she knew she would savor well after the dream was done. It permeated her senses and filled her with more of that lust with which she had become so familiar. Before she knew it, she was opening her mouth, inviting him inside. He eagerly accepted with gentle swipes of his tongue against her lips and teeth. He took her breath away, and though she gasped, she would not break. Thalia wanted more of him. She breathed him in, taking his heat into herself. His arms enveloped her, the folds of his robe cloaking her in darkness and hiding them from the world.

"Dark prince," she said. It wasn't a question. She reached out for him and felt his hand close over hers then bring it to his lips. He kissed gently at the delicate bones. "Tell me your name," she whispered, watching the shape of his mouth as his lips lingered on the slope of her wrist.

"Names are unimportant," he replied, drawing her into his embrace. "You may call me your own. Prince, lover, or savior. It does not matter." She felt his arms slide around her waist, pulling her further into his darkness. His smell filled her, making it hard to breathe. Musk and ash, burning sandalwood—all those scents that when she caught a whiff of them in her waking world made her blood race and her sex tingle. "In your language, my name would mean nothing. It would be repugnant to your ears."

Thalia said, nuzzling into his neck and kissing at the bit of exposed flesh, "All that you are, whatever you are—I am forever yours."

He pulled away, threading his fingers into her hair and brushing it back *from her brow. She wanted to touch him, but her arms were so heavy. She was like a carnival puppet in his arms, only moving as he wished. "I would almost believe you, little thing." His hold was strong as he lay her down on the grass. "But you and I are only meant for dreaming."*

"I know that you're real."

"I am an illusion, Thalia. I have been selfish to let you dwell so long in this darkness. This dream world that can never be." He knelt beside her. "It is time for you to find your own path."

Thalia panicked. "What are you saying?" she gasped, sitting up. "You can't leave me!" She tried to reach out and take his arm, but he stopped her.

"Every time we meet, it gets harder to let you go. I fear that you will follow me too far and not be able to find your way back."

"I don't care," Thalia whispered. "I want to be wherever you are."

"You don't mean that!" he hissed, savagely pulling her body against his. He crushed his mouth against hers, holding her tightly so that she could not touch him. He held her so tightly she could feel the blood rushing to the site of the pressure. The hand that held her arm was thrust into the light, and she could see that it was strange, more of a talon that grasped her, its long nails and scaly flesh burning her flesh beneath its grip. She opened her mouth, offering herself freely to his invasion. Slowly his tongue slid along hers, tasting her, tasting him.

Gathering the curls at the base of her skull in his fist, he pulled her head backward, drawing a moan from her lips. He blazed a trail of kisses down her jugular vein, then nibbled gently as if her skin were the most delicious of delicacies. His fingertips trilled lightly across her collarbone. The path worn by his fingers was still warm as he continued lower. He'd never been so bold before, and though it was frightening, Thalia craved his touch. He paused, looking up at her, his eyes beseeching. "No..." he snarled. "I cannot let this be!"

"Please!" she said, taking hold of his cloak and watching it fade to smoke. "I would rather die here in your arms than return to that desolate place alone." Looking down, she noticed the clasp of her own chemise between her breasts. She pulled at it gently until the wisp of cloth fell away, leaving her naked and trembling beneath his gaze. "You cannot tell me that you do not desire this."

The prince did not answer but pulled back his own cloak. By some strange magic, the moonlight broke through the trees, casting light on her lover. He turned slowly, letting the light illuminate his face. His fiery gaze was heavy as he was finally revealed. One side of his face seemed to be made of ash and fire.

The skin was red and shimmering, reflecting the moonlight like some glistening, burning liquid. At the gradient of his cheekbone and the corner of his right eye, it appeared to crack and fall apart, revealing flame beneath the skin. As the mantle of black smoke fell away, Thalia could see that the distortion continued down his body. The scars carved harsh lines in his flesh. The longer she gazed on him, the more grotesque his disfigurement grew. "Is this what you wanted to see, little one?"

"I am not afraid," she replied, but the trembling of her hand as she reached for him betrayed her.

"I am merely a magician, Thalia. But my illusions are shallow."

"What illusion?" she whispered, her mouth searching for his again. "I don't understand."

"The real me is a monster, and I cannot let you pledge yourself to such a creature." He took her hand, pressing it to his heart. More of the blackened and burnished skin appeared beneath her hand, growing outward. "You will always have my heart, little thing. But our time is done."

"No... please!" she cried, but he was already fading. The dream world began to crumble around her. "Don't leave me!"

"Goodbye, Thalia." She opened her eyes to watch him fall into ash at her feet.

⚜

Thalia pushed back the hood of her cloak and looked up in the gray skies to cool the burning in her eyes. She would not allow herself to accept that he was really and truly gone. She wished she could understand what she'd done. Was it Markus? Had her failure to save him caused the dark prince to abandon her? She could hardly blame him. In the month since Markus's death, her emptiness had completely consumed her. Her dreams that had once been a refuge were now a mere void of darkness where she could only search for something she would never find again.

It had started to rain intermittently, and if the sky was any indication, it would soon be pouring. *Perfect*, she thought. There is no situation that apparently can't be made worse by rain. Her stomach rumbled, reminding her she hadn't eaten in days.

Esa had raised Thalia from infancy. Her mother had died in childbirth while the tribe was journeying across the continent, desperately seeking shelter from the harsh mountain winter. The old midwife had tried to save her mother, but by the time she reached their encampment, Thalia's mother was dead. Her father, the most famed dragonslayer of Tarkin, had hated Thalia from the moment she first drew breath. He had called the child murderess and refused to even hold her. Esa had told her once that if she'd been left in his care, she would have died of starvation and neglect. The old woman had saved her life, but Thalia had inherited her father's love of the hunt and realized her calling early on. Upon hearing of her father's death, she had left Esa's cozy cottage in Isling and journeyed to her kin in Tarkin and made them teach her to slay. Thalia rubbed the raised mark on her wrist. It itched as if to taunt her for running away, but she didn't care. She would never hunt again.

"Oy, love! Don't have enough sense to come out of the rain?" Thalia's head snapped up to see a young boy on the road gathering kindling.

"Pardon?"

"You're soaked clean through! Don't you know you'll catch your death?"

Thalia smiled and nodded. "I don't have much choice, do I?"

"I'm guessin' not, lovey," he said, bending down to pull at a gnarled root on the path.

"Why are you out here?"

"Gatherin' some scrap wood for me fire," he said. "So's I guess I don' have much choice either. Gotta stay warm."

"Indeed," she replied. "Is this the road into Isling?"

"What's left of it."

"What do you mean 'what's left of it'?"

The boy didn't answer but pointed up the road. The trees made a dark canopy as the road wound its way toward town, but just past the next bend, Thalia could see that the trees were broken and scorched, lying across the road like the blackened bones of some enormous beast. She could smell the stench of fire on the wind. It should be a comforting scent, but it had turned sour in the rain. "What happened?"

"Dragon," he replied simply, tying his sticks to sling over his back. "Last month."

"A dragon? There hasn't been a dragon this close to the capital in ages."

The boy shrugged. "Isling must be cursed, love. The Wyrm of Gwynfir they call it. Come down from the mountain some years back and started burnin' fields and farms. Then it started comin' toward town. Never this bad though." Thalia's heart clenched in her chest so hard that she doubled over coughing. "You okay, love?" the boy asked, dropping his bundle and coming over to pat her on the back.

Thalia grabbed the boy, kneeling. "There's an old woman. A midwife named—"

"You mean old Esa?"

"Yes! You know her?"

"Of course," he chuckled. "Everyone knows her."

"Is she all right?"

"'Course she is," he said. "It'd take more than dragon fire to kill that old bird." He pointed toward town. "Her cottage is right where it always was. Probably the only one that didn't get a stitch of ash…"

Before he could finish, Thalia was running down the road. She needed to get to Esa. She needed the reassurance of the old woman's embrace. Suddenly the world had become very cold, and while she wouldn't admit it to herself, Thalia, who had always been a solitary soul, needed the warmth of another.

It had been at least ten years, but Thalia's feet seemed to know their way despite how the village had changed. The streets were mucky, and she nearly fell three times trying to run, almost as if something were holding her back, but she finally made it. She pushed back her cloak and smoothed her hair. What if the old woman didn't recognize her? What if she was angry that Thalia had gone and hadn't even bothered to write and tell her that she was well? Suddenly she was entertaining the notion that she might not be welcome here anymore. Of course, there was only one way to find out.

A pounding at the door startled Esa. "Who could that be this late?" she wondered, pulling her shawl tightly around her shoulders. It was unusually cool for the late summer. Dark magic was afoot. She padded across the rushes and peeked out of the keyhole. "Thalia," she whispered, disbelieving her old eyes. So her visions were true! Indeed, the old magicks were at play. She opened the door to see the small girl standing in the rain. "By the gods, child! What's happened to you?" The girl looked like a drenched rodent as she stood there.

"Please, Esa... I had nowhere else to go," Thalia said, bowing her head to the old woman.

Esa stepped aside and rushed her inside. "Of course, child. Come in before you catch your death out there!" Thalia came inside and dropped her shoulder bag and crossbow at the hearth. Slowly she peeled away her soaking jerkin and coat and knelt by the fire. Neither woman said anything for several minutes. It had been years since last she saw the girl that she loved as her own child. As Esa observed the girl, she could tell that the years had not been kind. Her face was dotted with mud and soot. Bruises highlighted her delicate features, and blood stained her hands. Her shoulders were slumped with exhaustion and an all-consuming sadness. Thalia was broken.

"It's been long since your last visit, child."

"I am sorry, Esa. Things have been difficult." The girl stared into the fire, watching the flames lick and leap at the hearthstones. Her heart was broken; the old woman could sense it. She was lost in the world and hoped that she might find comfort at the foot of the only mother she'd ever known. "I've tried to come to Isling so many times. Much has changed."

Esa smiled. "No need to make excuses, child. You're here now." She pushed a cup of tea into Thalia's hand. "Drink this while I fix you something to eat. It will make you feel better."

Thalia nodded and sipped at the warm liquid. She said nothing for a time, just stared into the fire and clutched the teacup as Esa chattered away about the dragon attack on Isling. It wasn't like her. The child used to be so full of life. It troubled the old woman as she threw a rasher of bacon on the stove. "No, it won't," the girl suddenly said.

Esa looked up and turned to the girl. "Pardon?"

"It won't make me feel better. It is likely I will never feel better again." With that, she burst into tears, the teacup slipping from her fingers to crash on the hearth.

"Oh... Thalia," Esa started, pulling the pan off the fire and going to the sobbing girl. She gathered her in her arms, pressing her close against her generous bosom. "Shush, child... tell old Esa what's troubling you so."

"I lost him, Esa," Thalia sniffled. "He was depending on me to take care of him. And I failed! The boy is dead because of me!" The words were painful, and they spewed forth like a blistering venom as she related the tragedy of Markus's death. "I couldn't stop him. He just... he ran away from me. And I thought he was ready..."

"Shh... there, child. Sometimes things happen that we cannot control."

"I'm so... angry! I want to kill them—all of them—but I can't bring myself to fight. For the first time, Esa... I am afraid." She threw herself against the old woman again, her bitter tears soaking into her shawl.

"Hush now," Esa scolded, brushing the heavy, golden curls from Thalia's brow. "What you need is a rest. In a few weeks' time, your heart will heal."

Thalia shook her head, wiping her eyes with the back of her hand. "No... I'll never hunt again."

"Of course you will, darling child," Esa replied, rising from the stool and getting the girl another cup of tea. It was a special brew that would quiet her mind and let her sleep. "Drink this, and I promise, you'll feel much better in the morning. There is nothing that cannot be made better with a good cup of tea."

Chapter Eight

It had been a month since Tristan's meeting with Queen Mab, and much had happened. The decimation of Isling and his last meeting with Grafton had left the king ailing and weak. Raving about a curse upon his house, he had taken to his bed at his son's insistence and not emerged in a fortnight. Everyone expected that Tristan would be named as successor any day. Christophe was not the mighty ruler he once had been, and allowing him to continue could spell disaster for Osghast. Already, hordes of wild men had been attacking the borders and burning out farm villages. Tristan had sent out several legions of knights to various outposts to combat these barbarians, but they were becoming bolder, and soon open war would be upon them. The dragon had been quiet, at least. But everyone seemed to be waiting, as if they were afraid that any moment the dragon would appear to finish its work, obliterating the entirety of Osghast with a mighty exhale.

"Sire, the spring festival cannot go on while the country is in such a state," Grafton sniveled as he struggled to keep up with Tristan's long strides. "Inviting all of the people into the city is lunacy! Why not just feed them all to the dragon and get it over with? Or the Eastern Tribes?"

Tristan chuckled at Grafton's cowardice. "You worry far too much,

Grafton. The festival will go off without a hitch. It must. The festival is the crux of my plan to save Osghast."

"Sire?"

He paused, turning to the round little man and pointing out the window toward the vast countryside surrounding the castle. "Do you see all that, my friend? That is the kingdom of Osghast. It has been strong for a thousand years and will be strong for a thousand more. Some say our people are blessed by the Fae. That our forest brings sustenance to them, and therefore, we are under their protection. That is old thinking, Grafton. Ancient superstition. This dragon curse, this plague upon our people must be fought like any other enemy. The people must have a reason to believe in the house of Laurenz once more. A show of strength is what we need!"

"But your father—"

"Is wasting away in his bed! He cares not, one way or another. Once I've proven my worth, he will be content to retire and leave the kingdom in my care."

"What does any of this have to do with the spring festival?"

Tristan scoffed, wondering how he got saddled with such an idiot as a confidante. "The spring festival was started thousands of years ago by my ancestors to gather all the kingdom's virgin maidens. Three were chosen: one to be sacrificed to the king, one to the Fae, and the last to the fire drakes of the mountain. Over the years, the ritual has become merely symbolic, as the dragons were long ago driven from this realm."

"You mean to sacrifice a virgin to the dragon?" Grafton stared at Tristan as if he'd lost his mind and should take to bed like his father. "Do you really believe that will sate the bloodlust of such a beast?"

"Don't be stupid, Grafton. I only mean to draw the dragon into the city with the promise of a sacrifice."

"The dragon? Here?" he asked, his eyes wide with disbelief and fear. "We've been lucky that it has remained in hiding since Isling!"

"Don't worry. We'll be prepared. Once the sacrificial lamb is chosen, she will lead the beast into a trap where I will dispatch it. Once I've taken the head, the people will insist that I be crowned, and we can all live happily ever after."

"And how do you propose to do this? You know absolutely nothing about dragon slaying."

"But I know people who do. Trust me, Grafton. In a few months, all this will be but a bad memory, and dragons will once again be the stuff of myths in Osghast."

⚜

Thalia awoke disoriented. The sun had barely peeked over the horizon. There were tears on her cheeks, and her eyes felt swollen and gritty. She'd been crying in her sleep over her prince. He had forsaken her, just like everyone else had. Her father, all of her kin... Markus. And why shouldn't they? She couldn't save them from the fires of their fears. Her father had been right all along. She was nothing and should be content to be nothing. A murderess condemned to walk alone forever. At least no one else would have to die. Perhaps she should draw up enough courage to throw herself into the sea and be done with it. Would her prince be waiting for her in the afterlife? Or maybe it was as Esa had always said and that the soul just traveled in death from one vessel to another. If that were the case, maybe her next life would be better than this one. Maybe she could right all her wrongs.

"Thank heavens you're awake!" Esa rushed into the room, setting down the dim lamp and pulling clothes from the trunk at the foot of the bed where Thalia lay. "Get up, child!"

"What is it, Esa?" she croaked, rubbing her eyes.

"You have to leave this place! Quickly! You must get up and dress yourself now." The old woman grabbed her by the wrists and pulled her from the bed. She was surprisingly strong, and Thalia stumbled to her feet.

"Please, Esa. Just let me sleep a while longer. I'm so tired..."

"There's no time!" Before she could elaborate, they could hear commotion out in the street. Both women rushed to the window and peered out, trying not to be seen. Up and down the street, royal guardsmen could be seen pounding at the door of every cottage. There was shouting and crying as young women were pulled from their homes and rounded up in cage-like carts. Rain added to the chaos, throwing up showers of mud as the women were dragged along, most crying out and reaching for their families.

"What's happening?" Thalia mumbled, watching as a girl that couldn't have been more than twelve was wrenched from her father's arms.

"I don't know. It started at dawn. Guards from the king's castle in Thane started dragging all the unmarried girls out into the street. By order of Prince Tristan! Now do you see why you have to go?"

Thalia nodded and began grabbing at her clothes strewn over the room. She dressed quickly. "Put out the light. Maybe they won't think we're home."

Esa nodded. "You can slip out the back. Hide in the forest until nightfall. By then the whole thing should blow over." Thalia groaned with the weight of the pack on her shoulders and pulled the cowl over her head. She nodded, but something told the girl she would not be back to Isling. She started for the back door from which she might sneak into the alley behind the house. "Hurry, child!"

Thalia froze as the pounding on the door began. "It might be too late, Esa," she hissed, pressing her body against the wall. Her hand closed over the crossbow at her back, and she felt around for a bolt. She wasn't going down without a fight. "Open the door, Esa. Don't fight them lest they run you through. My life isn't worth yours."

"But—"

"Just do it!"

Esa tried to open the door slightly, but the burly knight on the other side kicked it wide open, throwing harsh daylight into the gloom. "Open in the name of the king!" the knight barked.

"You've no right, sir!" Esa shouted, putting herself between the guard and Thalia. "This is my home!"

"The lands and all the people in it belong to His Majesty King Christophe!" A tall man pushed the others aside, making his way into the cottage. Thalia was immediately frightened of him. His black eyes were cold and calculating. His hair was greased back from his shiny, pale forehead, and he had the mouth of a serpent. She cast her eyes down and saw that he was the only one of the knights wearing a chest plate that bore the crest of Laurenz. The captain of the royal guard. He read from a scroll. "All maidens of Osghast are hereby summoned to the castle for the Rite of *Sheakhol*. Citizens will draw to the capital in three days' time to witness!"

"*Sheakhol* hasn't been done in a thousand years!" Esa protested, holding on to Thalia tightly as the guards seized her. "A woman's sacrifice won't stop the dragon!" Thalia struggled in their grasp as they pulled her pack from her shoulders. Her heart sank as she heard the hollow thud of her crossbow hitting the floor. If they got her hands bound, it would be over. Thalia thrashed and kicked, trying to keep them from noticing that she still clutched a bolthead in her hand.

"Calm down, you crazy bitch!" one of the guards exclaimed as they pulled her toward the door. Thalia's boots made deep trenches in the dirt floor as she tried to slow them down. She hated when someone could best her strength, and these knights were not letting go.

"There now," the captain said, running a jagged fingernail across her cheek. "Maybe you won't be chosen for the crags!" The guards chuckled. Thalia used their distraction to wriggle from their grasp and lunge at the captain. She threw herself at him, using his size and awkward stance to overpower him. They fell, and she slashed at him with the arrow she held between her fingertips.

"You'll never have me!" she hissed. He recovered quickly from his shock and lurched forward, smashing his helmet against her skull and knocking Thalia backward.

"Thalia!" Esa screamed. She reached out for the girl, but the knights were strong. She could only watch as they dragged the dazed girl from the cottage, hanging limply on the arm of the captain. "Where are you taking her?"

"The capital at Thane," the captain replied. His tone was teasing. "Don't look so sad. Perhaps she won't be chosen." As soon as the captain cleared the threshold, he threw the old woman aside. "Either way, the dragon will perish."

Thalia's head swam, and she couldn't seem to focus as the captain dragged her across the muddy road. Screams and cries of young girls echoed in her ears. A knight took hold of her arms, jerking her away from the captain and heaving her into a large wagon. She tried to stand, but she was too disoriented and sat down hard on the mucky floor. There must have been a hundred women in the makeshift cage, some naked and others in their nightgowns. "Where are we going?" she muttered.

A rugged farmer's daughter hoisted Thalia to her feet and pushed her against the bars. "You'll get trampled if you lay there much longer."

Thalia nodded. Her head still felt heavy from her daze, and she could feel a large knot forming in the center of her forehead. "Thank you."

The woman scoffed. "Probably better to let you die, but this way at least you got a fighting chance."

"What do you mean?"

"They're taking us to the capital for *Sheakhol*."

"What's that?"

"Kind of a spell, really. The king will choose one of us for a dragon bride."

There was a collective shriek as the cart began to move and they were thrown against one another. "A dragon bride?" Thalia said once she could stand.

"It's just a nice way of saying sacrifice. One thing's for sure. One of us is going to die in the fires of the dragon's belly."

Thalia looked around at the faces of the girls collected in such close quarters. She knew that it was unlikely that the king would choose one and let the rest of them go easily. Even if he did, Thane was a half-day's journey away, and most of these women were peasants. They would likely not be able to make their way back to Isling. Most of them would probably never see their families again. Thalia's stomach turned thinking of it. "Is this the future you were so eager to leave me with?" she whispered to her prince as the cart trundled away.

Chapter Nine

Thalia had a sickening feeling as she stared around the room at the crowds of girls gathered from the village. They huddled in corners and held on to each other, trying to keep warm in the dank dungeons under the castle. Most were dressed in wisps of a chemise, made even more insubstantial by the rain water and splashes of mud that had drenched their bodies on the way from Isling. Some had spatters of blood across their youthful faces and scrapes where they'd fought with the guards. Thalia was struck by the fear in their eyes. Some of the girls were so young as to still have their hair in braids. Her heart went out to them as she watched them sob, still shouting for their mothers.

Sheakhol was an ancient rite that had not been performed in Thane for at least a millennium. It was said that the kings of old had appeased the Dragon Lords by offering a virgin bride each year at the Equinox. If what the guards said was true, one of them would be offered as tribute to the dragon that had been plaguing the kingdom. She smiled at the irony of her situation. For years she'd been the most fearsome slayer on the continent. The Huntress of Tarkin was the stuff of legends. How comical it would be for her to die chained to the cliffs outside of Thane as a dragon tore out her heart with its talons.

Thalia heard a small sound behind her despite the din of noise in the room. She turned to see a small girl huddling against the wall. She couldn't have seen more than ten summers. She looked malnourished, and her white blond hair was caked with mud. She didn't wear a chemise like the rest. Her shift looked as if it had been made from an old blanket or shawl. It hung off her shoulders and barely fell to her knees, revealing bloody scrapes on her legs. A wellspring of anger rose in Thalia's chest. This was obviously one of the unwanted children that wandered the towns, begging for food and shelter. Evidently the guards had just picked them up along the way because there was no one to protest. "She's just a baby," Thalia whispered. She wandered over to the girl and knelt before her. "Hello, love. My name is Thalia. What's yours?"

The girl was so frightened that, at first, she did not respond. Her eyes darted around the room as if looking for someone to be angry if she spoke. "Enke," she said finally.

"My name is Thalia," she replied. She offered the girl a warm smile, and the child tried to return it.

"I heard some of the other girls talking. They say that we're going to be taken to the dragon." At the mere mention of the word, the girl started to cry again. "They took me from the towns, away from my brother! He tried to stop them, but the guards were too strong." Her words trailed off in a torrent of renewed tears that shook her tiny body. "Are we going to die?" she finally spat.

"No, love." Thalia smiled and offered her hand to the child. "Everything is going to be all right." She looked around, standing on the tips of her toes to see if there might be some way to escape, but the walls were thick, and every iron portcullis had been lowered and chained. Then she saw it. A small, bent grate at the base of the outer wall. The opening was small, meant to allow water and waste to flow out of the dungeon and into the moat. Quickly, Thalia gauged the probability that the tiny girl could even fit through the opening. If she could bend the bars back just a little more, perhaps. She put a finger to her lips and began leading Enke through the crowd. "You must be very quiet." Thalia knew that if others saw what she was about to do, all would be for naught. Most of the women here were much too large to fit through, and the guards would hear them struggle. No, only little Enke would be escaping today. Perhaps if she could save just one...

As they reached the grate, Thalia knelt to whisper in Enke's ear. "All right, you must stand here. Try not to let anyone see what I'm doing." The little girl nodded, and Thalia turned to the iron bars. They were rusted and bent, making the metal weak. She looked around for something she might use as a lever, but she had no such luck. She would have to rely on her own strength. She pulled hard on the broken bar, but it wouldn't budge. Looking back over her shoulder, she could see little Enke, her frightened eyes all over. She heard the child gasp and a commotion on the other side of the room as guards began to file into the room.

"Thalia! They're coming!" she whined. All around them, girls began to shout and wail. They moved toward the blocked stairwells in boiling masses as if they might hide behind one another and avoid the guards. Thalia used the confusion and noise to her advantage. She began to kick at the bars with her heavy boots. Over and over she pushed at them with her feet. There was a squeal as they began to give way. It was all the encouragement she needed, and she continued to kick in earnest. Uncaring about the noise, she groaned with the effort.

"Hurry, Thalia!" Enke exclaimed. "They're coming this way!"

She ignored the warning and pulled at the loosened grate with her hands. She tugged with all her might until it bent enough to leave an opening just large enough for the child to wriggle through. "Come on, Enke! You have to go now!" The girl dropped to her knees and did as she was told. "Once you get to the other side, follow the trench to the base of the castle. You should come to a narrow ladder of stones that will lead you up to the aqueduct. You'll see a larger grate there with great streams of water. Can you swim?"

"Yes," she said. "My brother taught me."

"Good. Climb through the grate and swim as hard as you can to the surface. The current will take you into the moat and down to the river."

"But... what about you?"

"Don't worry about me, child. Now go!" She pushed the girl down and urged her through the grate and into the tunnel beyond. The girl whined and whimpered as the jagged edge of the bars cut into her skin as she wormed through the opening, but Thalia kept pushing her.

"That one!"

Thalia winced as she heard the deep, growling voice shouting behind her. She'd been seen. She could hear the boots and clatter of swords as the guard came toward her. None of that mattered. Enke was almost through. "Hurry, child!"

"I'm trying! My leg is stuck!" Thalia looked down and noticed that the edge of Enke's shift was caught in the bars.

"Stop that there!"

"Just pull it, Enke!" she shouted. The child did and pulled free of the grate just as the guard was upon them. With a final look back, Enke ran down the tunnel and was out of sight just as the guard's fist came down.

❧

Thalia expected to awaken in a prison cell. After all, technically she'd helped a prisoner of King Christophe escape. She didn't know much about the law in this part of the continent, but she was almost positive that the penalty for such an act was death by hanging. But as she struggled back to consciousness, she noticed that she was not in a cold prison cell but a bedchamber fit for a queen. Her head ached as she sat up. The guard had evidently hit her with some kind of object, and she was still somewhat dazed. A blurry haze clouded her vision, but she could see that she lay atop an enormous bed covered in a jeweled duvet. A fire roared in the hearth opposite, warming her body. The light was mercifully dim, but she could make out a mirror and a wardrobe full of silks and satin.

Thalia threw her legs over the side of the bed and stood up, stumbling toward the mirror. She groaned at the pain in her head and the muscles of her arms and legs where she'd pushed open the grate. She smiled, whispering a small prayer that Enke had gotten back to her brother; otherwise this would all have been futile. Her eyes focused, and she could see her image in the mirror. She almost didn't recognize herself. She seemed a shell of the woman she had been before Markus's death. Her frame was thin and frail, and her long blond hair hung in tangles. Her green eyes seemed to have lost the firelight they'd once had. Defeat and fear had taken their toll.

"I am afraid, prince," she whispered to her reflection. She spoke to him, knowing that he would not answer, but it made her feel better just the same. In her dreams, though she feared him, he had made her feel safe and protected. He would lay waste to any who tried to harm her. The shadow of his form spoke of his danger and ferocity, but he always spoke to her so kindly. She wished he would speak to her now. She wanted to wrap herself in the protective embrace of his voice. Thalia couldn't believe that he didn't really exist. That he was just something her mind dreamed up to cope with a miserable childhood. He was too real. His voice, his touch, the way he seemed to know every one of her dark secrets—it was all too material. When she woke from her most fevered dreams of him, she could even still feel his body, still feel his warmth wrapped around her like the gentle rays of spring-time sun. Surely some magical force beyond her understanding had brought them together.

"I don't know what to do. I fear that some terrible fate awaits just beyond these doors, but I can't see it. Please... please comfort me," she whispered to the dark. "You've always been there. Since I was a child, you've given me strength." She couldn't help it. Her words dissolved into bitter tears, and she sat down hard on the floor, sobbing into her hands like a child. What did any of it matter now? Markus was dead at her hand, and her prince had forsaken her. What difference did any of it make? Perhaps in death they could be reunited. She could taste his lips once more, all rose petals and ash. She could again feel the heat of his touch. "Perhaps death is better, sweet prince. Would you like me better if I were dead? Would you return? Is that what this is? Some kind of test?" Her eyes were drawn to the fire. It blazed brightly in the hearth, an inferno so large that a man could easily stand up inside the firebox. There was an old Tarkinian legend that said that all slayers were born of fire and that was why they had such a unique ability to kill dragons. It would also account for the strange birthmark she bore on her wrist. Perhaps she was to return to the fire. To die as Markus had. But still, her mind feared the pain. One who had killed so many of their kin would be a hearty meal for a dragon. He would take his time and pick the flesh from her bones slowly, then crush them between iron mandibles. She was terrified. For the first time since childhood, she feared a mindless serpent.

"I know that you can't hear me, prince. Even if you could, you would not answer. But if only I could understand what I'd done to drive you away, I could die in peace." She sniffled and wiped the tears from her eyes, feeling like a ridiculous child. She stared around her. If she hadn't been in such a predicament, she might be in awe of such a place. In her whole life, she'd never seen such opulence. Even the vaulted ceiling overhead was laid with a filigreed tile that sparkled in the firelight.

"Do you find your accommodation acceptable, my lady?" Thalia gasped, for a moment believing that her prince had indeed answered her plea. As she turned, her heart sank again at seeing what could only be Prince Tristan. She had never looked upon his face but had heard tales of his fine features and strength in battle. His hair was golden and shone like a halo about his regal brow. He looked familiar and might have been handsome if it weren't for his mouth. A slim and sneering mouth that turned up in an amused smile, evidently at seeing her timidity. "Can you speak, or have they brought me a mute? I was beginning to think my guards had killed you in the process. You slept for many hours."

"Majesty..." she stammered. "I... I did not see you come in..." As an afterthought, she remembered to curtsey and nearly fell on her head trying to.

"No, no, my lady," he started, rushing forward and taking her wrist gently to help her up. "You bow to no one."

"I'm sorry?"

"Why should you?" he said. Giving an exaggerated bow, he raised her hand to his lips and kissed the back of it gently. She smiled at the ticklish feel of his whiskers against her skin. "For you are the savior of us all."

"A savior? Whatever do you mean?"

He chuckled and led her to the edge of the bed and gestured that she should sit. "Of course. You have been given the highest honor that can be bestowed upon a commoner of Osghast. To save the people from the wrath of this pestilence!"

Thalia gazed at the prince. "I would hardly call a dragon pestilence, sire," she scoffed. "They are mindless creatures that care only for consuming death—ash and decay. Hire a dragonslayer and be done with it."

"Do you not think that we have tried that, my dear? Slayers from all corners of the continent have come to our aid. All of them have taken our money and brought back nothing but scales fashioned from silk and glass. Or they haven't come back at all. My father, King Christophe, believes as you do. That this is a mere animal that is just passing through and will soon move on with his food source."

"But you don't believe that?"

"Of course not. This beast is clever. And seems to be bent on some kind of revenge against our royal house. He's attacked up and down the border towns, each time coming closer to Thane."

"You think he's stalking the capital?" Thalia couldn't stop herself from laughing, but Tristan's expression was grave.

"I know he is. You see, he has other motives. This dragon seems to think he has some kind of claim on these lands, and he will stop at nothing to regain what he feels is his birthright."

Thalia's jaw tensed. "You think he's a Dragon Lord."

"It's the only explanation."

"But no one has seen one in a thousand years. Dragon Lords are Fae shapeshifters. In Faerie, they can take a human form, but in the world of men, they're trapped."

"I see you're well-versed in the legends of my people. This dragon is larger, stronger, and deadlier than anything a common slayer has ever seen. Even if they could kill him, they'd never find him. The Dragon Lord is cunning, hiding in the deep places of the earth. He can withstand fire and water. And he might hide in Faerie. But you, my beautiful darling... you are the weakness that our friend has not considered." Tristan brushed his fingertips along her cheek, a gesture that made Thalia's skin crawl. He was handsome, but there was something predatory and pathetic in those eyes.

"I don't understand."

"*Sheakhol*. Nyxyn, my counsel, is schooled in Ancient Magic. According to the old scholars, the Dragon Lord cannot resist the call of the rite. This evil plague of a beast will be helpless to resist the pull of *Sheakhol*'s magic. He will be drawn to the crags where you will be waiting."

Thalia's hope sank in her chest like a heavy boulder. "I *am* to be put to death for helping the child." She shook her head. "Perhaps there is a pestilence in this kingdom after all," she murmured.

Tristan barked a greasy laugh that chilled Thalia to the marrow of her bones. This man... this boy who would be king had become twisted and greedy for power. These men were dangerous. "You would be careful to whom you are speaking, my dear. I could have your head with the snap of my fingers."

"Then do it, if you are so eager. I do not fear death," she lied. "That child may have been an unwanted, but she did not deserve to die on the crags."

"I'm glad you're pleased. As soon as we became aware of your exceptional talents, I set the rest of them free. They're all probably back in their meager homes, warming themselves by a smelly old peat fire, unthinking about your sacrifice."

Thalia couldn't be sure, but she could see the lies dancing in his eyes. She didn't want to know what had become of those maidens, but she knew it wasn't good. "My talents?"

"Oh, of course." He reached out and grabbed her arm, pulling it out straight and running his fingertips along the dark mark on her wrist. It was only a birthmark, but the dark spot twisted around the tiny veins there and into the palm of her hand. It looked like a dancing flame that flickered in the dim light offered by the fire. "You're a slayer of Tarkin —the only marked slayer in your generation. Unless I miss my guess, you're the one they call Huntress."

Thalia nodded. "How did you know that?"

"Don't be so modest, my dear," he said, closing his cool, clammy hand over hers and patting it with mock tenderness. "Your gifts are well known throughout the land. A slayer with an almost supernatural ability to know what the beasts are thinking. Some have even called you a descendent of the Fae Queen herself, a born consort of the Dragon Lords."

"There is nothing magic about me, Highness. Other than my exceptional skill at getting myself into trouble."

His lips spread into a wide, toothy grin that sent a shiver of unease crawling over Thalia's skin. "On the contrary, my dear. You're a very lucky girl. You see, you have been given a unique opportunity."

"How so?"

"Well, you really have two choices. Assuming the dragon doesn't kill you."

"Why would you think he wouldn't?"

"I have reason to believe that, should you go willingly, the dragon will take you for his bride."

Thalia laughed. This time she could not help it. The ridiculous and desperate superstition of the prince was too much. "You've heard too many stories, Highness. Dragons, despite all your tales of the Fae and shapeshifters, are animals. Rare animals, yes. But they are animals nonetheless. They don't take brides. And they can be killed like any other if given the right opportunity."

"Opportunity is exactly what I was thinking of, my lady."

"I don't think I understand what you ask, Highness."

"You're the bait, child. You will lure the dragon in during the ritual. When he approaches, legend says that he will be vulnerable, trapped in the intoxication of Nyxyn's spell. The dragon will bow to you, opening himself up for your dagger." He pulled a dagger from his belt and offered it to her. Thalia took it fast, and before Tristan drew his next breath, it was at his throat.

"I could kill you easily, sire."

"But you won't." He smiled, his eyes traveling over her body. He made no attempt at subtlety as he sized her up. It made Thalia feel grimy, and the tiny hairs on the back of her neck stood up as if she were about to be ill. "If what they say of you is true, then your honor will not allow it."

Thalia huffed and stepped back, releasing him. "You're right. I wouldn't want to waste a good weapon with such bitter blood." It was an exquisite weapon, fashioned of the finest steel and folded many times by a skilled blacksmith. Carvings of ancient spells had been worked into the blade itself, and the hilt was the body of a raven.

"My father gave me this dagger long ago, Huntress. How appropriate that you should use it to ensure my place." He stared at the dagger as she turned it over in her hands, examining the craftsmanship. Thalia had never seen its equal. "Look at the striations in the blade. It was made to slice through flesh as easily as warm butter. And it is indeed unique. The only one ever crafted."

"It is a beautiful piece to be sure, Highness, but surely you don't think that a young girl will be able to slay a dragon with such a modest weapon."

"You don't have to slay the dragon. You only have to wound it. Distract the beast long enough for me to kill it. Use your unique talents to calm it. Trap it."

"Do you honestly believe that this will work? The dragon at the very least will tear my body from the chains and carry me, broken and bleeding, to his lair where he'll devour my flesh slowly."

Tristan grinned. "You may be right, Huntress. But my guard will be standing by to make sure he doesn't escape. Make no mistake, child. The dragon will die."

"That's so comforting," she grumbled. "If I do this for you, what then? Will you let me go?" She captured his gaze and held it. Thalia did not trust him. His eyes were cold, and though his voice never wavered, he was nervous. He was not certain that his plan would work, but he also realized it was his only chance.

"Better than that, my lady." He bowed, bringing her hand to his lips to kiss lightly at the scraped knuckles. "Should you succeed, I shall make you my queen."

Chapter Ten

When Tristan left, Thalia was more confused than she had been before. There was something niggling in the back of her mind. Something about Tristan's story didn't quite add up. She had heard the stories of the Dragon Lords as a child from Esa, but those were just stories. There was no such thing as a dragon that could change his shape—not even in the kingdom of the Fae. Most people didn't even believe in faeries anymore. Life was difficult but simple for the people in the far reaches of the kingdom like Isling and Tarkin. They didn't have times for daydreams of magical creatures.

And what of Tristan's offer? Imagine, Thalia of Tarkin—Queen of Osghast. The very notion was preposterous. The people of her homeland often thought of her as something otherworldly, but never a queen. Queens didn't have dirt under their fingernails or ratted tangles in their hair. Catching a glimpse of herself in the mirror, Thalia was sure she had both and much more. Her clothing was torn, her body covered with splotches of mud, and her hair was one big knot. No, Thalia was not made of royal stuff.

A knock at the heavy oak door brought her out of her reverie. At first, she was afraid to make any noise. Perhaps if she just kept quiet, whoever was on the other side would go away. But they knocked once more, and the door opened. A thin, regal-looking man dressed all in black entered, followed by two chambermaids. His arms were folded with one slender index finger tucked under his chin. He did not speak, but strolled up to Thalia, looking down his nose at her. "Well. This just won't do," he said with a sneer.

"I beg your pardon?"

"No, child. Don't speak unless you're spoken to," he replied. Thalia's mouth snapped shut so hard that her teeth clicked together painfully. "I am Balan, your groom. These are my assistants, Freya and Xyneth. We've come to prepare you for the ceremony."

"The prince means to dress me up before throwing me to the dragon, I see." She stared at Balan defiantly, daring him to silence her.

"Well, what sort of virgin sacrifice would you be looking this way? Even a hoary dragon wouldn't bother with you. You look like you ate one raw with your bare hands." Thalia could feel herself blushing and moved to cover herself. He snapped his fingers, and the chambermaids brought a large tub into the room and set it down in front of the fireplace. "All right, child. Come and take those filthy things off." When she didn't move, Balan came over and began pulling at her tattered tunic.

She immediately grabbed his hand and twisted his arm behind his back in one graceful movement. "Take your hands off me!" she snarled, pushing him forward so that he stumbled over the edge of the rug.

Balan brushed off his coat and glared at Thalia, obviously affronted that she would dare touch him. "Well, the prince certainly didn't choose you for your temperance!"

"He chose me because I don't suffer fools," she growled, smoothing the tunic over her thighs.

"Be that as it may, the ritual of *Sheakhol* requires that you're clean and pure," he snapped. "My job as His Majesty's valet dictates that I oversee any task he deems worthy. And today that task is making sure that you are fully prepared for the ritual that will take place at moonrise." He pulled a timepiece from his coat and stared into its face. "The sands tell me that we have just over an hour to make that happen, and I am never late, my lady."

"What difference does it make if I'm clean or wearing some ridiculous gown? The dragon will devour me either way."

"It matters because we all have our station in this world and things that are expected of us." Balan stood tall with his hands on narrow hips. Thalia could see that he was immovable. Though it pained her to acquiesce, she liked this man with his blustering and prickly tone. In his way, he was as much a warrior as she and just as determined in his quest, and she couldn't help feeling respect for him if not for his mission. "Must I call in the guards to tether you, or will you comply with my reasonable request?" His eyes sparkled with a glimmer of kindness, and this time he offered his hand.

Thalia allowed the valet to lead her to the hearth. The handmaidens were busy filling the copper basin with warm water. She could see the steam rising from it, and her resolve wavered. A warm bath was not a luxury that she had been allowed often as of late. It would help to clear her mind so that she might concentrate on the task ahead. If she were going to survive, Thalia would need to stay calm and think. Balan's hands were gentle this time as he pulled at the ruined fabric of her tunic, slipping it down over her shoulders and letting it puddle at her feet. She gasped at seeing her own haggard frame in the mirror opposite. She looked as if she hadn't eaten in weeks. Her skin seemed to drape around her bones like a shawl. Her breasts, which had always been a source of desire for most of the men she'd come across were no longer the shapely orbs that were almost too large for her elfin stature. Like everything else, they were bruised and drawn. Her skin had lost the youthful luster it had once had. Time had taken its toll on Thalia, and she wept to see it.

"Why are you crying, child?" Balan asked, pinning her hair up as best he could with the tangles. "If the rumors around the castle are correct, Tristan doesn't mean to let the dragon kill you."

"How can you be sure?"

Balan smiled. "He's much more interested in killing the dragon than appeasing it."

"Why do you say that?" she asked, allowing him to support her weight as she pushed her leggings over her hips. She was trying very hard not to concentrate on the fact that she was now completely naked in front of this stranger with nothing—not even a few locks of hair—to hide herself.

"Tristan is vying for power. He wants to be king."

"King Christophe is still alive, is he not?"

"Yes, but Tristan feels that he is weak. He wants his father to retire to the country and give him control. He thinks that if he can kill the dragon, his father will abdicate and give him the throne." He turned to one of the chambermaids and nodded to the pile of clothing. "Burn those."

Thalia watched as the girl gathered up every possession she had left and took them away. It was true that they were ruined, but now she felt that she was tied to nothing else in the world. "Does Tristan really believe in the Dragon Lords? Perhaps this is just a show of strength to the kingdom."

Balan chuckled and helped Thalia step into the tub. "Tristan knows that the Wyrm of Gwynfir is not a normal dragon. And Tristan has more reason than most to believe in the lore of the Fae."

"He is superstitious?"

"He is no stranger to Queen Mab. He nor any of his kin. It has always been so." He held her hand as she sank into the warm bath. She sighed audibly as the water rose around her. The water was scented with rosewater and precious oils that calmed her senses and made her mind lazy. The panic and worry of the day seemed to slip from her skin with the droplets of moisture. "Some say that the dragon that plagues us now is a Fae curse, wrought by Mab herself to torture Christophe."

"Why would she do that?"

"He was her lover, of course." Balan took a soft sea sponge from the basket beside the tub. He dipped it in the fragrant water until it was full and then squeezed it over Thalia's skin, getting it wet. Over and over he did this until the initial layer of grime ran into the tub. "Some said that she was wildly jealous of the queen, Tristan's mother, and laid a curse upon the House of Laurenz until Christophe agreed to go with her into Faerie to live forever."

"The curse being a Dragon Lord?"

Balan nodded and cleared his throat. "Freya," he called. She brought a vial of golden liquid, and he gestured that she should sit. The girl knelt beside the tub. She squeezed a bit of the liquid into the sponge and used it to spread the thick soap over Thalia's skin. It smelled of sandalwood, and despite her initial reaction to resist, Thalia closed her eyes and let the girl wash the blood and dirt from her body. Soon she was lost in the gentle strokes of the sponge along her shoulders and down each arm. Slowly the girl worked the cleansing oils into her skin, scrubbing away at the sorrow and pain and fear that the last few days offered. She could feel Balan's fingers in her hair as he pulled at the pins and tangled curls. They tumbled down over her shoulders as he nudged her to lie back. With a small silver pitcher, he gathered water and poured it carefully over her head, getting her hair wet. It was thick and took a few tries, but the warm water felt so nice running over her scalp that Thalia nearly groaned with pleasure. His fingertips were hypnotic, massaging more of the sweet-smelling soap into her hair. She began to drift, lost in the sensation of these expert sets of hands trilling over every part of her.

"I can do this myself," she murmured, not really wanting them to stop.

"Tonight, you are a queen, my lady. Let us take care of you," Balan said.

She was nearly asleep when he spoke again. "You may get up now. Quickly." Remembering the wormwood, he helped her to stand and steadied her on her feet. "There's no time to waste."

As he led her from the bath to the hearth, Xyneth returned with masses of white fabric draped over her arms. Thalia felt like a marionette as they pulled the gown over her head. They worked her arms into the sleeves, and Freya held her upright while Balan pulled the bodice strings tight. She stared at herself in the mirror while Xyneth combed her wild golden hair into place and wove tiny flowers into it. Looking at her reflection, Thalia could hardly believe her eyes. She'd never really been allowed to be a girl before. The life of a dragonslayer was difficult and left no time for things such as fine linen gowns or perfume.

"There. You'll do." Balan smoothed her hair and smiled. It was a sad sort of smile, like he knew that this was the last time he'd ever see her. He gave her shoulder a reassuring squeeze and whisked the other two servants from the room. "We'll just leave you to yourself for a while. The attendants will be here soon."

And just like that, he was gone. The silence in the room was a deafening blanket, and Thalia could hear the blood rushing in her ears. Out of the corner of her eye, she could see the silvery dagger that Tristan had left on the vanity. Perhaps it was just her imagination or maybe some lingering aftereffects of the wormwood infusion, but Thalia thought she could see dark magic emanating from the small object. She picked it up and turned it over in her hands. Her own face was reflected in the gleaming blade. The blade was long for a dagger and slightly curved at the end. She could see tiny serrations that would rip and tear at flesh. The hilt was intricately carved with the head of a raven. The eyes of the bird were tiny, deep red rubies that glistened in the firelight. This was an instrument of ritual yes, but also an instrument of death. And it was bloodthirsty. Tristan had told her to wear it holstered to her thigh, but Thalia didn't want it that close to her skin. Looking around, she found an extra ribbon that was left over from her hair. She used it to tie the heavy dagger into the folds of her skirt, hidden but within easy reach.

"It's time." Thalia's heart thumped hard in her chest as Balan's voice broke the silence. Behind him in the doorway were several attendants dressed in black, including the nasty guard that she'd attacked back at Esa's cottage. As she passed him by, she paused to grin at the thin scar across his cheek left by her arrow.

"Not so brave now, are we?" he snarled.

Thalia didn't allow his threatening tone to diminish her pride. She held her head high, ignoring his words but knowing that he'd eventually live to regret them.

Chapter Eleven

"Everything is in place, Highness." Tristan turned to see Grafton standing in the archway. "The moon rises quickly."

"Good," Tristan replied. He pulled his breastplate over his head and allowed Grafton to buckle it tightly at his sides. He ran his fingertips over the image of the dragon that had been carved into the leather. "This was my father's armor, Grafton."

"Aye. I've seen it many times, sire. On your father."

Tristan nodded. "When he was strong. Before I had to take over his responsibilities. When he was a good king." He looked up at Grafton. "My father used to hold me on his lap and tell me tales of his adventures. Stories of war he'd waged to expand the kingdom of Osghast all the way to the mountains of Gwynfir. How his ancestors had worn this same armor to drive out the Dragon Lords and avenge the ruin of Ellythin. Now, I will wear this armor to rebuild that which the dragon has tried to take from us. This will be a good night, Grafton."

"Are you certain, Highness?" Grafton's beady eyes revealed a glimmer of uncertainty.

"Do you still doubt me?"

"It isn't exactly doubt, my lord. But have you considered that if you do not succeed—"

"Don't succeed? Why wouldn't I succeed?" Tristan snapped. "It's a foolproof plan. Nyxyn will draw the dragon in, the girl will incapacitate it, and I will swoop in at the last second to take its head. Simple."

Grafton shook his head. "And dangerous. What if the dragon does not come?"

"Nyxyn assures me that the ritual will not allow that."

"And what if he tears the girl to shreds?"

Tristan chuckled. "What if he does? She is nothing to me."

"She is a dragonslayer in Tarkin! The stuff of legends in the borderlands! If she dies, they will retaliate!"

"Don't be ridiculous, Grafton! From the stories I've heard, Huntress is an outcast of her tribe. The girl's only function is to wound the beast. Weaken it. Distract it long enough for me to swoop in and take its head."

"But what of the girl? You must be aware that the dragon will immediately devour her."

"As long as he is distracted for a few minutes while he feasts on her body."

"Your compassion is overwhelming, Highness."

"Compassion? Will my compassion for one peasant girl save the entire kingdom? I think not. Compassion and sentiment is what got us in this position to begin with, Grafton. My kingdom—"

"Don't you mean your father's kingdom?"

"Pardon?"

"Your father. It's your father's kingdom." Grafton lay a paternal hand on the prince's shoulder. "As of this morning, King Christophe was still ruler of Osghast."

"Not for long, my friend," Tristan replied, shrugging away. "My reign begins tonight."

❧

The streets of Thane were eerily silent in spite of the crowds that lined them, Every citizen was present, all carrying lanterns to light the path to the crags. The moon was full, hanging high overhead like a great eye staring down on the town. Perhaps it was. The gods were lingering overhead, trying to decide their fates. The notion made Thalia even more frightened as she stood at the gates of the castle. Balan and the two handmaidens stood just behind her, ready to carry the impressive train of her gown as she made her way through the streets. Balan had explained that she was being bestowed a great privilege. Thalia wasn't sure being torn apart by a fire-breathing dragon was any great privilege.

"Come, my lady," Balan said behind her. She took a deep breath and closed her eyes. In her mind, she could see her prince. He would walk with her to the end and stay with her on the crags until it was over. Perhaps then they could dwell in darkness together. Forever.

Her slippers made no noise on the crude pavement as she walked down the long avenue and into the town. Prince Tristan and his advisor and a magician called Nyxyn led the grotesque wedding party. As they approached the town, she could hear the people chanting. She couldn't make out the words; they were in some ancient dialect, but it sounded like singing and screaming all at once. She closed her eyes again, and the starbursts of their fires exploded in the dark, making her feel dizzy. She stumbled, and Tristan was there. He took her arm and steadied her. He flashed her that predatory grin and gave a wink that turned her stomach.

All too soon they came to the cliffs' edge. The noise of the waves was deafening. Even more ominous was the feeling of disorientation. The only light now was that of the moon behind the clouds. She could not see the water, only hear it and feel the vibration beneath her feet as it slammed into the rocks below. The magician began to read from the ancient leather-bound tome that could only be a grimoire. Thalia wanted to cover her ears as he shouted the words into the quickening wind. The language was ugly and distorted. It sounded like the tongue of demons—a growling and hissing of syllables. Lightning creased the sky, lighting up the narrow stairs that would lead down to the crags. Balan stepped forward and gave a slight bow before taking her wrists and binding them with silken rope. As he finished, he leaned forward and kissed each of her cheeks. Funny, he almost seemed apologetic.

Thalia looked around as the lightning flickered again. The townspeople had followed them this far and stood around the cliff, watching and waiting. She bit down hard on the inside of her cheek. People were all the same. The spectacle of watching these men sacrifice her body to the dragon was both horrific and too tempting to pass up. They wanted to weep in disgust and terror as her blood splattered their faces and her innards rained down from the sky as the dragon enjoyed his meal.

All at once the chanting began again. This time it was furious and almost sexual, panting and moaning into the storm. Balan took her arm and began to lead her down the uneven stone stairs to the altar. Nyxyn was already there. He continued his spell as Balan lifted her arms and fastened them into the loop overhead. It was a precarious place, and she could see the groom's hands shaking as he struggled to keep his balance on the narrow precipice. He knelt carefully and fastened her ankles to the cuffs attached to the stones. As the lightning lit up the horizon again, Thalia gasped. She was dangling from the rock face with nothing to hold her back. There was a pop and a whiff of sulphur as fire blossomed from the torch in the magician's hand. Another whispered word and the flames raged high. The flames sparked and flickered, turning blue. He stabbed the torch down into a hollow place in the rock. Then all went silent save for the low sound of the chanting behind on the cliff and the crackling of the strange torch flame.

"What happens now?" Balan asked the magician.

"Now we wait."

Thalia watched as they ascended the stairs again. Neither looked back.

⁂

She wasn't sure how long she'd been there. Her eyes fluttered open, and she realized that she must have fallen asleep at some point. Or passed out. Her arms and shoulders were screaming with pain as she swam back to consciousness, and her face was burning from the wind and salt spray that assaulted her as she hung there in the dark nothingness. The regal gown clung wetly to her frame, and she shivered with the cold. The moon had sunk from view, so it must have been hours that she'd been here. The torch had long since burned out.

Perhaps Tristan's little ritual hadn't worked. After all, *Sheakhol* was a Fae secret that was meant to call the Dragon Lords to their marriage beds, and this beast was not a Dragon Lord. He couldn't be. They were an extinct breed of magic, gone from this world for good. And fire lizards did not respond to magic spells. No, Tristan just meant to leave her out here to die on the crags as a symbolic show of strength. It was ridiculous.

"Are you out there, King of All Dragons?" she called, her voice dripping with contempt. "Are you afraid to face me? The great Huntress of Tarkin! Well, are you? Come out, you witless wyrm! I am not afraid!" She hoped they could hear her, safe up there in their little enclave. Perhaps they would think she had gone insane. Perhaps Tristan himself would come to see if she were mad. She would kill him with the dagger he'd so discreetly placed upon her. All it would take is one slip of the knot at her wrists. Balan had left enough slack so she could break her bonds easily.

Suddenly, her thoughts were interrupted by a hollow rumble like thunder. She looked up, thinking how absurd it would be to be struck by lightning at this point. But the sky overhead was calm. The rumble came again, and this time Thalia felt it in her chest. A breeze, warm and humid stirred the water below, and she could feel the spray on her feet. She saw something out of the corner of her eye. A shadow moved behind the clouds, and her heart began to pound. She could smell it before she saw it. A burning smell like the leaves in autumn as they decayed on the forest floor.

When the dragon emerged from the clouds, she heard the crowds of people on the cliffs above scream and their feet pounding the earth as they ran. It circled overhead, and as its wings flapped, she heard that heavy rustling again. Thalia looked up. It was larger than any dragon she'd ever seen. No wonder Tristan assumed it was one of the lost Dragon Lords. Its body was impossibly long, at least a half-league, with a wingspan to match. She could see the muscles working in its shoulders as it beat its leathery wings against the wind. Its scales were quite black, save for a glowing of what appeared to be red veins running through them. She gasped as it shrieked into the night, announcing its arrival. It was a guttural screaming that struck terror into Thalia's core.

Suddenly, she wasn't so brave and began to tug at the bonds. Who cared about Tristan's bargain? This beast was well above her abilities. This was some kind of witchcraft!

"Dammit, Balan!" she hissed, trying desperately to slip the knot. The more she struggled, the tighter the bond. He'd tricked her! They'd all tricked her! Balan was a practical man. Was it so surprising that he took little stock in Tristan's planning? He wanted to appease the dragon, believing that it was the only way to save them. "Help!" she screamed. It was pitiful, but what else could she do? "Help me, please! Someone up there!" Of course, no one came. She was their sacrifice. Their savior. Her death would save them, and there was no one willing to stop it now.

The dragon dove, skimming along the water. Its body kicked up waves of salty spray that stung Thalia's eyes. She felt the cutting air as it grazed past her, pulling up to light on the rocks overhead with a crash. She pulled back with a shriek as jagged shards of rock rained down. The townspeople screamed as it began to climb up the cliff face, its talons raking at the stones. Thalia closed her eyes, listening to the beast's heavy breath as it sniffed her out. If she didn't move, perhaps it would just move on. Tristan's plan would have been foiled, but she wouldn't die in the furnace of the dragon's belly.

As Thalia was waiting, thinking the spell must have failed, Tristan was coming to the same conclusion. "I thought you said the dragon couldn't resist the spell, Nyxyn!" The prince was furious and slammed his fist against the marble rail of the observation tower. "It's been hours, and still the virgin is bound to the crags with no sign! None!" He'd risked far too much to have this blow up in his face. The eyes of every citizen of Thane were fixed upon the skies, waiting for Tristan to slay the Dragon Lord. They stood there in the courtyard below, staring out at the cliffs. Already he could hear their voices carried on the wind. Already they had begun to doubt. No ancient magic or rite was going to save them. Perhaps they would be so frightened that they would move their families out into the border towns.

Or worse, they would align themselves with the tribes of barbarians or even the Illyrian knights. Tristan knew that the king of Illyria much desired to rule his rival on the continent. Many times, they had negotiated peace treaties and narrowly avoided open war with them. This sort of exodus could be just the chink in the wall that would lead to a war from which Osghast would most likely not emerge victorious. His father had seen to that with his foolhardy weakness.

"Patience, sire. Gwynfir is some ways away," Nyxyn answered. Tristan despised him. A weakling archaic fool. A relic from ancient days. He'd been an idiot to trust magic.

"The fabled Dragon Lords fly with a speed like a hurricane, you said. Why should it take so long for his wings to carry him?"

"I do not know, sire. But I did the spell exactly as it was written!"

Tristan rounded on the smarmy little man. His bald head and ragged robes and the crust of black dirt under his fingernails were annoying in and of themselves. As soon as he was king, Tristan's first order of business would be to dispose of the disgusting little troll of a magician. "Then perhaps all your wondrous magical feats are just parlor tricks!" he hissed, jerking Nyxyn by the robe.

Suddenly, the roar of the dragon broke the silence of the vigil below. Tristan threw Nyxyn aside and rushed to the balcony's edge. Looking down over the courtyard, the townspeople were scattering like angry locusts.

"Dragon!"

"Look out!"

"Mercy!"

Their words traveled on the wind of its wings to Tristan's ears. Just underneath, he could hear the little slayer, screaming from where she was bound. She cried for help that would never come. Tristan smiled. The little coward. Tarkinian or not, she was only a woman. His mouth watered imagining her writhing on the rocks below, chained to her fate. Her body would be dripping with sweat by now and her hair hanging in ratted coils around her face. Once this was over, he would have the little Huntress. If she survived, that is. "To the crags!" he shouted.

The guards assembled out of nowhere. Their heavy armor clanked as they readied themselves for the attack. At first there were only streaks of fire across the sky. It circled, hovering over them, just out of arrow's range. It was studying the melee below. Would it pick off the townspeople or come after Tristan?

Tristan descended the jagged stone stairs to where his guards were gathered below. "The dragon is mine! Draw it away from the town and bring it to me!" The guards scattered, Tristan behind them. They emerged from the gates just as the beast hit the cliff face. There was a terrible clatter and roar as it climbed. First one muscular leg, then another as it dragged its body over the side of the cliffs. It crouched low to the ground, sniffing out the body of the one who had called him. It slithered and hissed, throwing bursts of fire at the fleeing people. Tristan could see the thing's eye, glowing gold and contracting with the light. It was stalking its prey. There was no sign of blood or remnants of the girl, and Tristan narrowed his eyes in confusion. She was supposed to distract it! The heavy blade of steel he'd given her would pierce the scales, slowing it down, but clearly, she was not holding up her end of the bargain.

Guards lined each battlement, their arrows notched at the ready. An initial volley served to garner the dragon's attention but did little to harm it or even slow it down. It had made its way over the cliff. "Aim for its wings!" Tristan shouted down to the captain as he ran toward the fight. The dragon shrugged off the arrows as a minor annoyance, blocking them easily with its iron scaled body. The first wave of guards ran in, attacking whatever they could manage to reach with their swords. The dragon shifted around and threw them to the side with a swipe of its great tail, breaking their bodies as if they were toys. As the archers above continued to spray the beast with iron bolts, the dragon took flight. A great, heaving leap that shook the ground beneath their feet and shattered a minor bastian, spilling guards into the bailey below.

"Draw it away from the city!" The screams of the guards were desperate, and suddenly Tristan began to think he'd made a terrible mistake. Out of the corner of his eye, he could see peasants bursting into flame, running toward the edge of the cliff and throwing themselves down and into the sea below. Guards being crushed beneath a foot,

their bones audibly shattering. Tristan could smell the burning and death and blood. Turning back, he ran toward the castle. He pushed aside townspeople as they ran to and fro, trying to fight their way into the keep. There was another crash, and the dragon roared as it slammed against the outer wall and began climbing its way up the turret.

Tristan rounded the corner in the chaos and Nyxyn knocked him off his feet. "Run, sire!" he shouted.

"You!" Tristan growled, grabbing the man by the collar. "It's looking for you, you idiot!"

"I don't know what you mean," he sniveled as the prince pulled him off his feet. "The dragon was supposed to take the sacrifice!"

"And he'll get one," Tristan snarled, dragging him toward the tower stairs. Nyxyn struggled as Tristan pulled him over the stone steps. His body bumped along the path as the servants rushed about, practically trampling them. Tristan could hear the dragon hissing and breathing fire overhead. The castle shook with every movement, and the screams of the guards below were deafening. The once peaceful Thane had erupted into a hell on earth for which Tristan was responsible. He would not let this be for naught. Suddenly, the unintelligible hissing of the dragon grew and morphed into something like speech that quieted the cacophony. All movement ceased, and it seemed that time stood still. Tristan could feel the low growling deep in his chest as the dragon spoke. It was thunderous, and everyone dropped to their knees, holding their ears. He didn't understand the words, but their meaning was clear.

Suddenly, a shattering of masonry and oak girders sounded overhead, sending an avalanche of debris raining down on their heads. In the confusion Nyxyn slipped away, and Tristan let him go as he fought his way to the top of the tower. As the dust cleared, he peered up and saw stars glistening overhead. "Gods," Tristan breathed just as the dragon reared back, showing itself for a brief moment. With one more hissing word, it pushed its head into the gaping maw that had once been the turret and breathed a stream of fire down into the castle. Tristan pressed his body against the stone wall, using his armor to offer protection from the flames. Others were not so lucky, and he saw them set ablaze before falling from the crumbling tower to crash on the ground below.

Tristan drew his sword from the sheath at his back. Large and heavy, his father's sword had been forged for one purpose, and he meant to put it to good use tonight. Gathering his courage, he raced up the staircase, carefully avoiding the places where stones and mortar crumbled. As he emerged into the night, the dragon was perched on the side of the turret like a watchful raven, its head held high, proud of the destruction he'd wrought and daring anyone to defy him. "I do not fear you, Dragon Lord!" Tristan shouted, brandishing his weapon. Looking around, he realized that there were no more guards to defend him and no more distractions of screaming peasants. Anyone left alive would be hiding in the keep or the dungeons by now. Tristan was on his own. "Time to prove your worth," he whispered before lunging at the beast.

The dragon turned just as Tristan slashed downward against its clawed foot. The serpent hissed, whipping around to bring the barbed tail down upon him, but Tristan was faster. He dodged the blow and rolled across the stone floor. In an instant, he nimbly got to his feet. He avoided another swipe of the tail and managed to pull a shield from the arms of a fallen guard. He used it to shield his body as the dragon reared back and spit flame. The shield was heavy, and the dragon's breath was so hot that for a moment Tristan feared that the metal would melt around his gauntlet.

"My turn," Tristan snarled as the beast coughed its last. He taunted it, beckoning it closer as he darted here and there. The dragon got down on its haunches, stalking him. It rather reminded Tristan of a great bat, crawling along the sill. More of that rumbling speech. The prince knew that the beast was talking to him, as crazy as that might seem. "What's the matter, beastie? Don't like the present we had for you?" He had no idea what to do next. There was no way he would be able to slay the dragon unless its breast was exposed, and no dragon would do that willingly. What he needed was a distraction. A sideways glance offered Tristan an idea. A bit of the wall left behind would get him higher. He needed to be above it. With a great leap, Tristan made it to the wall. He landed precariously, dropping the shield. It clattered across the ground. The dragon swept it aside with its wing, throwing sparks. "Come on... come to me then," Tristan shouted. Higher and higher he climbed, the bricks beneath him quaking under his weight. They wouldn't hold him long. The dragon sat up and reared back. It had tired of playing with Tristan and wanted to be done with it. Before it could open its mouth, Tristan had leapt onto its back. He came down hard with the edge of his sword. The blade slipped between the black scales, and there was a satisfying suction as it pierced the flesh beneath. The dragon hissed and spat, thrashing about, trying to throw off his attacker. Tristan smiled and pulled the sword back and thrust again, this time clipping the edge of the wing where it joined its back. The dragon roared and unfurled its wings. This time it was not surprised; it was angry. The beast threw back its wing and twisted its body in such a way that Tristan was thrown the ground. He howled in pain, his skull connecting with the hard floor beneath. His eyes clouded, and he tried to shake it off. He gripped his sword, but the dragon encroached upon him, kicking it away with an almost gentle brush of its tail. "Go on, then," Tristan said. "End this!" The dragon crouched over him, one sharp talon stepping down on his shoulder. He cried out in pain as the beast's head lowered to his level. It growled, baring its teeth as it leaned in.

"Over here!" The feminine voice startled the dragon and Tristan both. The prince turned to see the Tarkinian girl limping toward them. The dagger he'd given her was clutched in her hand. She hissed and growled at the beast. The sound was eerie, like the speech of a serpent. "Come for me," she said again. The dragon backed off of him and looked toward her. His head cocked to one side as if he were studying her. "Well, come on, then!" she shouted. "I'm what you came for, aren't I?" It hissed and spoke back. Tristan spied his sword, lying just out of reach. If only he could stretch his arm just a little farther. "I am the virgin bride! I am the tribute of *Sheakhol*. The one you want!"

The dragon's body was strangely agile as it turned, creeping toward her slowly as if confused. Tristan used the distraction and heaved his body to the side, grabbing the sword. There was a great percussive noise as the dragon took flight once more, streaking into the night sky until it was out of sight.

Everything was silent. Tristan and Thalia stood there, staring as the contrail behind the beast dissipated. "Well... little Huntress," Tristan said, his heart pounding so hard in his chest he could scarcely breathe. "Seems there's more to you than meets the eye."

Before she could respond, the dragon appeared out of nowhere. With a single shriek it descended, grabbing Thalia in its horned talons and flying away into the darkness.

Chapter Twelve

*"*D*o not be afraid. No harm will come." Thalia's eyes fluttered open, and she found herself gazing into the pearlescent eyes of her prince. Once more his form was more of a ghostly mist than material. As he brushed his fingers along the crest of her cheekbone, he felt more like an icy breeze, and for a moment, Thalia was convinced that she was still there, cowering on that cliff face.*

"Am I dead?"

"Of course not," he replied. "You are very much alive."

"Then why are you here?" Her own voice sounded foreign to her ears. As if she were speaking through a murky sea. "Have you come for me?"

"I've come to tell you that all is not lost, little one. Things are not always what they seem."

"I don't understand."

"You will. Now. Open your eyes."

N o one could have been more surprised than Thalia was when she awakened, still alive. The last thing she remembered was the massive talons of the black dragon closing around her waist. After that, everything went dark. Dreams of the shadowed prince mixed with images of blood and death devoured her mind, keeping her in darkness. Thalia tried to sit up, but her shoulders screamed in protest. She was acutely aware of being cold. Looking around, she could make out dark, polished stone. She reached out, her fingers grazing the cool, wet surface. Was she somewhere underground? Her eyes focused, and she could just make out the outline of what appeared to be a boulder jutting out from the smooth wall. A cave then. And there must be water nearby. She could hear it dripping into a pool somewhere close. "Hello?" she called out. "Is there anybody there?" No one answered save for that steady dripping.

Slowly Thalia got to her feet. She brushed the dirt from her gown, glad to see it was still intact. There was no blood, and she did not feel any injury. Evidently the dragon had decided not to kill her just yet. Thalia would prefer that he just hurry up and get it over with. She did not fear death nearly so much as the anticipation of it. Finally confident on her feet, she decided she might as well explore.

The chamber where the dragon had apparently left her was enormous. As she looked up, she realized that she could not see the ceiling. Funny that a dragon would live in such a place as this. She walked on expecting to see a treasure room full of gold, but there was none. No treasure or piles of broken skeletons lying about. No stench of death. This was most unusual for a dragon's lair. Perhaps Tristan had been right. Perhaps this beast was no ordinary dragon. She passed a waterfall that emptied into a small pool. The water was so rich with minerals that it was thick and white like milk. Soon she came to a split in the cave wall. One passage was quite dark. The other was lit with a stream of light from above. *Perhaps this is the way out*, she thought. She continued down the path, relaxing as the air felt much lighter here. There was no trace of the sulfurous steam that so often accompanied dragons. After walking for what seemed like hours, she began to be aware that the path had turned and she was climbing. She could feel it in her thighs that ached with the exertion. "Where am I?" she wondered aloud. Finally, she turned a sharp corner, and the path narrowed to a marble corridor. The tiles were cold beneath her feet, and as she looked down, she could see her reflection in the polished stones. Perhaps it wasn't a cave after all. She came to a door, simple but sturdy. She expected it to be locked, but when she turned the knob, it opened easily.

As soon as the door opened, she could smell the dragon, an earthy scent like burning leaves. It was not unpleasant, but it filled Thalia with dread. She crept in as quietly as she could, wincing as the door creaked. She stepped into what appeared to be a ruined throne room. Charred tapestries hung from the frescoed ceiling. The floor had been inlaid with a jeweled mosaic that was tarnished and missing pieces. She had to be careful not to step on the jagged tiles with her bare feet. The forest floor had begun to take over with scrub weeds and tree roots coming through the crumbling stones. The only light was from a fire pit in the center of the room. And there, lying outstretched beside it, was the black dragon.

Thalia stopped short, her body still as stone. Had it heard her approach? Another beat and she could tell that it was sleeping. A great rumbling sound, almost like the purr of a lion reverberated off the walls. Its wings were folded around its body like a shroud, and its tail stretched out motionless behind it. Thalia almost laughed in spite of herself. This dragon looked like some great mastiff lying in front of a fireplace. "You certainly don't look frightening now," she whispered, stepping closer. If the room had been much smaller, the beast wouldn't have fit. It was clear from the crumbling walls to one side that he'd had some difficulty getting inside in the first place, and his body was stretched from one end to the other with only a little clearance over its head. She'd never seen a living dragon from this close before, and she had to admit she was curious. In the dark before, its scales had appeared quite black, but in the dim light of the fire, she could see that they were multicolored like the inside of an oyster shell. They sparkled in the dim firelight. Thalia wanted to touch them but was afraid of waking the wyrm. Would the scales feel wet or dry and coarse like a lizard?

The wind outside howled around the ruined turrets, and Thalia shivered as the cold seeped through the walls and into her bones. The fire had nearly died, and only a few embers still glowed. She hugged herself tightly in an effort to warm her body. It was of little use. She looked around for something to poke the fire. A loose branch hung down from a tree that had grown in through the wall. She tiptoed over, taking care not to step on the noisy, crackling leaves underfoot. She stretched for the branch, but it was just out of reach. Thalia looked over her shoulder to make sure the dragon was still sleeping. "Just one... little... jump," she said with a leap. She grabbed the branch and pulled it down. Unfortunately, her weight wasn't quite enough, and the flexible branch snapped backward, smacking Thalia in the nose and making her sit down hard on the stone floor. "Shit!"

"Are you having difficulties, little mouse?"

Thalia froze. She gripped the branch in her hand, prepared to use it to defend herself. She was afraid to turn around as the only other living thing in the room was the dragon. "Uhm... well... I..." She tried to get to her feet, slipping on the leaves and pebbles and sitting down again. "Ouch," she muttered.

"Come into the light, Mouse," it growled. Thalia heard a great rustling and thump that she could feel in the floor underneath her. Slowly she turned to see the dragon standing up, stretching like a large cat and shaking the sleep from its head. It even yawned with a rumble like thunder. "Don't be afraid. You're far too small to satisfy an appetite such as mine."

Thalia stood up and walked slowly toward the beast, dragging her branch behind her. Now that she had it, she realized that it was much too flimsy to do any real damage. Or indeed to stoke the fire. "You talk?"

"Don't you hear me speaking?" the dragon replied. It sat low on its haunches watching as Thalia crossed the room.

"Yes, but... I..."

"You didn't know dragons could speak. Common mistake. It's true that *most* dragons can't speak, but I am not most dragons." Thalia could feel herself beginning to smile, and she bit the inside of her cheek. How odd for a creature such as this to be arrogant. Arrogance was a human trait. She should have been terrified, but found she was only amused. "You find me amusing?" he said, plucking the thought from her brain.

"Well... I suppose."

"Don't suppose. You should be sure of yourself, Slayer of Tarkin." He spat these last words with a dose of venom that cooled Thalia's blood.

Thalia gasped, stopping short. How did he know? Her heart pounded in her chest as she realized that he had understood the game from the beginning, despite Tristan's best efforts. "You think I'm a dragonslayer?"

"I don't think it. I know it, silly mouse."

"But..."

"You slept for a long time. I had plenty of time for examination. You have scars along your back and side that suggest you've been scratched by talons. I've never seen a bird so large as whatever got you. So you've fought a dragon before. On the inside of your thigh you have a healed-over burn that could only be from dragon fire. And, of course, you have the mark on your wrist."

Thalia's color deepened. "Perhaps I was attacked." She unconsciously put her hands behind her back. "And you can't blame me for wanting to defend myself."

"Do not lie, Mouse. It does not become you. But have no fear. I won't hold your past murders against you if you'll extend me the same courtesy. Now. Come here so I might see you better." As she approached, the dragon sniffed the air, taking in her scent. "Hmm... you smell of the Fae."

"Is that good?"

"I've no idea. Perhaps. Fae are very tricky. Ungrateful little beasties." He quieted, staring down at her with his head cocked to one side as if concentrating very hard. It made Thalia very self-conscious, and she shuddered again. "Are you cold, Mouse?" Not knowing what else to say, she nodded. "Well, why didn't you say so?" Without another word, he turned his head and breathed a plume of fire into the pit beside him. Immediately the coals inside ignited into a spectacular column of flame. Though she was afraid, Thalia moved closer in an almost involuntary movement. She was desperate to find warmth and held her hands out in front of her. "A thank you wouldn't be inappropriate," the dragon said.

"Oh," she said, feeling her cheeks blush hot with embarrassment. "Thank you."

"No need to be embarrassed. You are, after all, the slayer of Tarkin and not used to being gracious to dragonkin."

"You said yourself that you're no ordinary dragon." It was a bit disturbing that he could almost hear what she was thinking. She made a note to ask him about it later if she lived that long. Thalia had never encountered a dragon that could read minds.

"Indeed, I am not." He settled back down with a lazy sigh. Thalia stared at the enormous creature. He was definitely the largest dragon she'd ever seen. And certainly the most intelligent. She'd never encountered one that could speak, much less one schooled in etiquette. Now that the fire was high, she could see the dragon and was fascinated by its body. Glints of color shimmered on his scales in the changing light, but they did not look wet. Underneath, they lightened to the color of ashes, but there was a dim illumination visible beneath the armor. It must be burning beneath the skin. Perhaps this was where he drew his fire from. As she drew closer, she could see that his wings were like those of a bat: leathery with a hard ridge of veins that extended from the sharp talons. A number of horned protrusions highlighted his sharp, serpentine face that was surprisingly expressive. Suddenly, he opened one enormous eye and stared at her. Thalia could actually see the muscle in his eye expand and contract as it focused on her. She got the distinct impression that he was staring as his eye narrowed and his entire body stilled. Finally, he spoke. "Do you plan on standing there gawking at me for the rest of the night?"

"Well... I really just..."

"Or perhaps some tiresome escape attempt?"

"Of course not!" she replied a bit too quickly.

"Well, that's probably wise. No one will come any closer to Gwynfir than Isling. And your own sovereign has already decided your fate."

"What do you mean?"

The dragon sat up once more on his haunches and yawned with a rumble she could feel in her own chest. "Surely you're familiar with *Sheakhol*. That ridiculous sacrificial rite you were subjected to."

"Of course I am," she said with an air of superiority. "The spell unites the dragon and his virgin bride."

"Poetic isn't it?"

"It's barbaric."

The dragon laughed, a deep gravelly tone that was both warm and frightening. "Humans are such delightful little hypocrites."

"What are you talking about?"

The dragon whipped around, stretching its long neck to curl around her body. "Did you think that I could not smell the hilt of my brother's dagger? That my keen eyes could not see it hidden in your skirts as you lay sleeping on the floor?" His teeth were much larger this close, and Thalia shuddered. She could smell the bitter scent of decay on his warm breath. "Do not think me a fool, dragonslayer!"

"Of course... I would never..."

"No," he growled, his enormous body slithering around her as she tried to back away. "You wouldn't."

"I only... I was chosen..."

"Chosen?" he asked.

"Yes. To be the sacrifice."

"And why is that, I wonder?" Thalia stumbled backward, falling over his massive tail and sitting down hard on the stones. "What makes you so special?"

"It was only coincidence."

"No such thing."

"My father was a great slayer of Tarkin, that's true."

"Ugh," the dragon scoffed with obvious exasperation. He lay down once more. "Boring."

"Pardon?"

"Your ridiculous lies and tricks. They won't work. I'm not some mindless reptile skittering along the stones at Thane. Tristan was obviously trying to use *Sheakhol* to lure me into the city so I'd take his little dragonslayer to my lair where she would, in turn, slaughter me while I was vulnerable. Am I wrong?"

"I..."

"Of course not. So here you are. The only thing I haven't figured out is why you haven't tried to use your dagger yet."

Thalia gathered her courage. It was the only way she was going to survive this ordeal and get back home. Home. The thought of Esa and her warm fire pit made fresh tears spring to Thalia's eyes. "Perhaps I'm just waiting for the opportune moment."

"Perhaps *I* am," he said with a grin that showed all of his teeth. His meaning was not lost, and Thalia recoiled. He laughed a great, growly noise at seeing her bravery fall short. "Not to worry, Mouse. I'll not be eating you today."

"But why not?"

"You'd prefer to be eaten?"

"Well... no. But what makes me so special?"

"I'm a Dragon Lord. I don't have to explain myself to one so lowly."

Thalia narrowed her eyes. "Lowly?"

He turned that great reptilian head toward her again. He seemed to be examining her body language. Studying her reactions. "Surely you don't think yourself greater than I." The dragon raised up to his full height and spread his wings. The ends of his horns brushed against the impossibly high ceiling, and his claws left deep cracks in their wake. "My strength surpasses any force imaginable! My breath of fire can raze even the greatest of kingdoms to the ground. My wings can shake the very foundations of the earth with the slightest gesture! My mind is so keen that it can pluck the thoughts from your head. I can see your past, present, and future. This is why you are lowly, Mouse. Humans are merely food. Or pets."

Thalia lay on her back before him, propped on her elbows and staring up at him with awe and terror. He could crush her with a mere flick of his talon, but she dared not show fear. "Your arrogance is quite a performance, my lord."

"You would do well to watch your tongue," he snarled. "Lest your words be carved upon your tomb." Thalia stood up, her heart pounding as she brushed the dirt from her gown. She was fascinated, watching the muscular frame move beneath the iron scales that slipped over one another. She could see that he had a deep wound between his shoulder blades that had begun to weep blood down his back.

"You've hurt yourself," Thalia murmured, hugging her body to try and keep warm in this dank, dark place.

"It will heal," he growled. "It would take more than the impotent blade of my brother to kill me."

"Brother?"

"Oh yes... the great Tristan of Osghast is my brother. My father, believing me a monster, cast my body out. It was only by the mercy of the Fae that I survived. If you can call being forever banished from the world, cloaked in a sheath of scales and horns mercy."

"If he is your brother... surely he will..."

"What? Show mercy? Take me into the kingdom as his equal?" he roared, turning on her with a dexterity that frightened her. "Your naïveté is charming, Mouse. My brother and father cast me out, and now I will take my vengeance upon them!"

"And what of the people? Those innocents of Osghast..."

"Those innocents who would chain a lone, terrified maiden to the rocks to either be eaten by a hungry dragon or slowly die as the cormorants feast upon her wind-burned flesh in the slimmest hope that they might save themselves!"

"They were frightened!"

"They are weak!" the dragon shrieked, startling her. "They fear what they do not understand, and that makes them dangerous. Better that I rid the world of their ineptitude. Your people... the kingdoms of men. They are a virus! A plague upon this earth that should be eradicated." The dragon bowed down on his haunches until he was staring into Thalia's eyes. The fire and ice intensity of his gaze burned into her, and though she was afraid, she could see something there. Something lurking beneath that was so human and familiar. But that was impossible. "A cleansing fire could be the medicine this land so desperately needs."

"There are good people there," she said, trying to hide the tremble in her voice. "You are a Dragon Lord. You could guide them..."

"To what end? Do you know why it would be pointless for you to run away, little one? Not because I would stop you."

"I wouldn't..."

"Surely you realize that should you escape, no one in the whole of Osghast would offer you friendship or shelter for fear of incurring the wrath of the Dragon Lord. In fact, if you were found, the citizens of

Osghast would throw your body on a blazing pyre to await the lord that would come to feast upon your bones. You see, *Sheakhol* doesn't just attract one particular dragon, it attracts many."

Thalia's heart pounded in her chest, and she abandoned all hope of hiding her fear as the dragon's body slithered around her like a serpent. "I... I don't wish to escape..."

"Go ahead! Run!" he shouted, his growling voice echoing off the stone walls until bits of the crumbling fresco fell at their feet.

"Please, my lord...," she whimpered.

"What are you waiting for? Run, tiny mouse! Run for your life!" His massive foot stomped the ground, shaking the room.

"No," she cried. The hot sting of tears wetted her eyes and soon they would fall. "I won't run."

"No," he said finally, his voice quieting. "You won't. These good people you speak of would beat you to a pulp and drag you to Prince Tristan and his idiot magician. These *good people* are cowards. Only looking after their own hides!" And now his voice seemed full of tears and loathing. "How else could they cast out one of their own? Even a dragon cannot be so cruel!"

"I... I'm sorry." She reached a shaking hand out to touch the leathery scales. He narrowed his eyes, watching in disbelief that she would dare.

The dragon turned away, folding his wings behind him. "Go. You will find appointments for one more... human. Up the stairs."

"But I..."

"Go!" he roared. "Out of my sight!"

Gathering her skirts, Thalia did the only thing she could. She ran.

Chapter Thirteen

❦

"What were you thinking?" Christophe shouted. He turned on Grafton. "It was you! You put him up to this!"

Grafton shook his head, fearing this old man who had suddenly been invigorated with rage. "Sire, you can't possibly believe that I would have purposefully tried to hurt the people of Osghast!" Grafton bowed and sniveled to him, practically kissing the old man's slippers. "My only intention has ever been to help you, my king."

"It seems you missed the mark. A dragon in Thane! The tower destroyed! Nearly a hundred dead! An innocent maiden from Tarkin thrown to the crags!" He whipped around, turning on Tristan. He stood there with arms crossed next to the fireplace. He didn't seem bothered by any of the events of the last several hours. "Is this how you intend to save our people, Tristan?"

"Father," the prince began. Honey dripped from his lips. Tristan had been manipulative since he was a boy. "Nyxyn thought that the dragon might be satisfied with a sacrifice. The way our ancestors dealt with these beasts."

"A magician? You thought a magician and his parlor tricks might deal with a dragon? Have you completely lost your mind?"

"Father, he assured myself and Grafton that he could stop the dragon! What would you have us do?"

"Keep my counsel in those matters of which you know nothing!" Christophe spat. The old man was quivering with restrained anger. His silver hair hung in sweaty tendrils, and his eyes were bloodshot. He turned on Grafton. "You! Out of my sight. Scuttle back to your gypsy shithole before I have you arrested for abetting this mess!"

Grafton gave a short bow and cast a livid glare toward Tristan. "As it pleases you, sire."

Christophe watched as the minister left, practically shuffling along the floor like the snake his personality so heartily emulated. How Tristan had allowed himself to fall in with the likes of Grafton. The man would betray them at the first opportunity. Such foolishness only strengthened his resolve not to retire as his son would wish.

"You shouldn't let this upset you so, Father. Your heart..."

"Yes, son. My heart is broken to think that my own flesh could be so stupid!"

"Father!"

"Yes. In trying to show our strength, you've made us a joke amongst every kingdom on the continent! And that's not the worst of it!"

"Oh please..."

"Oh yes, my son. Once word reaches Tarkin that a slayer has been sacrificed, what do you think they'll do? It will be an invitation for open rebellion!"

"Then let it come!" Tristan shouted. "The people need an example!"

"The people need a strong leader!"

"And who will lead them, Father? You? You're an old man, pining for a lost love like a pathetic adolescent. The last several months you've barely gotten out of your chair except to piss into the fire!"

"I didn't raise my son to talk to me this way," Christophe mumbled. When he looked into Tristan's eyes, he could see the hatred there burning brightly. It had always been so. When he was a boy, Christophe had tried to love him, but whenever he had gazed into his child's face, all he could see was Katrin. Tristan was a constant reminder of Christophe's sins. His birth had crippled their relationship from the start. As an adolescent, Tristan had been desperate to win his father's approval, but nothing had ever been enough. No matter what he did, Tristan could never bring his mother back. Soon after, the boy had stopped trying.

"You think Grafton is a revolutionary? Perhaps he is! Perhaps he and his kin will lead the way toward an open war we will not win! Show him that we will not stand for it, Father!"

"You are blinded by your thirst for power, Tristan. You will be king someday, but you are not ready!"

"And when will I be ready, Father? When there is no kingdom left to rule? Perhaps this is all your doing, Father! Perhaps it is *you* who is in league with the dragon!"

Christophe fell silent for a moment. Tristan's words had taken him aback. His mouth worked as if he were searching for the right words and falling short. "You've no idea what you're talking about! The past is full of old ghosts that you could not possibly understand."

"I went to see her, Father," Tristan spat. "The Fae within the Dark Forest..." Christophe turned, and for a moment, he could not speak. How much had Mab told him? This secret, their family's poison boil, had been bubbling under the surface far too long. "She said she knew you. That you had brought this upon us."

"Tristan..."

"No! Just tell me the truth!"

"Your mother," Christopher said. "She could not conceive, and Mab was the only hope we had to secure Osghast's future. She promised to help us, but fairies cannot be trusted. They are fickle friends. I had no idea what evil would befall us."

"Don't you *dare* blame my mother for your treachery!"

"My son... I tried to spare you this. But what's done is done. Leave the dragon be!"

"Leave him be! You killed my mother! Just as sure as if you'd run her through with your blade!"

"Tristan," Christophe gasped. "You must believe me. I did not know what was going to happen! I was desperate."

"This is why you've hated me! My whole life you've been the specter at the feast, lurking in shadows. You knew! You watched the towns burn one by one!" With every word, Tristan became more furious, backing his father against the wall. "You let our people die to protect your lies!"

"I've never... *hated* you, my son." Christophe reached for him, desperate for his forgiveness. He knelt as his feet, taking his hands as if desperately trying to hold on. The realization that Tristan thought—had always thought—that his father hated him was too much. "Everything I've ever done was to protect you. Your mother... she wanted a child so badly. And I needed an heir. I loved her, Tristan. I could never deny her happiness."

"So you made a deal with that Fae whore!"

"Believe me, son. I never imagined that Mab could be so cruel." He bowed his head. "That she would cause such misery. We were friends. I'd known her since I was a child. I trusted her! Your mother tried to warn me. She sensed that something was wrong, but I was too foolish to listen." Christophe broke down, crying openly at Tristan's feet. "Please, my son... please forgive me..." As he looked down on the old man, the prince felt nothing but loathing. His weakness ran so deeply that it outshone all else. "You're right, Tristan. I killed her with my lust and greed..."

"So what she told me is true? The dragon... it's my brother. My twin."

Christophe nodded, sobbing into his son's hands. "Gods help us, it is. The dragon is your brother."

Tristan shook his head, bringing Christophe's hands to his lips. "Rise, Father," he said, kissing the back of his father's knuckles gently. "Please... it is I who should be asking your forgiveness." He helped the old man to his feet and pulled him into a tight embrace. "I've been a fool." As Tristan held him, Christophe could feel the tension still there in his son's embrace. The hatred and greed that rolled off him in waves. "For not seeing what you really were."

"Tristan!"

The sharp blade slid between the king's ribs easily. White hot pain exploded in his side, and instinctively he tried to pull back, but Tristan held him tight. He wanted to scream for help, that his son had taken leave of his senses, but it was no use. The tip of Tristan's dagger pierced his lung, and no air could escape. The blood was already blossoming hot and wet from the wound. Christophe could already hear it dripping to the floor in a viscous syrup. "A groveling, impotent...," Tristan hissed, twisting the dagger so that it tore through organs and tissue. It was indeed an effective weapon. "...coward," he whispered, kissing his father's cheek as he let him down slowly.

"Long live the king."

Chapter Fourteen

Thalia burst through the first door she reached at the top of the ruined staircase. To her surprise, there was a bedchamber there. It was old and strewn with cobwebs as if it had been frozen in time and a transparent, shimmery cloth had been laid over everything. She could smell decaying flowers and the sharp stench of charred wood. An old fireplace, cold and full of ancient ashes dominated one side of the room. In the center was a large bed with the charred remains of drapes hanging around it. The coverlet was covered with dust, but Thalia could tell that it had once been magnificent. Like everything in this place, it told the tale of a lavish past. She'd never seen anything like it. Even before her life as a slayer with her tribe in Tarkin, Esa's cottage had been no palace. It was cozy and warm. In fact, she thought that someday she'd like nothing more than to spend the rest of her days there, but there was nothing lavish or resplendent about it.

"This doesn't make any sense," she said aloud as she wandered around the room. "No one has lived in these ruins for a thousand years."

"On the contrary. It's been more than two thousand." Thalia turned to see a chambermaid standing in the doorway. "But time doesn't mean much in this place." As the maid came into the light, Thalia was struck by her extraordinary beauty. Delicate features adorned pale alabaster skin. Every movement was a graceful dance as she moved across the room. She was familiar, but Thalia could not place her. Surely she would remember someone like this maid. "Does my appearance frighten my lady?"

"No," Thalia stammered. "I was... I was frightened... yes. But only because..."

"I know. Malik can be frightening. Of course, he's really just all bluster and arrogance. He's really not so bad once you get to know him."

"And you know him I suppose?"

The girl chuckled. It was a pleasant, tinkling sound that immediately made Thalia smile. "As much as anyone can know a dragon." The chambermaid began fluttering around the room brushing the dust and grime from the furniture and opening drapes. Golden light pushed through the gloom, and Thalia began to relax. Everything looked better in the day. "You've very pretty."

"Pardon?"

"You. You're very pretty for a sacrifice."

Thalia blushed. "I'm not sure what you mean."

The maid laughed. "It's just that I would not expect Tristan to give over such a pretty maiden to a hideous creature. In ancient times *Sheakhol* was really just a means to get rid of the poisoned lines. The deformed, prisoners, the mad. Of course, the Dragon Lords of old didn't care much. They only meant to devour them. The meat of a lunatic was just as tasty." Thalia felt her stomach turn. It didn't surprise her that Tristan would throw away those he deemed unworthy. She could sense an inherent evil in the boy who was so hungry for power over Osghast. What others might mistake for nobility, Thalia had known instantly was twisted avarice.

"So I am to be devoured?"

The maid chuckled again. "Heavens no, child. Malik would sooner destroy the spires of Heaven than hurt you, my lady."

"Malik?"

"The Dragon Lord. It is his name. Malik. Of course, he has a longer, Draconic name, but it would not be pleasing to your tongue, I'm afraid. At any rate, he will not harm you."

"Then why am I here?"

The maid did not answer but went back to her work. Thalia decided she'd probably rather not have that question answered just yet anyway. She wandered over to the window just uncovered by the chambermaid. It looked down over an overgrown courtyard that had once been a vast garden. The skeletal remains of rose vines and ivy crept over the stonework crumbles. An enormous oak tree bowed under the weight of a wisteria vine and its own branches that bent toward the ground. Thalia leaned against the frame and stared down at this secret wonderland that lay far below.

Thalia closed her eyes, and for a moment, she could see what it had been like before. Flowers bursting in a spectacular show of color, golden leaves of autumn trees that hung overhead and were strewn along the ground like a magnificent carpet. She could see herself there, reclining on a soft bed of heather with the warm breeze against her cheeks. And laughter. She could hear the infectious laughter of children carried on that breeze. And another an octave below. Then she could see them: a boy and girl, twins with hair like a raven's feather and eyes like fire and ice. It was a merry chase that ended when they saw her lying there. "Mummy!" they cried. "Come save us from the dragon!" Then another burst forth from the hedgegrow. A dark prince with cool eyes and a laugh that both taunted and comforted. He caught the girl child and swung her into his arms, kissing her cheeks until she could scarcely breathe.

"Oh my darling one," he said. "There is no escape!"

"This place was beautiful once, wasn't it?" Thalia said, snapping back to reality. The vision had left her breathless. She could still feel the soft heather in her hands.

"There is beauty in decay, don't you think?"

"Well, yes. That's not what I mean... this castle. It was beautiful, wasn't it?"

The chambermaid shrugged. "I suppose it was in its day. But that was long ago, mistress. Only the shell remains." The maid clapped her hands. "There. That's much better now."

Thalia turned to see that the room had been completely transformed. The silken coverlet and drapes were no longer charred but looked as good as new. A roaring fire burned in the hearth, and a vase of fresh roses and lilies had appeared on the dressing table by the bed. It was as if the room had suddenly been brought back to life. "How... what did you do?" she breathed.

The chambermaid smiled. "Funny how the light changes things."

"The light?" Thalia shook her head as if trying to clear it. Clearly the excitement of the day was wearing on her. It simply was not possible for a ruin to become a queenly bedchamber in a few minutes' time. There was very definitely something strange going on. "I think..."

"Here now," the girl said, taking her arm and leading her over to an armchair by the fire. "Just sit down and relax a bit. We'll need to get you out of that ragged gown and into something warm. I'll make you a cup of tea and then draw you a hot bath."

"I don't understand... this castle. These ruins. They were abandoned when the first of the Laurenz line was betrayed by the Dragon Lord of Gwynfir. How is it that this room is untouched?" She sat down in the offered chair and stared into the fire. "What sort of witchcraft is at play?"

The chambermaid smiled and brushed Thalia's hair back from her face. "All in good time, my lady. For now, just accept what is and rest yourself. My master would not like it if I let you get yourself worked up." Thalia wanted to say more, but suddenly she was so tired she couldn't think. A gentle ache settled behind her eyes, and she closed them. "That's it, my dear," the maid said. "Rest yourself now. I'll fetch you a nice cup of tea. Everything is made better with a good cup of tea."

*"*It's kind of ugly isn't it?*"*

"Malik!" Bella exclaimed, jerking the baby away from him. "Don't be rude!"

"Well it is! Look at its scrunched-up face. And it smells!" As if to emphasize his point, he pinched the end of his nose.

"She. Not it," Bella explained for the thousandth time. "You should never call a little girl 'it.'"

"It doesn't understand me," the boy grumbled, throwing a stone into the rushing brook. He was obviously bored of sitting here in The Veil looking at the baby. Bella could tell. Malik longed to be a child like the ones he watched from afar, loved and beautiful, but he was an angry child. He often let his dragon side take over, and his temper was ferocious. Here in the moonlight, Bella could offer him the illusion of beauty but nothing more. Consequently, he hated it. "What did you bring it... her here for anyway?"

"The poor thing was abandoned. Her mother died in childbirth, and her father cast her out." Bella cast a sideways glance in his direction, noting the boy's remorse that was evident in the slump of his shoulders. He'd been cast out by his own father. "You wouldn't have me leave her in the forest to die, would you?" Malik shrugged and stalked back to where his fairy guardian sat by the stream. He peered over her shoulder and down at the tiny girl child. "Perhaps one day she'll make a merry playmate for you."

"She's human, Bella. She'll be afraid. You know she will."

"Not here." Malik stuck his tongue out at the baby, making a silly face and growling playfully. To his surprise, she giggled and reached out for him. "See. I think she likes you."

"Maybe." The little one laughed at his voice again and reached out to touch him, but he shied away. "No, baby," he scolded. "Don't you know that humans can't touch dragons?"

She squealed and reached for him again. This time her movement was so violent that Bella stumbled, losing her grip on the baby. Malik was quick, grabbing the child's arm to keep her from falling. Bella gasped, bracing herself for the screams that would surely come. Dragonkin were hot. The fire boiling beneath their skin would blister delicate human flesh. But it never came. In fact, the only sound was the child's cooing.

When he jerked his hand away, Bella examined the spot. "Unbelievable," she whispered. There was no blistering, but a small brown mark that looked like flames curled around the baby's wrist.

"Did I hurt her?" Malik croaked. "Is she all right?"

Bella nodded. "Yes... I'm not sure how..." Evidently Bella's bewildered expression was wildly amusing for the child, and she began to laugh in earnest, tiny tears spilling over her cheeks. Soon Bella and Malik were laughing with her. The baby reached for Malik again, and this time Bella handed her over, carefully setting the infant in his arms.

At first he seemed almost afraid of the child, but soon he was holding her close and staring down at her. Almost spellbound by her beauty.

"It's all right. I won't tell anyone how the terrible dragon fell in love with a human baby," Bella teased.

Malik paid her no mind. He was too mesmerized by her eyes and the round bow of her mouth when she yawned sleepily. "I think I'll call you Thalia," he whispered. "It means fearless."

⁂

Belladonna started down the staircase, making sure that the door to Thalia's room was closed behind her. It would do no good to get lost in her memories today. There was work to be done and not much time to do it. As she continued down, the decay melted away like a wax candle in the sun. As she passed through corridors, the worn tapestries and faded drapes shimmered and repaired themselves. The sconces along the walls breathed to life, illuminating the castle and chasing away the gloom. The crumbling stones and mortar began to slowly heal, blocking out the light that shone through the broken chinks. It was as if she were breathing new life into the place with a brush of her fingertips.

Bella shivered as she entered a vast hall. The rugs on the floor were moldy and so distorted with dust that their patterns were obscured. The walls were crumbling, and the coals in the fire pit were almost nothing. There was also a very noticeable hole through which the dragon was able to enter and exit. He'd obviously been here; she could still smell the sooty scent of his scales. She continued out of the castle and onto the rocky cliff face into which this part of the castle had been carved. Looking down she could see his long, glistening form sunning himself on the rocks below the waterfall.

"A dragon caught off his guard is often a dead dragon," she called as she wandered down the stone steps to the stream below.

"I'm not worried," Malik growled, rolling over in the grass and tumbling into the stream. He disappeared beneath the surface for a few moments and then popped up again, blowing a spume of water from his nostrils and shaking his head. "Why are you here?"

"No reason, really. I just came to check on our new charge." She sat down on the grass and dangled her feet in the cool water.

"*Our* new charge?"

"Well, of course. I didn't want to refer to Thalia as *your* prisoner."

"She's not my prisoner," Malik replied, striding through the water. "I'm only keeping her here until it is safe for her to return to her home in Tarkin."

"And how long will that be?"

Malik growled, tiring of the fairy's endless questioning. "Until the people of Osghast are no longer under obligation to feed her to any traveling firebreathers."

"That could be decades, Malik."

Malik rose out of the water once more and heaved his great body up onto the shore. He stretched his wings and fluttered them until they were dry, spraying the fairy. "Was there some purpose in coming out here to bother me?" He raised his head, narrowing his massive eyes to stare at the ruined castle that seemed to be slowly repairing itself. "What have you done, Belladonna?"

She followed his gaze and shrugged. "Just tidying up a bit."

"I don't *want* it tidied up a bit," he snarled.

"Funny, I didn't ask you," Bella replied. "But you're welcome." She watched as the dragon moved with a grace reminiscent of the man underneath. "I actually came to thank you, Malik."

He chuckled. "Thank me? Whatever for?"

"For bringing Thalia here. For not letting her fall into Tristan's clutches."

"You knew I wouldn't," he replied, his voice gruff and bordering on dangerous. "You knew that I couldn't."

"We are all ruled by destiny. Even creatures like us." Belladonna rose and went to him. He bowed his head and allowed her to stroke his rough, scaled skin. "Her being chosen was not just coincidence. The Fates have more in store for you yet."

Malik laughed heartily this time. "I would rather those fickle bitches just be through with me, if it's all the same."

"You don't mean that."

"Don't I? What difference does it make if this woman has been brought here on purpose? Tristan wishes her to kill me in my sleep in exchange for being his queen. Humans are hungry for power. Even with all the magic in your arsenal, Bella, could you sway her from this path? And even if you could, look at me. What would she want with a grotesque and foul creature like me?"

"She can see your true face, Malik. I believe that."

"Even in Faerie she is afraid. Always, my human form fades with her touch, falling into ash before her. She is not of the Fae; therefore, your illusion is thin." His expression was so full of despair that Bella's heart felt heavy at seeing it. "She thinks it is only a dream. Why not just let her keep that?"

"There is more to Thalia than meets the eye, you know. She has a magic all her own."

"Whatever you say," he sighed, clearly tiring of their conversation.

"You doubt me?" She chuckled to herself and began to pace. "Remember when you first saw her? She was able to touch you."

"So?"

"So, don't you think that's a bit of a coincidence? Perhaps there's something more to her. Maybe she's the key to breaking Mab's curse! Magic, even Fae magic, is all about balance. If Mab can turn you into this creature, then there has to be a way to reverse it. Aren't you even the least bit curious?"

He turned away and rose up on his back legs, spreading his wings. "She is human. She cannot dwell in our world, Bella. And in this world, I am a monster. I could be her pet at best. She thinks I'm just an animal."

"She doesn't know what to think."

"No! I won't get my hopes up for something that cannot be. And all of your illusions and hopeful magic tricks aren't going to fix it."

"But Malik..."

"Keep her safe," he said and took wing, streaking across the sky to disappear in a wisp of cloud and smoke.

Chapter Fifteen

Strangely, the chambermaid had been absolutely right about the tea. As soon as Thalia drank it, a calm had descended. Her eyelids felt heavy as she made her way across the room. She was almost afraid to touch anything. Surely the furnishings were ancient and moldy. They would crumble in her hands, but the bed looked so inviting with its soft coverlet and piles of cushions. She pushed back the drape and lay down across it, sinking into the comfort of the feather mattress.

Thalia wanted to sleep. More than she ever had before. Not really because she was tired, but because she wanted to shut out all that had happened. The chambermaid had offered some comfort that the dragon would not harm her, but he had said himself that she could not leave. Was she to live in this strange fortress forever? She longed to go back to the warm hearth in Esa's modest cottage. She could make herself content to live forever in the tiny village of Isling, a midwife or healer. Perhaps even find a suitable mate and raise a passel of children. It was a safe and ridiculous fantasy that she knew would never satisfy her. One thing was certain: she could not go home now and probably never would. She would be trapped like a princess in a tower like in those horrible fairy stories she had loved as a child.

She closed her eyes, and Tristan's face swam into view. It wasn't an unpleasant face, and in another time and place, she might even have found him handsome. He had promised to make her his queen if she could bring down the dragon. Would he come to rescue her? Did she even want him to? There was something about him. His eyes were so cold and hollow. There was a greedy sort of evil lurking behind them that was dangerous. He was obviously desperate for power, but to what end? Thalia slapped her hands over her eyes as if she might chase the vision of the spoiled brat prince away. Suddenly his eyes were distorted, morphing into the gaze of her prince. He stared intently back through Tristan's eyes until finally the image shattered in a plume of smoke and fire that made Thalia gasp. "None of this is real," she whispered to herself as she surrendered to sleep.

⚜

"I thought I told you to stay away." Thalia opened her eyes and found herself in the familiar grove where she'd met him so many times before. The dark prince stood at the edge of the trees, a dour and ominous expression casting shadows over his countenance.

"How could I?" she asked. She stepped closer, and he dissolved in smoke, reappearing behind her on the other side of the circle. "You are so much a part of who I am. I would sooner pull my beating heart through a jagged maw than stay away from you."

He laughed at her words, and the sound cut straight through her soul. "Pretty words, but they are meaningless, little one. Do as I say, and do not stray to this place again."

"But why, my lord? Why do you send me away?" This time when she approached, he was still. She was able to stand before him close enough to feel the heat that radiated from his body. "I have never been anything but a slave to your will. I have loved you—"

"No," he snarled. "You have loved an illusion. Thalia, you are a child, treading on dangerous dreams and unrealized lust. I will not trap you in my world of darkness."

Thalia stared around them. The lush green of the forest floor and the inky blue dark overhead. The stars that shone above cast their light through the trees and illuminated the ground with a thousand tiny sparks. "I don't under-

stand. This world is the only place... the only place I've ever felt love. Warmth."

"It is an illusion!" he roared. She cowered, falling to her knees before him. "You were a child, and I was lonely and looking for a playmate. I never meant..." He knelt in front of her, their eyes meeting. His sadness was evident, and Thalia wanted to reach for him. She dared not. The last time she had tried to touch him, he had left her. "I never meant to let you stay. I never meant to love you."

"I don't understand..."

"If you could see me, Thalia... really see me, then you would understand. Perhaps I should show myself, and that would turn you away."

"I could never turn away from you. Please... I need you. Just as I always have." She took his hand, and this time he let her. It was warm, then running hot until it was burning in her palm. Thalia stared down at it, watching as the skin blackened and fell away to reveal scales of burnished scarlet beneath. His hand grew and elongated, a birdlike talon emerging from the wrist.

"Is this what you wanted to see?" he hissed, pulling her close and whispering against the cuff of her ear. He drew the tip of his claw along her cheek and down the plump vein at her throat. "Will the illusion be shattered?" As he spoke, his body grew against hers until his size was overwhelming. "Will you be repulsed by my true face? Enough to let me go?" As she slid her hands over his shoulders and down his back, she could feel his cloak fall away and the leathery black wings emerge.

Thalia gasped, watching as the pale flesh of her prince cracked and dissolved to reveal the beast underneath. His body grew and contracted. She could hear the bones break and reset themselves in strange positions. His face, which had always been a comfort, morphed and changed. A grotesque distortion of massive teeth and horned protrusions. He opened his mouth to speak, but all he could do was roar. A lonely, angry hiss and rumble that filled her with dread and despair.

"Is this... what you wanted to see?" he roared. "Is this... face... what you love?"

"I... I don't..."

He bent down, knocking her backward with the sudden anger and intensity of his gaze. She crawled backward along the grass as he advanced, stalking her like injured prey. "No! You don't! Scutter away, tiny mouse! Run!"

"But I..."

"Go now!" he screamed, breathing fire in a ferocious burst over her head.

⚜

Thalia woke with a start, sitting up in the enormous bed. Her head ached terribly, and she put a hand up to block out the harsh light from the fireplace. She could smell something all over her clothes. Putting a sleeve to her nose, she inhaled deeply, and it was so overwhelming that she nearly gagged. Burning flesh. She had smelled it many times. It was the smell of a body that had been bested by a dragon. "But it was only a dream," she cried. Or was it? Everything was so real. The prince. The dark prince from her dreams that she'd known since childhood—could he really be...? She shook her head. The thoughts tumbling around in her mind were too much to process. He'd revealed himself to be the dragon. Or was her mind playing some trick? Perhaps the dragon, Malik, was just on her mind and had invaded her dreams. But everything had seemed so real. As if she really had been walking into Faerie like Esa said. But she feared this beast to whom she'd been given, and perhaps that fear had colored her dreams.

The dragon's roar sounded overhead, and she rushed to the window, seeing it burst from the trees below and into the sky. Higher and higher it climbed until she could see its silhouette against the moon just as it disappeared. "This... this cannot be," she whispered before bolting from the room.

Down the corridor she ran, round and round the spiral staircases of stone to the marbled floor below. Desperately, she looked around for a way out into the darkness. Suddenly, it was as if the whole expanse of the castle had shrunk to a tiny casket that smothered her. But everything had changed. Each hallway opened on to another and another. As if someone were deliberately trying to disorient her. Where once had stood a ruin of an ancient kingdom was now an opulent palace where mosaics inlaid with jewels and gold adorned the floor and brightly embroidered tapestries lined every wall.

"Hello!" she called, finally coming to a halt in a great room. "Please! Someone answer! I'm frightened!"

"What's all the shouting about?" Thalia turned, and the chambermaid was standing by the fire. She'd been sure the woman hadn't been there before.

"You!" she said stomping toward her. "You've done this!"

"Done what, dear? I'm afraid I don't understand."

"Don't play dumb. You're… you're doing something to me…"

"I have no idea what you're talking about, dear. The master asked that I look after you, and so I have." Thalia wanted to crush the tiny girl with her bare hands. She was being deliberately silly. "I've tidied up a bit, if that's what you mean."

"That is *not* what I mean, and you know it!"

The chambermaid chuckled softly and approached Thalia as if she might be a crazed dog. "You're very tired, miss. Just imagining things. Why don't you let me fix you something to eat?"

"The dragon. Where is he?"

"He comes and goes in his own time, my lady." Thalia shrugged off her hand and dashed from the room. "Miss! Come back!" the chambermaid called after her, but she had to get away. Anywhere but inside this claustrophobic bubble of confusion.

Chapter Sixteen

Thalia was breathless as she made her way through corridor after corridor, looking for a way out of the castle. She ran through what seemed to be an inexplicable labyrinth of twisting staircases and darkened halls until finally she came to a heavy oak door. With all her might, she pushed against it, heaving the door open with a groan. To her surprise, it opened onto an expansive garden. Probably the one she'd seen from her room above. Everything was overgrown: vines crawling along the ground and over stonework, the remnants of rose petals and leaves crunching underfoot, and angry-looking, gnarled branches reaching toward the broken stones. But in corners and small cracks, it appeared that this garden was coming back to life just as the house had done.

Thalia passed through an arbor with skeletal vines that snagged at her hair as she ran into the forest. The darkness descended around her as the canopy overhead deepened. She was suddenly overwhelmed with the distinct sense that she was no longer in control of her own destiny. It was a claustrophobic sensation, and she had to get away. Malik was right: no one in Osghast would offer her shelter, not even Esa. So there was really no use in running away, but it was too hard to breathe in the castle. It was ever-changing, like the stones themselves were some great beast, waking up after a long winter nap.

She ran down the tattered old path, the wind whipping at her cheeks. Overhead the sky had grown darker and finally broken open in a magnificent downpour. The rain mixed with Thalia's tears, wetting her cheeks and drenching her ragged gown until it was soaked through. The fabric was so heavy that she finally couldn't run anymore, and she ended up sitting down under a tree. For how long she sat, she couldn't be sure. The emptiness and sadness consumed her as she sat there in the mud. Never in her life had she felt so abandoned. Being alone wasn't anything new to Thalia. When her mother had died, her father had laid most of the blame on Thalia. He had barely acknowledged her existence, and she had lived in solitude until it had become an old friend. Only Esa had been there. And the dark prince. He'd always been there, haunting her dreams since she was old enough to have them. Her only real friend and now... she feared the worst.

The rain began to fall in earnest now, and the cold crept into her bones. Thalia stood, knowing that she had to make her way back to the castle. It had begun to get dark, and the ancient trees looked like gnarled old crones reaching out for her. She tried to keep her eyes focused on the ground as the rain dripped from the ends of her straggled hair and into her face. She wrapped her arms around herself in a tight hug, desperately trying to get warm. Lightning crashed, and a thin, spidery bolt struck the tree just ahead. Thalia gasped as a heavy, blackened branch fell at her feet. She could smell the sharp hint of fire, and it roused her from weakness. She broke into a run, sprinting through the woods. She could see the dark outline of the castle in the distance, but the path seemed to be moving away from it. Her feet pounded on the ground, and the scrubby underbrush tore at her feet and ankles until they were bleeding. Suddenly, she stopped to look around and realized that she was in exactly the same place she'd started. There was even a scrap of her dress caught on the stump where she'd been sitting.

"Damn you!" Thalia shouted at the sky, throwing her hands up and stomping the ground like a child having a tantrum. She didn't know who or what she was screaming at, only that she was violently angry.

She wanted to tear at her clothes and skin until the blood came. Something that would release the fear and anger that boiled in her blood. And now to make things worse, it was raining, she was cold, and she was lost.

"What is all the shouting about?" a low, rumbling voice inquired.

Thalia's head snapped up. The voice was all around her, and she could feel it in her chest. She recognized it at once as the dragon's. Had he been following her all this time? "Hello?" she whispered.

"You've ventured far from the castle, Mouse. Are you running away?" His voice trailed off in a loud yawn that almost made her smile. "Because that would be so tiresome."

"Where are you?" she called.

"Just ahead of you. Keep walking forward toward my voice." Thalia considered his offer. Was she sure that she wanted to get closer to him to avoid being lost? Perhaps lost was the best place for her. "Come on. The path you're on will only take you farther into the forest. Some say this place is enchanted by an evil fairy."

"What do you mean?"

"Well, you'll think you're moving forward when really you're only walking in circles until you're exhausted, and she can steal your soul."

Thalia walked slowly, trying to keep herself from making any noise. No point in announcing her arrival. "That's a silly story."

"Yes. A fairy has no use for your soul. Come closer, Mouse. I promise I've not led you here only to devour your bones."

"How can I be sure?"

"If I were going to eat you, I could have done it back at the castle. I prefer my meals warm anyway." Thalia followed the low rumble of Malik's voice to a clearing where he stood. Seeing him this way was far different than in the ruined hall. Here he looked majestic and much larger. His wings were unfurled as if he were about to take flight. "There you are, Mouse."

"Yes. I... was lost." She swallowed the tremble in her voice.

He hummed. "This forest is a strange place at night. I was about to come looking for you. You rather ruined my plans, I'm afraid."

"What?" She was taken aback at his matter of fact rudeness.

"Yes. I had planned a most spectacular hunt tonight from which I would probably not return for a season. But alas, someone had to save you."

"I beg your pardon!" Thalia snapped. "I don't remember being asked to come here."

"But you did volunteer, didn't you?" She started to protest, but a look into his face indicated that it was of little use. He knew all about Tristan's plan. There was no point in hiding it.

"Only to save the life of another."

"I see." He looked up into the sky above. The rain was beginning to slow, but the drops splashed against his scales and in his eyes. He shook his head, throwing a spray of water from his wings. "I don't like the rain. Do you?"

"Not always," she replied with a shiver. "It's very cold."

"Indeed. Let's get above it, shall we?"

Thalia looked around as if she were unsure that he was speaking to her. "What do you mean?"

As she approached, Malik bowed before her, stretching his winged arm out before her. "Climb on to my back, Mouse. Let us get away from this angry place."

"Uhm... I... don't..."

Malik laughed heartily, throwing his head back. "A dragonslayer who's never flown before? You are indeed full of mystery, little thing."

"It isn't natural for a person to fly."

Malik looked around. "Is there anything about this that's natural?"

"Well... no."

"Then let us enjoy the strangeness. Now, up you get." He tapped his talon on the ground in a show of mock impatience.

Thalia started forward, but hesitated as she reached his wing. "What... what if I fall?"

"Silly mouse. I won't let you fall. Come on, lest I think you're a coward."

"I'm not a coward!"

"Then prove it." He sighed and turned his head, waiting for her.

She bit her lip and put a slippered foot on one leathery wing. "Are you sure this won't hurt you?"

"I think I can withstand one tiny dragonslayer. Stop stalling. I'm getting wet."

Thalia nodded and stepped up, going down on her knees to climb precariously up the scaly arm to his elbow. She slipped once in the stream of rain that ran between his scales, but he straightened the wing and caught her. With a gentle shudder, he tossed her gently to his shoulder. "It will be most comfortable for us both if you sit in the valley between my shoulder blades."

"Do I just..." She shifted around, trying to find a position that would make her feel somewhat secure on this very precarious perch. "Like a horse?"

"If you like, but do hurry. The storm is getting worse." Finding that the girth of his serpentine neck was too great, Thalia finally lay flat on his back holding on to the ridges of bone that protruded across his shoulders. "Are you finally ready, Mouse?"

She took a deep breath, trying to swallow the shuddering that would be evident in her voice. "Wait... are you sure...?" But before she could protest, Malik shot from the ground and into the sky above them. His ascent was so fast that the inertia made her head ache and her body feel impossibly heavy. She began to fear that she would slide down the beast's spine and be launched into the abyss from the end of his pointed tail. "Stop! Wait! I'm going to fall!" she screamed, knowing he probably couldn't hear her.

Ever higher the beast ascended, through the rain and lightning toward the roiling of the storm clouds. "Don't look into the rain!" the dragon shouted, his gravelly tone carrying over the wind and thunder. Thalia put her head down, praying that her stomach would stop rolling over. The noise was incredible, so loud that for a moment she thought her head might explode. And then, everything was still. Slowly Thalia picked her head up just as they burst through the clouds and into the endless midnight blues of night above.

When she dared to look, Thalia opened her eyes to the magnificent view of the storm from above. She could watch the lightning bounce from cloud to cloud reminding her of two great deities conversing. The ice crystals kissed her cheeks as the cold air rushed past. The sensation was exhilarating. Malik stretched out, leaning into the wind. His muscular wings beat the air slowly and steadily, like a heartbeat. "It's so beautiful," she murmured.

The dragon hummed in agreement. "Hold on," he growled before twisting his body into an impossible spiral back toward the ground.

Thalia screamed, gripping the scales at the back of the dragon's shoulders. "Slow down!" she shrieked, squeezing her eyes shut. The dragon laughed against the wind, showing off his prowess as he pulled up at the last second, unfurling his wings to slow down and level out. "Don't do that!" she said when she caught her breath. "You'll kill us both."

"You have such little faith, Mouse."

"I make it a point never to trust a dragon."

"Perhaps that's where you've gone wrong."

Thalia began to relax a little, pulling her knees under her body and sitting up between the dragon's shoulders. She was able to throw her leg over one of the spines that protruded from the soft space where the wing joined his body. It offered some security. It was a bit like riding a big horse. They soared along with the updraft, sailing above the storm and into the night. Thalia's head felt light, and it was almost as if she were the one with wings. She couldn't help but smile. Never in her life had she felt so scared, delighted and utterly alive all at once. The mountains rose out of the mist, hulking dark shapes in the distance. "Where are we going?"

"Away from the storm and the interference of fairies," he replied.

Thalia laughed nervously. "Fairies?"

"Oh, don't we believe in fairies? Better not to say that aloud, lest they hear you."

Malik turned his body slightly, and Thalia gasped, clutching at his scales as best she could. He turned toward the mountains, seeming to fly into them. She squinted her eyes shut, not wanting to look as she was sure he was going to crash them into the rock face. But with an inhuman grace, he avoided it and flew between the mountains, twisting in and out amongst the peaks. When he evened out once more, Thalia caught her breath and tried not to sound as terrified as she was. "Fairies are ancient myths. There may be some truth to them, but I don't put stock in their power."

"Yet you have no trouble believing in talking dragons."

It did seem ridiculous. "Perhaps I should open my mind a bit more, my lord." Malik snorted in reply and began his descent into the mountains.

The forest where Malik landed was a lush green expanse of overgrown trees. At the center was a massive waterfall that emptied into a stream that snaked and wound its way around the mountain, presumably to join with the rushing river that surrounded the castle grounds. "Where are we?"

"Gwynfir," Malik replied, bowing low so that Thalia could slide down from his back. "A much more palatable environment for a dragon, wouldn't you agree?" The canopy overhead was thick with foliage, only allowing tiny slivers of moonshine to glisten among the leaves on the forest floor. Thalia felt very small, but she could understand why this place was a comfort to the dragon. The grove where he'd landed was open, and she could see the mouth of an enormous cavern that would lead into the base of the mountain, just behind the waterfall.

"It's beautiful here."

"And hidden. As I said, this place is devoid of magical interference." He turned, taking care not to swipe her with is tail as he walked toward the cavern. Thalia was so fascinated by the graceful, yet clumsy gait of the dragon that she stood there watching for several moments. "Come," he commanded. "My home is this way."

"Home?" she asked. "I thought the castle..."

He said no more, but she followed him into the darkness. As they entered the cavern, Thalia could hear the thunderous roar of the waterfall crashing against the rocks above them. She had, at first, been afraid that it would be completely devoid of all light once inside, but the gentle glow that came from within Malik offered some illumination until they entered a sort of antechamber. With a breathy whoosh, the dragon spat a ball of fire at a pit full of wood, much like the one in the Great Hall of the castle. Thalia shivered as the warmth rushed around her. The room glowed with the firelight. Polished stone floors and walls stretched so high that she could not see their terminus in the deep darkness. Hanging down were dripstones in shades of orange and red. The path continued, but Malik made no move to go farther, instead settling down.

"So... this is where you keep your treasure, is it?"

"I beg your pardon?" he asked with a yawn.

"Your treasure. Don't dragons hoard treasure? Gold? Something like that?"

"I think you've read too many stories."

"I just know dragons." Thalia wandered about the room, marveling at the way the chamber had been literally carved into the base of the mountain. "But I suspect you're no ordinary, mindless serpent."

"Indeed," he replied.

"So what is this place?"

"It was once an entrance to a kingdom of dark elves. They lived beneath the mountains in a vast network of caves. Some said that they were fairies that had been banished from Mab's court."

"Why were they banished?"

"Giving magic to the kingdom of men. Anyway, once they were turned out of Faerie, their hearts grew stony and cold. Twisted. So they fled into the mountains with their dark magic."

Thalia nodded. She had heard this story before. The women of her tribe had told it to them many times. "The birth of the Dragon Lords."

"Quite right, my lady."

"Is that what you are?" Thalia uttered the question before she could stop herself.

"I'm not sure," he replied.

He looked into her face, his enormous eyes focused on her so intensely that it made Thalia feel self-conscious and another curious sensation that up to now she'd only felt in dreams. It wasn't exactly fear, but it was something just as dangerous. Something sensual and warm. This beast seemed to know her. There was a familiarity there that she couldn't place, but it was there just as strongly. Something in the way he looked at her. It was very human, even primal. When he spoke so gently, she was almost sure they had met before. She shuddered at the strange thoughts rolling around in her mind.

"Why so silent? Does my grotesque visage still frighten you, Mouse?"

"No... I... I'm just cold," she replied, hugging herself. "And your face holds no fear for me now. I suppose for a dragon, you're quite... handsome."

"No need for flattery, Mouse," he huffed. "Come closer, then." Thalia chewed at her lip and shifted from one foot to the other. She was nervously pondering his command. Perhaps he'd brought her all this way only to devour her in peace. "I'm not going to hurt you. Come." Thalia slowly meandered to where he lay on the cold stone floor. He resembled a lion lying there, his head resting on a single winged arm. He took a deep breath, and she could see the narrow spaces between his scales glow red. His other arm he curled into his chest, making a small well where Thalia might lay. He beckoned her closer with a nudge of his muzzle, and she lay down. He curled around her body and pulled her in close to where she could feel the heat radiating from where his heart beat slow and steady in his chest. "I told you I was warm."

Thalia smiled and lay her head in the crook of his arm. "Thank you," she whispered. "This is much better." She could hear the steady thrum of the dragon's heart. It was relaxing, and she could feel her own pulse slow, matching time with his. "Why are you being nice to me?" she asked after a time.

"Why shouldn't I be?"

"Well, I thought that dragons were..."

"Evil? Vicious creatures bent only on destruction and feeding their insatiable thirst for blood and ash?"

"Well... not exactly. But I'm a dragonslayer."

Malik hummed in agreement. "So if given the chance, would you slay me?"

Thalia pondered his question. Wouldn't she? Thalia had been raised from a small child to be a slayer worthy of her lineage. Her father had been the greatest in their tribe. Everyone had known his name as the most fearsome slayer in the entirety of the continent. He'd driven the rogue lords into the mountains and killed off their reptilian offspring until the threat had nearly been eradicated. At least in the cities. Slaying was a part of her soul, but she was so intrigued by this Dragon Lord. There was something so human beneath the armored skin, and

Thalia wanted to know him. "No. As you've said, my lord, you are no ordinary dragon."

"I'm glad you noticed."

Thalia lay there silently for a time, the only sound the roar of the water and the dripping of the groundwater down the glassy walls. For such a dark and damp place, it was very warm here. "I cannot help feeling that we've met before. It's your voice, perhaps." She yawned, stretching out along the scaled forearm. "Like something from a dream." Her eyelids were so heavy. The fear and uncertainty had taken its toll, and now all her body wanted to do was rest. She was simply too exhausted to be afraid of the dragon anymore. "Tell me about you. How you came to be in the mountains."

"I'm afraid it isn't a very interesting story."

"Humor me, my lord."

"I'm told that women prefer stories about love and magic. I'm afraid my story is one full of hate. I'll not bore you."

"Please," Thalia murmured. She was so tired, and this was the first time in days she'd felt truly safe. "Tell me anything. Tell me a story."

The dragon snorted and let out a grumbling snarl as he stretched out. "If it pleases you," he began. "A sad story, perhaps. A story about two princes."

"Is there a princess?" Thalia whispered, barely conscious.

"No, a beautiful queen. A beautiful queen who loved her king well. For many years, they longed for a child. But the beautiful queen lay barren, and the king fell in love with another: a dark fairy of the forest. She begged her human lover to stay with her in Faerie and even tried to trick him into falling asleep in her bed of starlight, but the king would not forsake his queen. The fairy mistress was jealous, as are all Fae-kind, but knowing how much he loved the queen, she agreed to help him. With a bit of Fae magic, the queen finally conceived, and the whole of the kingdom was overjoyed. On the night the queen was to give birth, she was in great pain and out of her head with fever. Something was wrong. She could feel it."

"She knew about the fairy?"

"Perhaps. Dark magic was afoot, and the queen was afraid. Her husband tried to soothe her, but to no avail. The queen brought forth the first son, perfect and wailing. He was beautiful. Everything that the couple could have hoped for. But the spell had not finished its work just yet. In a rush of blood, the queen brought forth another son. The second child was grotesque and deformed. A serpent-like body covered with scales and bony spines worked its way out of her belly through a gash made by its terrible claws. When the king saw the creature, he was repulsed! Surely such evil did not spring from his loins. He cast out the beast, hurling it from the highest tower and into the sea below. But the king paid a terrible price for his fickle and shallow nature. His queen was dead, and he was left a bitter and lonely old man with only his baby son to console him."

"Such a sad story," Thalia murmured, laying her cheek against the rough scales of his shoulder. She could feel tears swelling in the corners of her eyes. "Whatever happened to the other prince? The one who was deformed?"

"They say he fled into the mountains. The Fae took pity on him, raising the young boy to be strong so that one day he might reclaim his birthright." Malik said no more, and Thalia didn't want to press. She was so very tired. She fell asleep listening to the rumble of the dragon's heart and the purring hum of his breath.

Chapter Seventeen

When Thalia awoke the next morning, she was tucked into the warm bed at the castle. The crackling of the fire and the smell of brewed tea and bacon forced her eyes open. How had she gotten here? She was sure that she'd gone to sleep cradled in the arms of her prince. No. That couldn't be right. It was Malik, the Dragon Lord to whom she'd been sacrificed. He had saved her from the storm and taken her back to his lair in the mountains. Hadn't he? Perhaps it had been another strange dream. Thalia seemed to have those more and more lately.

"Rise and shine, mistress!" Thalia sat up to see the chambermaid entering the room with a steaming silver tray. Her mouth immediately watered at seeing the source of the good smells that had pulled her from sleep moments before. A plate piled with bacon, fruit, and cheese sat alongside a pot of tea and a small saucer with biscuits and jam. More food than she'd eaten in ages. "I've brought you something to eat," the chambermaid said, setting the tray over her lap. "You look starved." She wanted to tear into the food and completely devour it like a starving lumberjack, but she forced herself to be delicate.

"Not starved, but definitely hungry," Thalia said around a mouthful of bacon. "I'm used to it. Not much time to eat when you're running for your life or sleeping in a field."

"Running for your life?"

"Mmmhmmm." She spread jam on one of the biscuits and shoved it into her mouth, savoring the sweetness of the preserves. Her eyes fluttered in absolute bliss. This was like the breakfasts that Esa had made for her as a child. "Slaying dragons is a dangerous profession."

"Oh... a dragonslayer? That's a bit awkward."

Thalia chuckled and nodded. "What's your name?"

"Bella, miss."

"I'm Thalia," she said, taking another sip of the tea. "This is perfect. Just the way I like it. A hint of cinnamon. My mother... well, she wasn't really my mother. But she raised me. She always put a little bit of cinnamon in the tea."

"Thank you, mistress. I mean, Thalia." The girl smiled and went to the wardrobe in the corner of the room. To Thalia's surprise, she pulled out yards and yards worth of expensive fabrics. These were not moth-eaten gowns from ages past but new gowns that looked as if they had been made just for her. "I took the liberty of digging out some old clothes for you. Thought you'd be tired of wearing that old thing." Thalia looked down at herself and was immediately mortified. The fabric that had once been white was now a dull shade of brown from the mud stains, and the hem was completely frayed. It had been a couple of days since the ritual, and she hadn't had a warm bath or clean clothes since. "I've also drawn you a hot bath." Thalia nodded and watched as Bella buzzed about the room. The dress she pulled from the wardrobe was much more extravagant than anything she'd ever seen. As she draped it over the chaise, Thalia noticed the intricate embroidery and jewels worked into the folds of fabric.

"I... That dress doesn't really seem... like me," Thalia stammered.

"Oh, it will be fine. Besides, it's all I could find on such short notice." Thalia finished choking down the last of her breakfast and allowed Bella to take it away before leading her into the bath. The room was warm, and a large tub sat atop a small pit of smoldering coals. Thalia tensed, thinking that it looked as if the chambermaid was about to throw her in a gigantic soup cauldron. "Come on, then."

Without a thought for her own personal vanity, she pushed the gown over her shoulders and let the ruined thing puddle around her feet. As a hunter who had spent most of her life in cramped tents with others, she had no qualms whatever about being naked in front of this chambermaid. Bella smiled, seemingly surprised at the girl's lack of modesty. She stepped into the tub and sank all the way under the steaming, aromatic water.

"There, now. Isn't that better?" Bella asked, handing Thalia a towel as she emerged, sputtering.

"It's warm," she coughed.

Bella gave a curtsey. "Good. Well, I'll just leave you to it, then."

"Wait," Thalia said, pushing her dripping tendrils away from her face.

"Yes, mistress?"

"What am I doing here?" Of all the questions she'd had burning on her tongue, this was the one that had been niggling at Thalia since her first meeting with the dragon. Why hadn't he just devoured her and gotten it over with? Why bother being nice to her or having this chambermaid offer her food and clothing? Could it be that he was just fattening her up like a witch from a children's story?

"The king of Osghast offered you as tribute to the Dragon Lord..."

"Thinking that I would either slay the dragon or he would devour me. Neither of which has happened yet. You seem to be going to an awful lot of trouble to create this illusion of decayed grandeur, and I'm just curious to know how long I have to live."

"There are many different sorts of tribute, love. I don't think you're going to be devoured anytime soon. If Malik were going to eat you, he's had plenty of opportunity."

"Then I ask again—what am I doing here? Because if I'm just here to wander around an old castle, I'd rather just go home and take my chances with the townsfolk."

Bella knelt beside the tub and laid a calming hand on Thalia's arm. "Just calm down, girl. We all have our parts to play—"

"And what's yours? This castle is a ruin! No one has lived here for two thousand years, yet in a day's time, you've managed to make it fit for a king! Tell me what's going on!" Thalia stood up, splashing water over the lip of the tub.

"All right, mistress... just sit." Thalia hesitated but finally lowered herself back into the tub. "You've been brought here for a reason. But not the reason you think. And not the reason that Tristan thinks."

"What do you mean?"

"I suspect you already know this for yourself, but Malik is no ordinary fire-lizard. Nor is he a Dragon Lord."

"Then what is he?"

Bella paused and hung her head. "He is a prince of Osghast."

The laughter bubbled up from her belly in an uncontrollable wave until Thalia was gasping with it. Had she really heard Bella correctly? Imagine that... a dragon being the king of Osghast! "What are you talking about?"

"It's true," Bella hissed. "He was cursed by the Fae at birth! Cursed to be a monster that would be the embodiment of the jealousy harbored by Queen Mab!"

Thalia's laughter dried up, and she could only stare at Bella for several moments until finally she shook her head. "This is ridiculous," she started, rising from the tub and stumbling into the bedchamber. "I can't believe I've stayed here so long," she mumbled to herself as she pulled on the simplest of Bella's offerings. She wasn't going to sit there and listen to the ridiculous fantasies of chambermaids. The Fae were not real, and if they were, they existed far beyond this realm. "I need to get out of here. I don't belong. Nothing here makes sense..."

"Is it really so hard to believe? Malik speaks. He reasons. And I've seen him reading books on more than one occasion. Surely you can't still believe that he's a mere fire drake? A rare beast from deep in the mountain."

Thalia heaved a sigh and sank to the end of the bed, holding her aching head between her hands. "I don't know what I believe anymore. I can't even be sure if I'm awake or asleep. This all just seems like a dream. A very long, very strange dream." The room fell silent, and for a moment Thalia thought perhaps Bella had gone. But when she looked up, she could hardly believe what she was seeing.

The chambermaid pulled her hair down, and with a sweep of her hand, the form of a young girl sloughed away like an old skin to reveal the hunched, round visage of a familiar old woman. "I don't... Esa is that you?" Thalia whispered. "This must be some kind of trick." She shook her head as if trying to clear it. "I must be going mad," she murmured as everything started to spin.

"Of course it is, child," Esa said, reaching for the girl. Thalia stepped backward, not wanting to be touched by this... whatever this was. "Please, Thalia. It's me."

"No... I don't believe this..." she stammered. "This place... this castle must be bewitched..."

"Not this place," she said, groaning as her younger form melted away, leaving behind the pains of an old woman. "The only one that's been bewitched is Malik."

Esa stumbled, and Thalia rushed to her side, guiding her to the chaise by the hearth. "Esa, tell me what's going on before I lose my senses completely!"

Esa sighed, obviously hesitant to tell the truth. "My name is not Esa, it's Bella. Belladonna. I am a servant of the Dark Lady. Mab, the queen of all fairies. She trapped me here in this world long ago."

"Why?"

"Because I defied her. Malik was born of a curse that Mab wrought upon King Christophe. They were lovers, and he chose his human wife over her. So when he asked for Mab's help to conceive a child with his human wife, she tricked him with an onion, poisoned with dark magic. When Queen Katrin brought forth Christophe's offspring, one child was Tristan, distorted in mind, and the other was Malik, distorted in body. When Mab saw Malik, she insisted I destroy him. She knew that he would grow into a terrible beast, bent on revenge. I refused, and she banished me from Faerie and trapped me in this meager form. I can only go as far as The Veil, that misty membrane between this world and Faerie. All of this..." She gestured around the room. "The castle, my youthful form... it's all an illusion."

"You've kept him safe all this time?" Thalia could feel the tears burning in the corners of her eyes, threatening to roll over her cheeks.

"I've tried. The saddest part is that Mab was right about one thing. Malik has become twisted and cruel. His anger toward his father and brother have hardened his heart. There is only one thing that has been able soothe the storm that rages in Malik."

"What's that?" Thalia sniffled.

Esa smiled and squeezed Thalia's hand. "You, of course."

"I don't understand..."

"When King Christophe drove me out of Thane, I took shelter in Isling. As a midwife and healer, they called me to your mother's bedside when she lay dying, having just bore you."

"You took me in when my father abandoned me."

Esa nodded. "I raised you both."

"I don't remember..."

"He was as a dream for you, child. You've seen Malik's true face, haven't you?"

Suddenly everything fell into place. The familiarity. The strange dreams. Her whole life, every fragment started to piece itself together and began to make Thalia's head spin. She held her head remembering all the games, the teasing, the fevered dreams. The dark and beautiful prince that had been her only safe haven was also the root of all her fears. He was the scourge of these lands and the stuff of nightmares. The great Wyrm of Gwynfir was Thalia's greatest love. Suddenly she felt very faint.

"I know this is difficult, child," Esa said, reaching for her.

Thalia shook her head. "You have no idea," she snapped, jerking away. "You've been lying to me my whole life!"

"Would you have believed me?"

"At least I wouldn't have spent my whole life wishing for something I could never have! Now I'm trapped here in this... cold, hollow delusion with the two of you!" Before Esa could protest, Thalia was gone. She needed to be as far away from the old woman as she could get. Suddenly her entire life, the old life that she had longed to go back to even, was a ridiculous illusion.

Chapter Eighteen

It was customary in the kingdom of Osghast that when a king died, their body lay in state for a month to allow people from all over the continent to travel to the capital at Thane and pay their last respects to the dead. The castle and the entirety of the town was decked in black. Every building was swathed in black bunting and wreaths of Elderflower. Citizens were required to wear black and were not allowed to speak while on the street in a show of respect for the dead. At sundown on the thirtieth day, the body of the king was burned in the courtyard of the castle. The royal family, every member of court, and servants of the household stood watch all night until nothing was left but the embers. At sunrise, the new king was crowned, and the period of mourning was over. But King Christophe's death was anything but customary.

Tristan was an accomplished schemer. For a month, he'd waited to see if the little Tarkinian whore would make good on her promise to slay the dragon, but no word had been sent, and she did not return. He had heard whispers of the castle at Ellythin being remade. His father's confession had begun to trouble Tristan more and more. His father had warned him that the Dragon Lord had a claim to the throne. Tristan clenched his fists so tightly he could nearly feel the blood bubbling through the skin. He had not come this far to have his birthright stolen from him by a... *creature*! His plans hinged on the dragon's destruction. But with each passing day, it became clearer that the Huntress had not fulfilled her part of the deal. There were even panicked rumors that the girl had been seen in the forest surrounding Isling. *What if she had escaped? Would the dragon come back?*

Damn his father! His death had nearly spoiled everything. Tristan hadn't planned to kill him. But the rage had taken him over, and he just couldn't stop. He'd had to think of something, and fast. When it was done, Tristan had tucked his father into bed as if nothing was wrong, cleaned the spilled blood from the stones at the hearth, and gone to bed as if all was well. He was awakened early the next morning by the shouts of Balan and some of the chambermaids. They had found Christophe cold in his bed. The exquisite dagger lay on the floor at the bedside as if discarded by an assassin. It was a very distinct weapon with its superior steel blade and the exquisitely carved raven at the hilt. A weapon fit for a king of Osghast, his father had once told him. There was only one other dagger in the whole of the world like this one. The one Tristan himself had given to the little slayer.

It would be so easy to frame Thalia for the king's murder. So easy for the people to believe that an outsider and a woman could kill their sovereign. If the rumors were to be believed, then Thalia was alive and well. Perhaps the dragon had grown fond of her. Once she was arrested and imprisoned, his brother would come to save her. And this time, he would not fail.

"Sire. It is time." Tristan turned to see Balan and Grafton standing at his door. "The sun is peeking over the horizon." He nodded and allowed Balan to straighten his flowing robes. They were purple: the regal color of the royal house of Laurenz. His father had worn these robes many years ago and his father before him. If one looked closely, they could see the evidence of age and disuse though the seamstresses had been working on the repairs for the entire month of mourning. As Balan smoothed the train behind him, Tristan was aware of how heavy they were. Black brocade inlaid with gold thread decorated the lapels. A trim of ivory and gold fur decorated the hem, and tiny jewels had been worked into the embroidery. They were indeed kingly robes, but they only served to highlight the weight that now rested on his shoulders.

"Your Majesty," Grafton sputtered with a clumsy bow. "Long may you reign."

Tristan only replied with a terse grin. He did not like Grafton. Not one bit. It was true that the gypsy governor had helped him thus far, but Tristan knew if given half a chance, Grafton would turn. He was an opportunist. Tristan's first act as king would be to get the border towns under control. These governors had grown far too comfortable and autonomous. And then there were the outlying kingdoms. Whispers of a coming rebellion had been heard throughout the continent, and there was no way Tristan was going to let this pass by unnoticed. Yes, a show of the strength of Osghast would be just the thing to get them all in line.

The Great Hall smelled of fire. The ashes of the king were still smoldering on the pyre. Tristan wrinkled his nose in distaste thinking what an antiquated old ritual. The castle would smell of putrid smoke for weeks. As he marched slowly up the aisle, a chorus of trumpets heralded his coming. The room was packed with nobles and heads of state. Citizens and peasants stood in the back and spilled out into the courtyard. The stench of them blended with the smoke and rich perfume of the privileged, creating a thick mist of sickly sweet death. Tristan brought his handkerchief to his nose as he passed by them.

Nyxyn and the other members of the royal council lined the steps leading up to the throne. The ancient crown sat precariously on a cushion perched in the hands of Grafton. Secretly Tristan hoped he would drop the gaudy old thing so that he would have a reason to run him through in front of this crowd of spectators.

When he reached the throne, Tristan turned to face the citizens of Osghast. Grafton began to ramble on, going through some mindless speech about the transfer of power and remembering the loss of one so dear as King Christophe. Tristan's mouth cut a thin, pursed line as he stood there trying to look as if he were listening to any of this drivel. Now that he was king, Tristan planned to make it a point to get rid of all these politicians and their rhetoric. Their hollow words sickened him, and he could taste the bile in the back of his throat.

"Kneel before your people, Tristan, son of Christophe and heir to the House of Laurenz!" As he did so, Tristan noticed the mosaic that decorated the marble floor at his feet. A dragon, the ancient symbol of the Laurenz clan, stared up at him with ruby-inlaid eyes. They stared at him accusingly. The eyes of the dragon knew what he had done, and they promised vengeance. "But not this day," Tristan whispered.

"Sire?" Grafton hissed at his side.

Tristan gave a subtle shake of his head and bowed, allowing Grafton to place the heavy crown upon his head. "Now rise! Tristan, King of Osghast, Lord Regent of Thane!" As Tristan rose, the crowd gathered knelt before him, bowing their heads in reverence. Tristan felt intoxicated. A new power rushed through his veins, rising in his chest as he pasted a sincere smile on his face, taking in their accolades.

"My people!" he said. "I am humbled by your love and concern for the royal family at this time of mourning. Our city has faced much tragedy in recent memory: the death of Queen Katrin, the Outlander raids on our border towns, the fiery destruction of our homes, and now the death of our king. Some of it was brought about by the declining health of my father, some by treacherous parasites that seem to infect from every dark corner of the continent. But we have persevered. As we have for the last thousand years, Osghast has been the one constant. The rock on which the other realms have leaned for strength and protection. It is because of your faith and constancy that we have weathered these storms and will continue to weather them!" There was another deafening crescendo that echoed off the walls of the Great Hall. "My friends, in this time of tragedy, it brings me great pain to confide the reason we're all here today. The safety of our kingdom has been violated once more, but I promise you... it will be the last time. The great Wyrm of Gwynfir has plagued our shores for years now, burning towns all around our perimeter. Just one month ago, the beast grew bolder and entered our city gates. The damage to our capital was great, and many lives were lost, but something more sinister was afoot, my friends. The chosen bride of *Sheakhol*, the one we thought would be our savior, was in league with the dragon all along!" There was a gasp and a din of muttering and whispers throughout the room. "It was she who stole into my father's room and took his life! But fear not.

Your king will avenge his father! I will track the dragon and his treasonous bride into the mountains to restore order and peace to these lands!" The crowd was silent, disbelieving that their king had been murdered in cold blood right under their noses. "Go now," Tristan said. "Do not think on our misfortunes. A fortnight of feasting and joy awaits!"

Chapter Nineteen

In the end there was fire. Burning and smoldering, ashes of women and children blowing in the very air she breathed. Bella could smell it. There was death and decay around every corner, under every stone. The world as they knew it was drawing to an end. The path was narrow, the stones lit by the sliver of moonshine overhead, but she followed it to its terminus at the sacred lake. The lake that was barely more than a pond now. The scorched ground lapped at the only source of relief until the earth cracked open, and the forest, once teeming with life, was now a tangle of gnarled trees and poisonous air. She looked down and saw her bare feet padding toward her destination. They bled, the skin torn and raw from walking.

Now she was standing in the acidic water of the once-thriving lake. It stank of sulfur and the rotting flesh of the animals left behind. A ripple in the water caught her eye, and she watched as her reflection twisted and roiled, dissolving into a vision of a world torn asunder by war. A young king stood over his father, a dagger clutched in his fist. Blood ran in streams through the streets of Thane, soaking into the cobblestones. Wild men the height of small trees with the tusks of animals growled and roared. Gazing into the mirror of the dying lake, Bella could hear them, could smell the musk of them. They overran the streets, trampling weary knights, women, and children. The sky glowed with a sickening *orange light. The whole world was on fire, and the cries for mercy were deafening. But there was no mercy to be had. Osghast would fall, and the world of men would fall into a hellish dream from which no living soul would awaken.*

Thalia wandered through the ruined garden in the dusky twilight. Honeysuckle grew wild, nearly choking the ivy that grew over the crumbling stones. She could smell it on the wind, and she smiled. She could remember the taste of the sweet nectar on her tongue from when she was a child. Esa had once told her a silly story about how the fairies used the honeysuckle blossom for a teacup. Yet another fairy tale the old woman had spun for her enjoyment.

She'd spent most of the last month here, sitting among the overgrown vines and wildflowers, trying to make sense of her situation. Or lazing in the bough of the gnarled tree reading a book. The chambermaid had been scarce, and Thalia was grateful for that. She didn't want to talk to her about fairies or magic or how the woman she'd loved as a mother had just been a sick masquerade.

Malik had not returned to the castle since their night flight. Strangely, she sort of missed him. Of course, now that she knew who he was, she felt awkward even thinking of being near him. Over the years, she'd confessed many dark secrets from the dusty corners of her heart to him. Could her dark prince really be there somewhere underneath those scales in the midst of the fire?

Then there was the matter of an entire village razed to the ground at his hand. Thalia stared down at the mark that wrapped around her wrist. It was a constant reminder of her purpose. Was she not still the Huntress? She had vowed to protect people from dragons, not fall in love with them.

"Oh Thalia! Thank heavens you're here!" Bella looked almost comical as she ran down the ruined path, stumbling over tree roots. "I've been looking all over."

"I've been here the whole time," Thalia replied with a yawn. "That's what I do now. Lie around here as a prisoner."

"As much as I'd like to engage in another pity party with you, Thalia, this is important!"

There was the Esa she remembered. "What is it? Just spit it out!" Bella grabbed her arm and began jerking her toward the castle. Thalia stumbled and dropped her book. She tried to pull away to get it, but Bella kept right on dragging her inside. "What? Bella! My book—"

"Just leave it! It isn't important."

Finally, Thalia wrenched her arm from Bella's grasp. "Would you kindly tell me what in the world is going on instead of tugging my arm out of the socket?"

"Oh, it's terrible," Bella said, doubling over as she caught her breath. Evidently she'd been running up and down the stairs searching her out. "A vision... a terrible vision...the king..."

"What of him?"

"He's dead!"

While hearing of someone's death was never a cause for celebration, Thalia couldn't see why this was so earth-shattering. "What of it? King Christophe was old and, from what I hear, fairly ill. His death can't possibly be a surprise to you."

"Surely you can't have been idle so long that you've lost your senses!" Bella snapped. "Don't you know what this means?"

"That Tristan got what he wanted. Good on him."

"No, stupid child! That Tristan has killed his father! He'll come after Malik! And you! He cannot be allowed to rule Osghast! He will bring death! Do you hear me?" Once more Bella began rushing Thalia toward the stairs.

"Just calm down, Bella," Thalia began, pausing at the stairs and refusing to move farther. "Perhaps your vision was just a... I don't know, a bit of underdone food. Or too much wine?"

"Don't be stupid!" Bella exclaimed. "Dreams are rarely just dreams. You should know that better than anyone! Mab has sent me this vision to taunt me. Tristan has killed his father to gain control over Osghast. He thinks he knows what is best, but it's folly! I see darkness and death! War and disease!"

"This is all terribly dramatic," Thalia sighed, dragging herself slowly up the stairs. She really wasn't in the mood for the fiery passions of fairies. All she wanted was a hot bath and her bed. "But so what? Let Tristan lie in a pool of his own blood and piss. What difference does it make? He's a fool that deserves everything that happens to him."

"The difference is that Mab tried to tell me this would happen. If I didn't destroy Malik that he would burn this world. And she likes nothing more than to be right."

When they arrived at the top of the stairs, Bella was very forceful as she pushed Thalia into her bedchamber. She stumbled over the foot of the vanity stool and sat down hard on it. Before she could complain, Bella had rushed to the wardrobe and began pulling piles of fabric and lace and tossing them over the end of the bed. Thalia watched for a while with her arms folded until finally curiosity got the better of her. "What are you doing?"

"I'm not sure," Bella said. "Possibly making a huge mistake, but we'll see."

"I don't follow..."

"Look, fairies are magical creatures, and magic has rules. One of those rules is that magic is balance. Anything that can be done can also be undone. You and I are going to attempt to undo Mab's curse."

She couldn't help it. The laughter bubbled out before Thalia could stop it. "Me? There isn't a magical bone in my body! What good could I possibly be?"

"You've got me. And right now, you're the only hope we have."

"Me? I'm just... I'm just a slayer. There's nothing special about me at all."

"Nothing except your love for him."

Thalia's heart pounded uncomfortably against her chest, and suddenly there was too much air. "I... I don't love him. How could I? It goes against my very nature..."

"So why haven't you killed him? All you need do is destroy the dragon, and you could be queen of these lands. Tristan would give you anything you wanted, and you could live in comfort for the rest of your days."

Thalia stood and paced. Bella was right. Thalia could have killed

Malik at any time. In fact, it seemed that he'd been waiting for her to. She stared into the fire and watched the flames lick at the fresh logs. Perhaps the answers to all the questions that were swirling around in her brain could be found in the flickering orange light. "I could never love Tristan. He's..."

"Dangerous. That is why breaking the curse is so important. Tristan will throw this world into chaos. Now that he has ascended the throne, he will wage war not just with Malik, but with the outlying kingdoms. Osghast will fall. I have foreseen it and fear it has already begun. As full of rage and hate as he might be, Malik is the only hope for his father's kingdom. He must claim his birthright and ascend to the throne of Osghast." She stopped piling clothes on the bed and turned to face the dragon slayer. "And I've watched you all your life, Thalia. You've loved Malik since the day you were born. And he you. Mark me! That true and pure love will be what breaks the curse."

⁂

As she allowed Bella to dress her in the layers of silk and lace, Thalia thought that sacrifice was a concept not truly understood by most. Most would not put other people so far ahead of themselves that they were willing to accept grave consequences to spare the ones they loved. It was supposed to be painful, terrifying, and uncertain. Otherwise, it wouldn't be a sacrifice. Markus had understood sacrifice. He had loved Thalia so much that he was willing to sacrifice his young life to protect the life of his mentor. The more she thought about it, the more Thalia was convinced that Markus had understood his fate before he ran into the fray with that bull dragon that would ultimately take his life. He'd known that in that fight, one of them would fall, and he had not been willing to let Thalia be the one.

Now as she descended from the safety of her bedchamber to the castle below, Thalia realized she had never sacrificed herself in all her life. The Huntress was an arrogant machine. She'd gone into battle with those dragons never thinking for one second that she would not emerge victorious. It had never truly been a sacrifice because she had never felt the danger. Tonight, as she made her way through the labyrinthine halls of the castle, she could most definitely feel the danger. Tonight, she was a sacrifice.

The layers of heavy fabric weighed her down as she descended the stone steps into the bowels of the castle. Belladonna trailed behind her holding the skirts as if she were some twisted sort of bridesmaid. Perhaps that was indeed her function. After all, according to the mythology behind *Sheakhol*, tonight she would be made the dragon's bride. "Be unafraid," she said over and over in her head. Malik had been nothing but kind to her up to this point. If he'd wanted her dead, he could have eaten her a month ago. It should make her feel better to know that the human form of her prince lurked beneath that suit of scales, but it actually made her feel more uneasy. Thalia's intense attraction for her dark friend was infinitely more frightening than a dragon. He had awakened something inside of her, and she wasn't sure what was going to happen should it be unleashed.

"Are you certain this is going to work?" Thalia asked as they reached the doors to the Great Hall.

"Not at all."

Thalia whipped around, staring wild-eyed at the chambermaid. "You mean you've never done this before?"

"Well... I never really had much cause to test the theory. The onion that Christophe gave the queen had many layers. I can only assume that the curse gave the prince many layers."

Thalia sighed and hid her face in her hands. "I hope you don't mean that figuratively."

Bella smiled and pushed open the doors. Thalia braced herself for the chill of the ruined hall, but was pleasantly surprised. The stones at her feet had been covered with a rug that ran the length of the hall, and the tapestries upon the walls all looked as if no time had passed. No longer were they moth-eaten and faded but vibrant and beautiful, telling the story of a young king and his exploits. In the last one, two lovers embraced amid vines of ivy and roses. "Bella, who is this?" She turned to find that she was alone. The thunder of the doors closing seemed to accentuate her solitude.

The Great Hall was also changed. It seemed almost warm with the rugs, heavy drapes, and the distinct lack of holes in the ceiling. A blazing fire had been built in the pit, and massive and inviting couches had been arranged strategically around it. Malik lay in the corner, filling up half of the room with his enormity. Thalia felt sorry for him. He couldn't stand up straight here lest he bring down the walls, so he appeared to be hunched over. "Good evening, my lord," Thalia said, bowing low as he opened his great eyes. "You've been gone a rather long while."

Malik cocked his head to one side, staring at the girl as she negotiated around the fire, approaching him. Clearly he was confused by her sudden appearance. "Thalia, what a surprise. I suspected you would hide yourself away as much as possible. I told Bella that she might serve your meals in your chamber."

"Don't be ridiculous, my lord. Why would I deny myself the favor of your company?"

Malik heaved a harsh chuckle that was almost a snarl. "I can't imagine that most humans would feel obliged to keep company with a dragon. Especially not the fearsome and ferocious Wyrm of Gwynfir."

"On the contrary, my lord. I find your company rather agreeable. Would you mind if I sat?"

Malik shook his head, obviously somewhat confused by her sudden change of heart. He watched closely as she made herself comfortable on the chaise nearest him. It wasn't an easy task given the layers of garments Mab had forced upon her. Thalia would never get used to the niceties of court ladies. She was quite happy with the garb of a warrior: leather breeches and a tunic with her crossbow strapped to her back. The only accessory a dagger strapped to her thigh. Mab had insisted she wear a full gown: underthings, chemise, corset, kirtle, and surcote. It had seemed like a good idea at the time, but now that she was here she found that her movement was severely restricted. She also had the ridiculous thought that she couldn't put her arms down fully at her sides. The entire situation was awkward. "You seem a bit... encumbered."

"Your chambermaid insisted I dress like a proper lady."

"Bella has strange ideas about things. You will learn to ignore her."

"Indeed. Of course, she did let me in on a few tidbits of information that had escaped the breadth of my knowledge."

"Oh?"

"Yes. She informed me that the ritual of *Sheakhol* was not complete."

Malik chuckled. "How so?"

"Well, the ritual itself was designed to offer the dragon a sacrifice that would become the serpent bride."

"And so it did."

"Yes, but that was only part of the story, wasn't it?"

"I'm not sure I understand your meaning, Mouse." Malik stretched and stood as much as he was able, slithering to where she sat and wrapping his enormous body around the couch and draping his tail over the end. "But I like bedtime stories. Do enlighten me."

"According to legend, the dragon took the maiden, and if she went to him willingly with faith and love in her heart, then he would shed his skin and reveal the lord underneath. If she showed any fear or had evil intent, then the dragon would devour her."

"An intriguing story. I'm not exactly sure what any of this has to do with me."

"I will stay here willingly, for the rest of my days. I will live here with you and do whatever you ask of me. I will be your bride..."

"My bride?" This time the dragon laughed long and loud, shaking the stone walls with the force of it. "For a dragon to take a human bride... truly take her... would be, at the very least, unpleasant for the human."

The innuendo was not lost on Thalia, and she couldn't help but smirk. "That's why it is called a sacrifice, my lord."

"This is ridiculous..." he began.

"Am I not to your liking? Perhaps there is another woman in Osghast that you would find more pleasing?"

"No."

"Then perhaps you fear me? The great Huntress of Tarkin?"

"I fear nothing!" Malik exclaimed, clearly insulted.

"Then what have you to lose? I am the only one who will surely die in this exchange." Thalia stood and crossed her arms defiantly over her chest. She stared into the eyes of the dragon with a haughty resolve. Bella had explained that she would have to bait him into it. That he would be resistant. She could only pray that the fairy was right. "Come on then. What are you waiting for?" He growled deeply in his chest and slinked closer. She could tell by the way the dark slitted pupils contracted that he was examining her closely. He raised his snout, sniffing her out. Thalia willed herself to be still. She couldn't show any fear, no matter how much she might want to. He was so close now, almost on top of her. She could feel his heat, and it was almost overwhelming.

"Have it your way then," he snarled finally. Stepping back, he stood watching. It was a predatory stance. "Take off your dress. I wish to see my human prize," he said gruffly.

"Not so fast, my lord. Surely you haven't forgotten the ritual. For every layer I remove, you must match it."

"Hmm...and how do you propose I do that?"

"Your skin. Dragons are as lizards, are they not? Shedding a layer of skin as they grow larger?"

"Of course."

"Then for each layer of clothing I shed, you give me one layer. That's the way it must be done."

Malik laughed. "You're very strange, Mouse."

"Do you agree?"

"Fine. Whatever you want," he said with a sigh of derision. "If that is the way it is done, then that is how we must do it. Go on."

Thalia bowed and pulled the silver comb from her hair, letting her hair fall down over her shoulders. With shaking fingers, she began to unlace the bodice of the surcote. Bella had tied the strings so tightly that she had a difficult time getting her fingers beneath the knotting, but she was finally victorious. The heavy, embroidered fabric practically fell from her shoulders as the ties were loosed. She bent over, picking it up and throwing it aside. "Your turn."

The dragon raised up on his haunches, stretching his wings behind him. He raised a single talon, dragging it down the middle of his chest. Thalia was fascinated as the skin split, at first just a little and then cracking all the way down Malik's front. He growled and groaned as he twisted his body, working the tough and hardened scales away from his body. Once it had split in one place, it split in others until all of the skin seemed to slide from his body like water. Thalia stood back as the great, dried-out pelt fell away and disintegrated into ashes as it hit the floor. "Is that what you wanted to see, Mouse?" he rasped. Obviously, the molting was a difficult process.

Thalia nodded. Suddenly she was filled with a strange urgency. She wanted to see what was going to happen next. The kirtle was heavy, and she struggled with it. This must be why noblewomen had maidservants. Getting in and out of these clothes unassisted was no easy task. She finally managed to pull the yards and yards of linen and lace over her head, only getting lost once or twice. By the time she was able to throw it aside, she was almost certain that Malik was laughing at her. "You try taking off a heavy dress over your head sometime!" she snapped.

"A few well-placed fireballs could make short work of your clothing," he said with a sneer.

"No, thank you," she replied. "Quit stalling."

Malik nodded and once more began to peel his skin away. This time was more difficult than before as he gave a tremulous roar as the skin split down his back and gave way. Once more the pelt seemed to dissolve and blow away before it could hit the ground. Thalia reached out at one point, wanting to keep a scale or two for herself, but the skin was mere dust on her fingertips. When he was done, she could have sworn that he was smaller than before, but she dared not mention it.

Twice more they carried on their dance, each of them shedding their clothing until only one layer remained. Thalia stood in naught but the simple linen underthings that covered her most private of places. Her modesty and the chill of the castle were conspiring to kill her nerve, but as Malik shed another layer, she noticed that the iridescent scales had grown thin. Nearly transparent. Beneath she could see pale flesh. His eyes, which had once been orange fire with glints of green like an autumn forest, were now the strangest shade of aquamarine with flecks of gold. He panted and hissed, now so exhausted that he lay on the floor nearly unable to lift his head. "This is some ploy to kill me, is it not, slayer?" He tried to move toward her, but the pain of it was too much, and he collapsed at her feet.

"Well go ahead... stab me through the heart. Take back my head to your king!"

Thalia knelt, taking his head in her hands. "No... please, my lord. You mustn't give up." She stroked her fingertips along the ridge of his nose, feeling the loose skin there. "It is an evil curse that will take great pain to break. You must trust me." The weakened dragon closed and opened his eyes in reply.

"Then let us be done with it."

Thalia stood, trying to keep from trembling as she slowly pulled the final slips of fabric away from her body until she stood before him naked. Straightening her spine, she was almost displaying herself for him. Her mind raced with what might happen next. Perhaps Bella had been mistaken, and she had gone through this for nothing. Had put Malik through this for nothing. Looking down at the creature, he no longer seemed fearsome but pathetic. Weak. A draft of breeze kissed her skin, and she shuddered. "It... is your turn... my lord..." she stammered. Her teeth were chattering now, and she was sure that if the dragon didn't devour her that she would die of a fever in a week's time.

"Come closer, Mouse," he rumbled. "My body," he panted. "It seems wracked with fever, but I will warm you." Using all the strength he had left, he raised up and opened his arms. Thalia went to him and allowed him to wrap her up in the muscular wings. His body swirled around her, offering a protective embrace that quickly chased away the cold. She slid her hands along the scaly shoulders and found that the scales were not hardened or wet, but soft and warm like a man's flesh.

"I know you," Thalia whispered. As she said it, his skin split once more and began to fall away. Where it opened up, a silvery steam emerged, wrapping around them like a glistening veil. Suddenly, Malik broke away from her with a roar unlike anything she'd ever heard. His body twisted and contorted, rising into the air as if carried by the mist. She was thrown backward with the force of the breaking spell and struggled to keep her eyes open. She wanted to see him. She needed to see if it was true. With a bursting of light, the dragon was gone, leaving behind a man. He lay there on the cold stone before her. His naked flesh was marked with scarring left by the shift, but as Thalia watched, it healed and disappeared, leaving behind perfect alabaster skin. His black hair fell in waves over his shoulders. The sharp edges of his cheekbones, the downturned strangeness of his eyes, and slope of his nose were reminiscent of the dragon's face, but indescribably beautiful. She wanted to laugh or shout with unadulterated glee at seeing him finally in the flesh. Fully awake. The dark prince she'd known all her life.

Chapter Twenty

Thalia wasn't aware of how long he lay there, unmoving. For a moment, she thought that perhaps he hadn't survived the change from dragon to human, but the steady undulation of his chest reassured her. "My lord?" she whispered finally, creeping toward him. He didn't respond or even move. "Are you well?" As she got closer, she could see the final pelt of his dragon form, laying mangled on the floor behind him. It had not disintegrated like the others. She knelt down, running her hands along the discarded scales. Instead of dry and crumbling like a snakeskin, they were thick and soft like leather. She tried picking it up, but it was so large and so heavy that she nearly fell down.

"Stealing my scales, are you?"

"Um... no..."

"Who could blame you? They'll probably fetch a fair price in the market towns. Armor made of dragon scales is a rare thing indeed in these times." He tried to sit up, using his arms and legs as if he were still a quadruped, unsure where to put them to make his body do what he wanted. Thalia went to him, kneeling to help him to a sitting position.

"Be careful, my lord."

"Why won't my legs work? Why is my body betraying me?"

Thalia grinned. "You've never used it before."

"This is preferable to my old form?" he grumbled as he tried to reach for Thalia's cloak still laying on the floor. His fingers were clumsy as he attempted to grasp the fabric between them. "I can't even lift this cloak!"

"Here, my lord... let me help you." Thalia pulled the heavy cloak around his shoulders. She knelt in front of him so close that she could feel the heat still emanating from his body, as if the fire of the dragon was still there within, burning brightly. This close, she could really see him, and his gaze was arresting. It was so overwhelming that she immediately felt dizzy and her chest ached. She held the cloak around his throat. The breadth of his shoulders was such that the fabric offered little protection from the chill of the room, but perhaps it would stop his shivering. His eyes cut deeply, and they did not wander from her face. He was studying her, gauging each reaction with a clinical eye.

"You know me?" he asked.

"Of course, my lord," Thalia answered, faltering under the heavy gaze of the dragon prince. "I have walked with you many times." She paused, her words sounding silly and childish to her ears. "In my dreams."

"Are you certain it was a dream?"

She shook her head. "No. No, I'm not. I'm not certain of anything anymore."

"Perhaps you were wandering," he began, his voice a rough growl deep in his throat. It was obvious that this new form was very strange to the prince. "Wandering in Faerie. A place where those of your kind can only venture in sleep."

"Perhaps," Thalia replied with a thin smile. His gaze was more than she could take, and she looked away, moving her hands away and backing off.

"Are you still afraid of me, Mouse? Even in this... pitiful state?"

"You're hardly pitiful, my lord. You'll find your strength soon enough."

"And when I do, will you still be afraid?"

"More than I have ever been." Thalia was suddenly very aware of her nakedness and crossed her arms over her chest in an attempt to cover herself.

He laughed again. "I'm surprised. You've known me your whole life. There's really no point in fearing me now. Come, help me to the chaise." He pulled the cloak from around his shoulders and offered it. "Perhaps this will make you feel more comfortable." She was now very aware of *his* nakedness, and the notion of comfort dissolved. She put her arms around his back, allowing him to lean against her as they stood. His body was heavy, and she felt dwarfed by his stature. Slowly the couple, looking like some great beast, moved together toward the wide sofa by the fire pit. They collapsed awkwardly in a tangle of limbs and fabric. "Oh, sorry," Thalia stammered.

"It seems I will have to learn everything again," Malik growled. "This helplessness is not amusing."

"You will be an expert in time, my lord," she said, straightening his legs across the chaise before kneeling on the floor in front of him.

"Mm…" he hummed. He stared down at his limbs, fascinated by their structure. Raising a hand to his face, he seemed to examine the lines and shapes: the sinew connecting bone to muscle and the intricate arrangement of the joints. "My skin is smooth," he said. "I thought it would be rough." He held out his hand, and Thalia took it. She ran her fingertips along the veins at the back of his hand. The skin there was very smooth indeed, from the delicate bones at the knuckle to the pads of his fingers. She stretched out his arm and held it in front of her. She traced the purple vein at his wrist and followed it up his arm to the inside of his elbow. "You are extraordinary, my lord."

"Hardly," he said. "I am a useless collection of bones at the moment."

"Lovely bones," she murmured. It was almost involuntary as she picked up his hand and brought it to her cheek. She needed to feel the heat of his flesh against her own. To be sure that this time he was real. That he wouldn't dissolve into ash and leave her awake and cold once more. He made no move to stop her as she brushed his fingers along her cheek. Finally he tipped her chin back, forcing her to look up at him. "I know you," he whispered. "Thalia." A strange flutter thrummed at her center as he said her name for the first time.

"Yes," she replied, looking down through her eyelashes. "All our lives."

He smiled, his eyes twinkling with a light she hadn't seen before. "I warned you not to wander too far into your dreams, lest you become trapped."

She nodded. "Is this your idea of a trap?"

"Perhaps."

"Then I've no wish to be sprung." Kneeling up to face him, she pressed his hand to her chest. "Let me warm your hands, my lord, so that they might find their strength."

❧

The sensation that a person has when touching another had always been a mystery to Malik. The cold, hardened scales of a dragon did not offer much in the way of feeling. The smoothness of flesh, the heat of blood or the thrum of a heartbeat was alien to him. Yet, when he was able to touch Thalia for the first time, it was like coming home. His cold, reptilian heart began to beat with a new rhythm in time with hers. A pleasing warmth set in, and before he knew it, his mouth was against hers.

Their kiss was awkward. Malik had no idea how to move this unfamiliar bit of flesh. It was small and eager. His teeth were no longer sharp; he had no breath of flame. He only knew that he wanted to breathe her in. He wanted to take some of her warmth inside of him and let it take root. For a moment he was still, merely acclimating to this new closeness, but before long Thalia took over. She was an excellent teacher, and he was ready to learn. Parting her lips, she caressed his between them. A gentle nibble that coaxed him to do the same. He caught on quickly, his body remembering so many encounters locked in Faerie. His palm cupped her cheek, and he pulled her in. This time he was assured and deliberate, teasing her mouth open with his tongue and invading with a slow persistence. She tasted of purity: rain and wind and sunshine. All of the things that had been so mythical to one as grotesque and hated as he. Finally, he was assured of their reality, and he wanted more.

Malik pulled back slightly, gauging Thalia's reaction. She was barely breathing, her eyes still closed. "Open your eyes," he whispered, his lips so close to hers. "I want you to see me."

"I'm afraid," she replied. "What if you dissolve in ash and smoke? Like all the other times." She brushed her lips against his once more. "I can't lose you again."

"Open your eyes." She gasped as he pulled his body upright, again towering over her. For a moment her fear flared once more, and she cowered. He would not let her escape so easily. Slithering and predatory, he stalked her as he slid down from his perch. He used his body as only he knew how, and Thalia moaned softly, unable to keep her arousal at seeing him this way at bay. Every movement and catch of breath gave her away, and now he was starting to enjoy it. Being the animal. He overtook her quickly, taking her wrist and pulling her up against him. The wisp of cloak around her shoulders fell away, and she was once again naked in his arms. "Am I real to you now?"

"Yes," she stammered, brushing her cheek against his.

"Still want to be rescued?" he teased, winding his arms around her waist and crushing his mouth against hers.

"Rescue me," she said when she was able.

He grinned and kissed her mouth again without a moment's hesitation. Slowly his fingertips trilled along her spine and into her hair. The silken mess tangled around his fingers, and he tugged gently, using it as leverage to deepen their kiss. Every breath was his as he breathed new life into her. He kissed her until she was breathless and could no longer resist. Her arms wound around him, and she held him tight. "Thanks be to the gods," she whispered. "I knew if I was patient, someday you would be here."

"I never left you," he murmured against her ear. "No matter how hard I tried, I couldn't leave you."

"Then make me your bride. And we'll never be alone again."

Malik's hands slid down to her hips, cupping her bottom and pressing her body against his. He was instantly overwhelmed by her softness, a quicksilver surge of arousal that fled straight to his cock. He groaned with its intensity. Thalia grabbed his hand, pulling it to her breast and closing it over the generous swell. She guided his hand, teaching him to caress it gently but with just enough pressure to draw a moan from her lips. His thumb brushed over the nipple, and she seethed. He stared at the tiny bead of flesh as it swelled and hardened beneath his fingertips. A stiff morsel of flesh like a tiny fruit. Malik's mouth watered, and he needed to taste it. Gripping her breast gently, he brought it to his mouth, closing it over the center and lapping at the prickly areola. The taste was every bit as decadent as he'd imagined it would be. Thalia gasped, and for a moment he thought he'd done something wrong, but she brushed her fingers through his hair almost holding him against her chest.

Malik drew his hand along her collarbone and down the slope of her chest between her breasts. She arched her body backward until she was lying on the ground before him, her legs still straddling his hips. He wanted to look at her, to see her flesh for real this time. It was pale and perfect. There were old scars here and there. They had healed over, but as Malik examined them, he could tell that they had been made by the scratch of talons or the grazing of teeth. Just over her hip was a place where the skin was so thin that he could see the blue veins beneath. She'd been burned. Badly. By dragon fire. Malik's heart clenched in his chest as he ran his thumb over the place. "Thalia… I'm so… sorry."

"Don't be silly. You've nothing to be sorry for," she said.

"A dragon did this."

"Yes," she conceded. "And this." She put an arm behind her head, showing a deep gash along her side. "And this." She threw her leg aside to show him another streak of red at the inside of her thigh. "These are my battle scars, Malik. But you didn't make them."

"But my kind…"

"They are not your kind. Those beasts I hunted and fought for so long—those were animals. Fire lizards. You are a Dragon Lord. With a human heart." As she said this, he leaned over, kissing the scarred flesh at her side. He followed the path of her ribs to another small scar just over her navel. "You've nothing in common with them," she whispered.

"Oh, I don't know," he replied, lapping at the deep scar on her thigh. It was so close to her sex that he could feel the heat coming off of it. "The thought of eating you alive did occur." With that he bit down into the supple flesh of her thigh. Thalia squealed as he nibbled gently at the marked skin like a hungry beast. "Devouring you slowly," he growled, tracing the slope of her pelvis. "Until you're begging for mercy." He was surprised to find that though his true form was weak and unfamiliar, every sense was heightened. He could smell and taste his delicate prey before he'd even attempted to touch her. Her scent filled him with desire. It was the smoke and ash of his heart and the bitter spice of his soul he could smell on her. She was a piece of him. The piece that he'd held deep in his dragon heart since the day she was born.

"It is not your mercy I seek, my lord," Thalia whispered.

His mouth watered. The arousal burning within was almost disturbing in its intensity. As if he feared that he may actually eat her alive as she'd always feared. Just a small taste. A flick of his tongue across the fleshy bit that concealed her womanhood. Thalia gasped, jerking her body backward as if to get away from him. "Did I do something wrong, Mouse?"

"Yes... I mean, no..." She stammered, but this time was different. The shudder in her voice revealed fear but not a mortal fear. This was more of uncertainty. Embarrassment and the unknown. "No one has ever touched me that way before."

Malik raised his eyebrow, amused by her confession. "No one?"

"I kept myself for you, my lord."

"A lover in a dream?" he chuckled softly. "You are very strange, Mouse." His words only made her more uneasy. Her cheeks positively glowed in the dim firelight. At once he could see that he'd hurt her feelings. "I'm sorry," he said. Now it was his turn to be embarrassed. "I didn't mean... it's just that, you're so beautiful, Thalia. The thought that you saved yourself for me... I fear I could never live up to your expectations of me."

"And what of you?" she asked then clapped a hand over her mouth. "Sorry... that was rude."

Malik smiled. "I think we can dispense with the niceties. And it wasn't rude. Let's just say that being a dragon doesn't offer much opportunity for the joys of the flesh." He bowed his head, unable to look at her. "Such a form. Who could love a dragon? That incongruous collection of scales and bone."

"But in Faerie..."

"In Faerie, all I could do was think of you, lover. No one else would do." He glanced up, their eyes meeting as she lay back once more.

"Then let us learn together."

"Yes," he said, his voice taking on a serpentine hiss. "Teach me every inch of you."

❧

In her most fevered dreams, Thalia had never imagined herself capable of such pleasure. Malik said to teach him every inch of her, but there was no need. He knew her body like his own soul, knew exactly where to touch, where to kiss, and where to whisper his breathy words. His tongue slipped over the swollen and sensitive lips of her sex until she mewled beneath him. They burst open like the petals of a morning glory, inviting him inside, but for now, he was content to tease at the gates. Over and over he brought her so close to the edge that it felt like falling, only to pull her back once more. So long ago, when she had first become aware of herself, she would wake from her dreams of him so humid and hot between her legs. It was a frightening sensation that would lay heavy in her womb all day, but his kisses promised that this time she would not go unrequited. This time there would be release, but not until he'd wrung every drop of slippery arousal from her.

"Malik," she moaned, tangling her fingers in his thick, untamed curls. "Please don't make me wait."

"Don't be impatient, Mouse," he teased, crawling up her body. He blazed a trail of kisses up her midsection and around each breast. "I intend to hear you screaming my name over and over. But not until I am fully seated inside you. I want to feel every throb and shudder." These last words he said against her mouth, offering his tongue so that she could taste her own essence. Thalia wrapped her arms around his neck and pulled him close. She could feel his cock pulsing and hard against the hood of her sex. Throwing her leg over his hip, her body moved almost of its own accord. Just one tiny push and she would be complete, but Malik was never one to be coaxed. He would possess her in his own time. With a snarl of dominance, he grabbed her wrists, pinning them down to the floor behind her. The cold, smooth stone was a comfort to her burning flesh.

Malik cupped her face gently in one large hand, his thumb brushing across her lower lip as he moved her head aside to gain access to the plump vein just under the jawline. He bit playfully, nicking the skin with the points of his teeth and then suckling gently. Thalia could hear her heart pounding in her ears. She could feel the dragon still hiding within him, and the danger was thrilling. It made her sex thrum and tingle that much more. Then his mouth was against her ear as he whispered to her in some strange language. She couldn't understand the lazy, rasping words, but she didn't need to. The way his body tensed and his manhood twitched was all the translation she needed. He pulled back, breathing heavily as he stared down at her. Those icy blue eyes darkened the longer he gazed. They were hypnotic, and Thalia knew that there was no turning back. She blinked slowly, reassuring him that this was what she wanted. All she'd ever wanted. Leaning in, he captured her mouth, drawing her tongue into his.

"Make me your bride," Thalia gasped as he pulled back. Without thought or hesitation, he pushed inside of her. It was slow and deliberate. Thalia tensed, waiting for the sharp sting of lost virtue, but it never came. She was ready to be his. So ready to leave her old life behind and become one with the only man who could ever be part of her soul. When Malik finally broke past the thin slip of flesh, there was no blood or violence. Only a peace that Thalia had wished for all her life. For a moment he was still, breathing against her shoulder. His eyelashes fluttered against her skin, and she could tell he was holding back. "Is there something wrong?" she whispered.

"I don't want to hurt you, Thalia." The low snarl of the dragon was evident there in his voice.

"I am not afraid." She crushed her mouth against his as she wrapped one leg around his waist. With her heel, she nudged him closer. She wanted him to move. She needed to feel the delicious friction of their bodies sliding slowly against one another. He obliged, sliding deeper inside until they were sealed together, hanging on to one another as if they might fly apart at any time. It was an awkward dance at first, neither really understanding what was involved. Then suddenly, their eyes met, and instinct took over. Slowly they made love in a pulsing rhythm, each allowing the other to learn just how the other wanted to be touched. Thalia stroked her fingers through his hair and down his spine as if to be sure that the smooth flesh was not a mere enchantment. He withdrew, nearly slipping from her folds and then thrusting back inside. Over and over he plunged deep into Thalia's core, his passion growing with every intake of breath. She whimpered as a burning ache set in and gripped him tightly, pulling him closer. She wanted to hold him inside until he was part of her. Those secret muscles that throbbed within seemed to reach out, clutching and gripping his cock tight until they were both groaning with the sensation of it.

When she came, it was a shockwave that shook her whole body. She could only hold on to Malik tightly, whispering his name as she crested the wave of ecstasy. He made no noise, save for a low growl as he reached his own climax. They lay entwined, losing all sense of time and space as they panted against one another. His body was so heavy and warm atop hers, she didn't want to lose the feeling of safety he offered. "Welcome to your new body," Thalia said, then giggled.

"A warm welcome, to be sure."

Chapter Twenty-One

Thalia rolled over on her back, smiling as the morning sun streamed through the windows and warmed her cheek. She was hesitant to open her eyes at first, afraid that it had all been a dream. A very vivid, sensual dream. Of course, as she stretched, the muscles in her thighs gave definitive proof of his reality. Once Malik had brought her upstairs, their evening had passed in a languorous blur of lovemaking, conversation, and finally sleep. Thalia thought that the sensation of falling asleep in the arms of one's lover, talking until the words ran dry, was the ultimate bliss. She'd never wanted it to end. Even now she could still feel him moving between her legs, his rough cheek brushing against the virgin flesh of her breast and his manhood filling her completely. Just the thought of it was enough to set off another shudder that rolled over her entire body and settled over her sex, making her long to have him inside her again.

Grudgingly, she opened her eyes and was relieved to find Malik still lying beside her. He lay on his belly, arms crossed under his head as if he were still a dragon. His long, unkempt dark hair fell over his cheek, moving as he breathed lightly. He was just on the edge of wakefulness but still fighting to hold on to some dream. Thalia wondered what he might dream about. Was he still a dragon, or was he wandering the green fields of Faerie? He seemed content, and she smiled to think she might have something to do with that.

Thalia brushed a gentle hand through his hair, smoothing it back from his pale brow. He stirred a bit but did not wake. She didn't want to wake him, but the thought of his arms around her again was just too inviting. Leaning closer, she pressed her lips to his forehead and lingered a moment. She loved the taste of his skin. Thalia smiled when he still didn't wake and began planting kisses along the arch of his neck and down the slope of his shoulder. He growled and rolled to his back, nearly hitting her with his elbow. The muscles along his side were a glorious configuration of living flesh. She couldn't help but touch him, tracing the lines and trilling her fingertips over each rib. Examining his body this way only made her want to explore further.

Slowly Thalia kissed her way across his chest, pausing to roll her tongue around each flat, dark nipple until it beaded between her lips. With a sneaky glance, she noticed that he was still not awake, though he made a soft, growling sound as she nipped at his skin. "Are you awake, my lord?" she whispered as her lips fluttered across the line of hair below his navel. He only responded with a stretch that allowed the coverlet to slip down, exposing his belly all the way to where the soft line of hair became coarse and wild, just at the base of his cock. She chewed at her lower lip, wondering if she might dare to pull the covers away. Thalia sat up and crawled over him, straddling his thighs then sitting back on his knees. He made no move to stop her, so she slowly pulled at the fabric until he was fully exposed. Her mouth watered. She had been so enthralled with the new sensations he'd wrought upon her last night that she hadn't really seen him until now.

Bending close, she examined his manhood. Such delicate construction for so crude a purpose. She watched as her breath against it caused a slight twitch that became more noticeable as the ends of her hair swept along the insides of his thighs. Then a single, tentative kiss. The skin was so smooth, and Thalia was fascinated by the pulse of blood rushing toward the warmth of her lips. It made her want to kiss him again and again, feeling his sex come to life, waking even as he slept. Finally, she couldn't help herself and took his cock into her mouth. The size of it was a little overwhelming, and she pulled back, swirling her tongue around the length. When she reached the tip, she nibbled lightly and rubbed her tongue against it, collecting the tiny drops of liquid that had already collected there. The flavor had a smoky, bittersweetness that only made her crave it more. Before long, she was devouring him, taking as much of his manhood into her mouth as she could. She wanted to pleasure him as he had pleasured her.

This time when she cast her eyes upward, Malik was watching. Those multi-colored orbs were fixed upon her as she took him into her mouth again and again. He made no sound, only watched with one arm behind his head for several minutes. After a time, he growled and wove his fingers into her hair. He tugged gently, just enough to make her scalp tingle, and when she looked up, he beckoned her to come to him. His cock slipped from her mouth, and she crawled up his body. "Kiss me," he rasped, and she obeyed. The taste of his mouth mingling with the silky essence that still lingered on her tongue made Thalia's heart beat faster. She felt sexy and alive. And possessed by him. Then his hands were on her hips as he positioned her over his cock. She couldn't wait, and before either could breathe or protest, she was sinking down, burying his member deep within. Once more she felt complete, and she nearly cried with relief.

He guided her movements, teaching her how to roll her hips back and forth and rewarding her efforts with a groan of pleasure. She tried to pull back, but he held her in place with a tight grip on her pelvis. It forced Thalia to grind her sex against him until they were both mewling with desire. Finally, it was too much, and he held her tight, rolling her over and pinning her to the bed. It only took a few rough strokes before both were shouting the other's name as they found release.

"I love you, Malik," Thalia whispered when she could speak. "Gods help me, I do."

"And I you, little mouse," he panted. "I think I've loved you all along."

Thalia shifted, burrowing into the crook of his arm to stave off the cold. He was so warm, as if the dragon fire still bubbled deep in his core. It was a comforting heat that made her feel lazy. "This is indeed a strange magic. I keep wondering if it's just a dream."

"If it is, then let us sleep forever," Malik sighed.

"Do you think Bella knew? When we were children, I mean. Do you think that she knew that I could break the curse laid upon you?"

"I think she hoped. I'm not sure Bella plans anything too far ahead."

Thalia giggled and laid her head on his chest, her ear just over his heart. It beat strong and fast. It was the same heart she'd felt in the dragon. Was the dragon gone forever? "I still can't believe... I'm nothing special at all. Just a slayer from Tarkin."

Malik chuckled and embraced her against his side, his large palm resting on the curve of her bottom. "You are a sorceress, my lady."

⊗⊗⊗

Belladonna stood on the battlements in the morning sunlight, feeling hope like she hadn't felt in many a long year and fear like she had never known before. The ruins of the castle Ellythin rose from the mist offered by the sea spray below, hardly any sign of its scarred past left behind. Her enchantment had eradicated the decay and sadness that had held the beauty of this place at bay for so long. The king had come home and brought with him a bride. Their love had sown new seeds of life. Life that would begin here and spread across the continent. Thane, Isling, the borderlands: each city would rise into the light under Malik, their rightful king. The time had finally come for him to seize power from the house of Laurenz.

Christophe, like his father before him, had been weak. Both were more interested in spending their spoils of war than defending them. Content to sit back and watch the kingdom fall to ruin while they amused themselves with mistresses and mead. Tristan thought himself noble because he was aware of the rebellions that were rising in the east. Tribes of wild warriors that were making their way across the borderlands would soon be knocking at his door. Even his pet, Grafton, had already been bought by these chieftains. Tristan's answer was to eradicate them and populate their regions with Osghastians. But the people of Osghast were starving. Isling and the other market towns were struggling to keep up with the demand of their trade posts overseas and leaving their people with nothing to eat. Other kingdoms around the continent were already finding alternative trade routes. Tristan would stupidly bring open war upon them, but to no avail. They were outnumbered, and their armory was primitive. Their only hope was Malik, a wise king that was the very embodiment of power. No one would oppose a Dragon Lord, and his magnanimous rule would unite the people. Bella had foreseen it. Malik would see it done. As she stared out over the ocean, she could smell the dawning of a new age mixed with the stink of encroaching darkness. It was overwhelming. She closed her eyes and said a small prayer that she was not too late.

"Could it be a fairy that I see standing here? Unguarded and daydreaming."

Bella gasped and turned, seeing Malik standing in the archway. "Is… is it really you? Or just one of my more convincing illusions?"

"I'm afraid not," he said as he strode toward her. His gait was careful; he hadn't quite found his footing yet. But his occasional limp did nothing to diminish his strength, and Bella's heart swelled again with hope. "Not even you could be so clever a sorceress."

"Oh, Malik!" she gasped, running to him and throwing her arms around his neck. To her relief, he embraced her tightly and laughed with her. "I can't believe it!"

"I find that hard to imagine."

"Of course I never doubted my own power, just the resolve of poor Thalia to put up with your odious disposition." She embraced him again and was, at once, struck by the strength that still lingered in his frame. His height, broad shoulders, and sharp features were so reminiscent of his dragon form. It gave him such a strange beauty that also hearkened to the boy she'd known so long ago.

"Perhaps she doesn't find me odious."

Bella smirked. "Evidently not. I can smell her perfume. You can say thank you anytime, you know."

"For?"

"For rearing your perfect partner, of course."

Malik snorted and stumbled as he pulled away. "I will eventually get the hang of this walking thing, yes?"

"Of course. Though I suspect your trouble walking this morning has very little to do with spending thirty-odd years as a dragon." Bella giggled as he cut his eyes at her. "Though if you're having so much trouble, I shudder to imagine how Thalia is coping."

Malik did not respond as he stepped up on to the battlements and stared over the cliffs below. "I haven't ever seen the world so close," he breathed, closing his eyes as the chill morning breeze kissed his face. "Always from high above, or lurking in shadows. Outside looking in." He turned his gaze to Bella once more. "I'm not sure I can do it. Be part of the world. Or if I even want to."

She stepped up beside him, winding an arm around his waist and laying her head against his muscled arm. "You must forgive them, Malik. The people of Osghast need you. The whole of the continent is about to fall into ruin…"

"Why do I care?" he snarled. "Why should I bother saving them when I was cast out—a treasonous monster unworthy of acceptance? No one has ever helped me!"

"You mustn't be selfish. And think about it, Malik. What would you have done in their position? Your father was crippled with grief over your lost mother. It was mercy that stayed his hand from crushing you right then and there."

"He was just too much of a coward to do it. He could only throw me from the tower like a bit of old rubbish!" He rounded on the fairy so quickly that she stumbled and fell to the ground before him. "Such blind compassion for one who betrayed your queen."

"Yes, he betrayed my queen. But Mab betrayed him as well, tricked him into magic he could never have understood. And don't you understand? If this world dies, devoured by darkness, the Fae will die as well. I will be trapped here. Forever. And forever is a very long time, Malik."

"Still a selfish little pixie." Malik sighed and began to pace along the wall, his gait growing more confident. "What makes you think that my brother will abdicate to me, Bella?"

"He won't have a choice."

"Indeed, he will. He has the favor of the people. No one will know who I am. And even if they did, they wouldn't be too keen to allow the great Wyrm of Gwynfir rule over them."

"They will not defy a Dragon Lord."

Malik shook his head as if trying to shut out her words. "You said yourself—I am no Dragon Lord. In case you hadn't noticed, I'm not a dragon at all. I'm... an abomination."

"Malik..."

"No!" he growled. "Haven't you stolen enough of my happiness? I'm not interested in being king! Let my brother have it. Go to him yourself and advise him if you must, but this... this has *nothing* to do with me! Nothing to do with Thalia! Just let us be. Why can't you just let me be happy?" His eyes were pleading, and Bella felt sorry for him. Sorry that she had to lay this task upon him. Sorry that he'd been born into such a predicament.

"Please, sire..."

He turned away, storming toward the doors. For a moment he paused, as if moving this new body was exhausting work. "Do not call me that," he growled.

"But that's what you are, Malik! You are the son of Christophe, an heir to the throne of Osghast. You must leave this solitary existence behind and embrace who you are."

He rounded on her quickly, his eyes blazing, and for a moment, she believed he might turn back to his dragon form here on the battlements. "You have no idea who I am or what I am! While I am grateful for your kindness, I owe you nothing! You nor any of my kin." As he stalked toward her, Bella cowered before him. Something about him was now more frightening than he had been as a dragon. His resolve was stronger. He would fight for Thalia, and he saw waging war with his brother as nothing more than a danger to their future together. Malik would not allow her to be taken from him. No throne could compete with his true love. Her heart sank as she realized that there was nothing she might say to sway him. "I'm afraid that I'm no savior."

"The world will burn, Malik! There will be nothing left for you or Thalia!"

"You mean nothing left for you!"

"Or anyone!"

Malik stepped back, pacing like a pent-up beast. She got the distinct impression that if he hadn't backed off, he would have hit her.

"I... I hate you for putting me in this position!" he snapped. "And I won't allow it! I won't put her in danger."

"She's already in danger, Malik. Don't you think Tristan will come for her? He doesn't just give up..."

"He got exactly what he wanted!"

"Don't you understand? You are an heir! He knows that as long as you live that his power is in jeopardy!"

Malik turned his back, waving her off. "Leave me alone, Belladonna."

"Malik..."

"Leave me!" he roared, storming away from her words and obligations.

Chapter Twenty-Two

Thalia pushed her food around the plate with the tines of her fork. She'd been sitting here for over an hour watching the sky grow darker with an impending storm and waiting for Malik to join her. Bella fluttered around bringing tray after tray of food and finally sat down beside Thalia. "Where could he be?" she sighed.

"I'm sure he just lost track of the time, dear," Bella replied, pouring more wine in her goblet and then Thalia's.

"Oh no... please," Thalia said, putting a hand over her goblet. She'd already had enough wine tonight to make her eyelids heavy and her speech slow. "But he's been gone for ages. When he left me this morning, he assured me that we would have dinner together."

"He's been alone so long. You can't expect him to adhere to social niceties like dinner times." Thunder crashed above them so loud that the glass in the windows rattled. Both women shuddered.

"I know. I just have this feeling that there's something wrong. Did he say anything to you when he left?"

Bella shook her head, taking another long swallow of wine. The fairy, while usually talkative and bubbly, had been acting strange all day. While Thalia explored the many rooms of the castle and the overgrown gardens surrounding it, she had barely seen her. Several times as she looked out the window, she saw Belladonna standing on the cliffs, looking out as if keeping watch for someone, but when Thalia had questioned her later, she would only shrug and change the subject. "I'm sure he'll be back before long. He's only been human for a day. There is much of the dragon still there."

Thalia sighed and played with her food a little more. Then an idea dawned. "Do you think perhaps he went to Gwynfir?"

"He couldn't even if he wanted to. Not without his wings. The path leading to the mountain's base has long since been destroyed. It's only accessible from the cave near the summit. Only dragons go there."

"He took me."

"Of course he did. It was the most intimate thing he could think of before he changed. Showing you his home. His real home. The only place he's ever felt safe."

Thalia stood up so fast that her chair fell backward. "But it's not his home anymore. He should be here!" She rushed from the dining hall and into the foyer beyond, nearly falling over her skirts.

"Thalia! Stop!" Bella called as she ran after her. "You can't go running out into the forest! There's a storm coming!"

"Maybe he's hurt..."

"That's ridiculous, Thalia. What would make you think that?"

"Something's wrong! I just know it! I can feel it. Malik is in trouble!" Before she could protest, another clap of thunder hit, and Thalia fell to her knees. As Bella tried to help her up, they began to realize that the noise wasn't coming from the storm, but from the sound of many horses clomping up the jagged pass. They ran to the windows and threw the drapes aside. It had already begun to rain, and it was pitch black. Lightning flashed, illuminating the rocky path that led to the castle doors. A small regiment of royal guards was advancing on Ellythin.

"What on Earth?"

"Tristan. He's sent them to rescue me, presumably." As she said it, there was a thud against the door and then a repeated banging. Thalia heard the wood splinter with the impact. "They're trying to break in."

Bella grabbed her arm and began pulling her toward the staircase. "Come, Thalia. We must hide!"

"Idiot," she grumbled. "As if I would need rescue."

"Perhaps that is not his purpose!" Bella hissed. "There are more sinister forces at work here, and we would do well to avoid them!"

"What about Malik?" Thalia said, stumbling over the rug in their haste to get away. "We have to warn him! Whatever they want, it obviously isn't good."

"Malik can take care of himself. Besides, I think they're coming for you, child."

Suddenly, the doors burst open in an explosion of wood. "Lord of Ellythin! Come forth!" Thalia recognized the guard from Esa's cottage, the one with the greased hair and the leather chest plate.

Evidently, he remembered her too, grinning toothily as she placed herself between him and Bella. "Hello, poppet."

"What do you want?" Thalia said, trying to sound more confident than she felt. She cast a glance sideways, hoping to see some object that she might defend herself with. Back at the dining table, there were knives, but the few steps back seemed like leagues.

"We've come to take you back," he said, taking a step toward them.

"I see," Thalia said. She swallowed hard to mask the tremor in her voice. Bella was gripping her arm tightly. "The prince…"

"King."

"What?"

"Prince Tristan has ascended to the throne, my lady. But you already knew that, din'tcha?"

"I've no idea what you're talking about."

The captain nodded and waved more guards through the doors. "The king was concerned with your safety, miss. Sent us to collect ya."

"Well… he's very kind. But as you can see, I and my… my… servant are quite well. Do tell the king that his kindness didn't go unnoticed." By this time there were ten guards surrounding them. This was obviously not a rescue mission. Their swords were drawn, and none of them seemed concerned that a dragon was going to appear and destroy them.

The captain said no more but nodded toward his men. Before

Thalia or Bella could react, they were upon them, grabbing and pulling at them roughly. The guard rushed forward, taking Thalia's arm and attempting to pull her toward him. She rounded quickly and elbowed his chin, knocking his head backward hard enough that she could hear the crack of bone. She scrambled away, jumping on the back of another guard that was busy trying to hold Bella.

"Get hold of them, you idiots!" the captain shouted, blood dripping from his lip.

More guards rushed in, pulling Thalia away from the other guard. But she was quicker, catching them off guard as she bashed her head against the forehead of the first and driving a knee into the guts of the second. They obviously weren't expecting a girl to be able to fight them, and they both stumbled backward. "Bella! Run!" Thalia screamed as she ran toward the dining room, knowing that one of those knives was her only hope. Before she could lay her hands on a silver hilt, the captain was upon her. With a hard kick to the middle of her back, he sent her sprawling forward against the table. The wind was knocked from her, and for a moment, she couldn't catch her breath. She tried to push back, but the heavy captain loomed behind her. As she tried to rise, he grabbed her by the hair and bashed her head against the table in two quick strikes. It didn't knock her out, but she was disoriented. Enough that he was able to turn her roughly so that she was lying beneath him. His hot breath smelled of mead and blood, and it turned her stomach as he breathed over her. "Let me go!"

"Not just yet, poppet." He leaned over her, sniffing as if he were some kind of animal. "Such a pretty thing. I bet you're unspoiled, too."

"Leave me alone," Thalia growled, kicking out desperately but unable to connect. She could hear Bella shrieking in the next room, and she wished that Malik were here. His dragon form would make short work of them. As the captain of the guard pressed his body against hers, licking at the side of her throat, Thalia managed to free one of her arms and reached back, struggling to grab at one of the utensils. Just as she closed her hand around the hilt, he grabbed her wrist, crushing it against the table until she lost her grip.

"Still the little fighter, eh?" he growled before his fist came down across the bridge of her nose.

Everything went dark.

⁂

I t was apparent that something was wrong as soon as Malik crested the hill. Ellythin rose in the darkness, outlined against the deep blue. He raised his head and sniffed the air. Despite his new form, the dragon senses still remained, and Ellythin smelled different. He sprinted across the ragged gardens and around to the doors. All over the ground were signs of struggle: broken stone, bits of cloth, and other debris lay here and there. The doors hung on their hinges, missing splinters and scraped up from either a battering ram or hooves. He recognized the sharp scent of horses and sweat. His heart beat hard in his chest, and he burst through into the foyer.

"Thalia!" he called, his voice echoing. "Thalia! Come down here now! Bella!" He held his breath, listening for any small noise. But there was none. He took the stone stairs two at a time, running from room to room searching for them and calling their names to no avail. The castle was completely empty. As he sniffed at the air again, he couldn't smell any blood, and that eased his mind somewhat. Perhaps they had just gone looking for him. But why would they go out in the storm? Even now, there was rumbling in the distance and lightning flashed, threatening to tear open the sky once more.

"Malik!" Bella ran toward him, stumbling over her feet in her haste. Her dress was torn, and her face was ashen with an almost feverish look. "Thank the gods," she panted. She slammed against him, weeping into his chest.

"What's going on?"

"It's Thalia. Tristan's men... they came to the castle. He sent them to arrest her."

"Arrest her?"

"Yes," she nodded. "King Christophe is dead, and they think Thalia murdered him!"

"What?" He grabbed her by the shoulders roughly, shaking her. "Where is she?"

"Please, Malik... I tried to help her! I tried to fight them off, but there were just too many of them! I had to get away..."

"You used your magic to save your own skin and not Thalia's!" He could feel the anger rising up from his middle, and he wanted to strangle the life from the witless pixie.

"No! I had to, Malik! I had no choice. They would have killed us both, and there would have been no one to tell you what became of us!"

The rage receded, and Malik relaxed his grip on Belladonna, shoving her backward and starting to pace nervously. He raked his fingers through his hair, mumbling to himself. "I shouldn't have left. I knew something like this was going to happen."

"Don't blame yourself," Bella said.

"Then who should I blame?"

"The only one responsible. Tristan. It's Tristan who has brought this upon us! I told you he was dangerous."

"Oh, so now it's my fault for not destroying him sooner?"

"No, Malik," she said, laying a calming hand on his shoulder. "But it is up to you to fix it."

"What are you talking about?"

"We have no choice now, my son. You must go and confront your brother. It is the only way to get Thalia back."

He rounded on Belladonna with an inhuman roar making her cower as if he might still breathe fire. "How do you propose I do that? Sneak in like an assassin? I'll get us both killed. Tristan has an army of guards that are waiting for me to do just that! They know I'll be coming for her, and they'll be expecting it. The whole thing is a trap! I can smell it!"

"But you're..."

"I'm what? I am *nothing* now! How can I fight the entire Osghastian army by myself? In case you hadn't noticed, I left behind my dragon form when the curse was broken! I shed the skin and left it lying on the floor of the Great Hall, along with whatever strength I had!"

She started to say more, but paused, almost holding her breath. Malik could tell that some devious scheme was working its way into her brain. He had seen this look many times over the years. The Fae were not strong. They had to rely on their wits and their magic to outsmart their opponents, and that's what Malik needed now. No longer could he rely on brute force. He would have to think his way through this, and it was in Bella's best interest to help him.

"What is it?" Malik said finally.

"Show me where you shed your skin."

Chapter Twenty-Three

When Thalia awoke, the only thing she was aware of was pain. A deep, splitting pain between her eyes that radiated around them like a mask of burning pressure. She was pretty sure that her face was swollen beyond all recognition. When she reached up to touch her cheek, she nearly screamed in agony. She could taste the blood on her lips, and the side of her face felt cold and sticky. Slowly, her vision began to clear, and after a few attempts, she was able to sit up. She was in a small, round room with a tiny window. It was dark and cold with no furniture to speak of. The floor on which she lay was rough stone, and as she got to her knees, it scraped against them. She was still wearing the modest gown that Bella had helped her into, but the flowing silk was stained with blood and dirt from the floor.

"Where am I?" she murmured to herself, half-crawling toward the tiny window. It wasn't much of a window, just a slit in the bricks so that she could see down into the courtyard below. She recognized this place. It was the castle in Thane. The place she'd been brought before the ritual that united her with Malik. The grounds were bedecked with bunting in the royal colors: proof that what the guard had said was true. A new king had been crowned. She could also see the distant battlements that had been destroyed by the dragon more than a month ago. A crew of peasants was laying bricks to rebuild the fortification, but the scarring was still there as well as scorch marks and blackened trees dotting the gardens.

"They call this the 'Screaming Tower of Thane.'" Thalia turned to see Tristan and the captain of his guard enter.

"How quaint," Thalia replied, turning back to the window and staring out at the horizon.

"Do you know why?"

"No idea, but I'm sure you'll enlighten me," she sighed, already tiring of Tristan's wicked king routine.

Tristan offered a thin-lipped smile. He was clearly insulted that she wasn't the least bit intimidated by him. He held her gaze, and for a moment, she was struck by his resemblance to Malik. They were twins indeed, but not identical. Tristan's golden hair almost matched the sun-kissed color of his brow. It was the mark of a hunter, and Malik's hunting had been done under a cloak of iron scales. They were like two halves of the same coin: one light, one dark. "Most think that it's because this is where the queens of old would give birth. But no, I'm afraid it's much more sinister than that. The castle was constructed some five hundred years ago by the only queen borne of the house of Laurenz. Queen Magira was thought to be the most beautiful woman in the whole of the continent. As the only offspring of King Charon, she became Queen of Osghast at the tender age of thirteen."

Thalia yawned. "How nice for her."

Tristan ignored her rudeness. "As we all know, young girls can be very jealous of one another, so when construction began on the castle, she insisted that the royal architect include a tower right in the center of the building that was higher than any that had ever been attempted. It was to be lined with heavy limestone bricks, brought from the mountains. No one was quite sure what use she had for such a thing, but as Magira was queen, no one questioned her motives or why the tower had to be so high."

"Well, towers are generally watchtowers, and at that time, there would have been many dragons..."

"Well, that's what everyone thought," Tristan continued. "Until the day of the spring festival. People came from all over the continent for reveling. As was the custom, all the young, unmarried maidens came into the square for a ritual dance. Traditionally, this was the time at which all the unmarried men would choose their brides. Just before the dance began, Queen Magira entered the square, bowing to each of the girls. As she walked through the crowd, she would stop at the most beautiful maidens and place a kiss on their foreheads. One by one, the girls who had been kissed were gathered up by the guards and led into the castle and high up into the tower. This tower. They were marched up the spiraling staircase to this very room where the guards barricaded them inside and set the entire room aflame. It is said that the screams of the dying maidens could be heard all over the continent, but because of the height of the tower, no one in the street below could smell the burning flesh."

As Thalia stared around the room, she could see that the bricks were blackened and glossy like obsidian. She ran her fingertips along the walls and noticed that there were tiny striations that had been gouged into the bricks. She held up her hand, matching the pattern of the marks. "Mercy be upon me," she whispered.

"Oh don't worry, my lady," Tristan chuckled. "I would never be so barbaric as to burn you alive. Though, the penalty for killing a king is probably less merciful..."

"You know I didn't kill anyone!"

Tristan sighed and gestured to the guard with a smug wave. Thalia cringed as the door slammed behind the guard and then the ominous clicking of the lock. He paced around her, as if giving her a clinical examination. Perhaps he was searching for signs that the dragon had marked her in some way or left his scent behind. It made Thalia feel dirty, and she crossed her arms over her chest, concentrating on being unbothered. "Yes, Thalia. I know you didn't. I know you didn't because I did."

Thalia gasped, his blunt admission hitting like a kick to the belly. "You?"

"Oh, don't look so surprised. I wouldn't be the first crown prince to seize power from his father with violence."

"How could you?"

"You're far too sentimental, Huntress. Call it a minor indemnity.

My father was dying slowly, succumbing to weakness and bringing the entire kingdom down with him. It was inevitable that I take control before he lost everything."

"You lying, murderous little snake…"

"Must we resort to name-calling? It doesn't become you. I was only doing what was necessary to ensure all our futures. And it was clear that he wasn't going to bow out gracefully. Believe me, Thalia. I tried."

She scoffed. "I can just imagine your trying."

Tristan feigned hurt, clutching his chest and giving an exaggerated bow at her feet. "You wound me, my lady. To think that you could paint me a villain. Perhaps I am, but I can assure you that a few small sacrifices are just a cross I will have to bear for the good of my people."

"The good of yourself," Thalia spat, jerking back from him as he tried to lay a greasy palm on her shoulder. "And what do you mean 'sacrifice'? Surely you aren't thinking of attempting *Sheakhol* again." She swallowed a smile of her own, thinking of how this time would be pointless.

"Oh, I don't think that will be necessary. He'll come for you himself. Assuming he still wants you. I can't imagine why, but seeing as how you haven't been destroyed after all this time."

Thalia turned away, her head high in defiance. "Malik would never be so stupid as to come here for me." She glanced over her shoulder, hoping that he couldn't hear the doubt in her voice. It wasn't stupidity that would draw Malik back to Thane. It was love, bravery, and honor. Three qualities the sniveling child-king would never understand. "Your traps are very obvious, Majesty."

Tristan gave a snort of disdain. "There is no trap. A trap would imply that I want to capture your precious dragon alive." He started to say more, but paused, pressing a finger to his lip and pacing. Finally, he spoke. "You know, perhaps the Fae witch was right."

"What are you talking about?"

"Oh Thalia," he said, walking around and placing his hands on her shoulders and rubbing slowly down her arms. It was an almost sexual caress, and Thalia cringed. "No need to be coy. Mab told me everything. About the curse and how to break it. She told me about you, you know."

"About me?"

"Oh yes, little Huntress. She told me that you were the only one who could destroy the dragon. I didn't believe her myself, at first. Of course, there's more than one way to destroy a dragon. Making him an impotent pet would certainly do the job. And how perfect. You make him fall in love with you. I kill my father and blame you for it. Arrest you and throw you in the Screaming Tower and wait for him to come. By now he's just a stuttering weakling. He'll be so easy to kill, Thalia."

She shook her head, trying to block out his words. Had it all been for nothing? It seemed now that she'd saved Malik only to make him vulnerable. "No one will believe you... I didn't kill King Christophe."

Now his arms snaked around her, and he spoke softly against her ear. "Do you think anyone cares? I'm the king, and you're just a dragonslayer. A dirty little tribe child. They will believe it because it is easy to believe. People aren't interested in the truth. They're interested in justice..."

"Justice is truth," she gasped, trying to pull away from him.

"Oh, you poor darling. Justice has nothing whatever to do with truth. Justice is finding someone to blame. And here I thought my little gift had gone to waste after that ridiculous ritual."

"What are you talking about?" she asked, finally pushing him off and backing away.

"The dagger I gave you to injure the dragon. I told you it was one of a kind." He pulled a dagger from a sheath at his side and held it out to her. "That wasn't exactly the truth." She didn't want to touch it. She could feel an evil energy radiating off of the steel. This weapon was the twin of the one he'd given her, right down to the slight curve of the blade and the placement of carved feathers on the raven at the hilt. He held it out to her once more. "Take it. I implore you, Huntress. It isn't everyone that gets to touch a blade that has tasted the blood of a king. It's quite a beautiful piece of craftsmanship. The serrations in the blade leave a *very* distinct wound."

Thalia's blood turned to ice in her veins. She wanted to grab the dagger and plunge it right into Tristan's heart, but then she really would have killed the king. Right now was not the time. That guard was right outside the door, and there was no other escape route. She'd be found out immediately and most likely executed on the spot. She would have to bide her time. He'd trapped her much too easily in his web of deceit. "What do you intend to do with me, sire?" she said, her voice nearly a whisper.

"I can't risk Malik thinking you're dead." He sheathed the dagger and smiled. "Ah, hope. The great motivator. The key is for him to think that there is hope that he can save you. He'll come to the castle, and I'll be waiting."

Thalia laughed bitterly. "All your scheming. All this time thinking that you're the hero of your own story." She stepped closer, their noses nearly touching. She would show Tristan no fear. "You're pathetic. And it will come home to roost. I promise you that."

"I shall truly enjoy killing you when the time comes, my lady."

"Funny, I had the same thought."

Chapter Twenty-Four

❧✦❧

"Are you certain this is going to work?" Malik had his doubts as he pulled the dark cloak around his shoulders. What Bella was proposing was absolutely preposterous. Of course, he had to admit that her logic was sound. Why else would the other skins dissolve into ash, leaving only one heavy pelt of scales lying on the floor? And leather armor fashioned from dragon scales was rare but not unheard of. But being able to take the dragon form at will? The thought seemed a bit odd even for a fairy.

"I'm not particularly certain of anything," Bella replied, stroking the muzzle of the enormous black stallion that would carry Malik back to Thane. "Only that Thalia must be saved and Tristan must be overthrown."

Malik grasped the saddle and heaved himself astride the horse's back, giving no sign of his former awkwardness. Rage had forced him to acclimate to these new dimensions. Yes, he was enraged. So many years he'd spent outcast and alone, and now that he'd finally broken free, no one was going to take that away from him. Not even a king ravenous for power. "All I care about is getting her back," he snarled, looking down on Belladonna. "Thalia is all that matters."

"Just be careful."

"Don't worry, Bella," he said with a smirk. "I know my way home."

She reached out and took his hand and gave a gentle squeeze. "He knows you're coming."

"Then his death should be no surprise."

With a kick to the flanks, the horse reared up and took off down the path through the darkened wood. *It is quite a strange feeling to be astride a beast instead of the beast itself,* Malik thought. He felt a sense of power and control very unlike how he'd felt as the dragon. At no time in his many years trapped in that awkward and lumbering form had he felt in control. The rage was always there, just on the edge of explosion. But this was different. While he was angry and felt a desperate need to save Thalia from his scheming brother as well as avenge himself, a calm had descended. His brother would be expecting him to burst in recklessly. Malik didn't need Belladonna's fairy clairvoyance to tell him that there would be guards surrounding the castle and an army of knights standing at the ready. He would have to employ stealth rather than strength to rescue Thalia.

As for taking up the mantle as king of Osghast, he still wasn't interested, despite Bella's protestations. He was willing to do whatever was necessary to save Thalia, but as soon as it was done, he fully intended to leave. He would flee the continent, run away to the ends of the earth if he had to, but Osghast was full of memory, and he wasn't interested in settling old scores.

The stallion given him by Belladonna was fast, as if it might be another bit of her magic. Its large black muzzle spewed heavy plumes of steam as the animal pushed itself faster, but it never seemed to tire. In fact, as they raced against the sun, the beast sped up. At this rate, he would reach the castle before dark. Which was good. He would need the cover of night to storm the keep. Especially if his brother was as cunning as he thought. Malik would be completely outnumbered, even if he had a dragon form.

The path before him began to narrow, and the terrain grew murky and uneven. If he didn't slow, the horse would surely break its leg. He pulled up on the reins, but his steed didn't seem to notice. "Whoa," he shouted with another sharp tug. The horse let out an angry whine and jerked his head. "Dammit, Bella," he growled. Leave to his fairy godmother to stick him with a crazed horse. The horse reared up once and took off through the forest, leaving the path. It leaped over blow-downs, crisscrossing between the trees. Malik felt a warm wetness sliding down his cheek as low-hanging branches whipped his face. It was a testament to his agility that he was able to stay astride the beast. "Stop!" he shouted again as if the horse could understand. With one more savage pull of the reins, the horse reared up and threw Malik with an angry snort before running off. He got to his feet quickly and ran after the stallion until he realized it was no use. "Bastard! You'd better not run back to Ellythin! I'll feed your worthless carcass to the wolves!" he shouted after it, kicking at the dirt.

"Halt!"

Malik slowly turned, hands in the air, to see a line of guards behind him. The Laurenz crest adorned the sleeves of their ragged tunics. "Drop your weapons!" the leader barked.

Malik glanced at the steel blade hanging at his side. "That doesn't seem fair," he replied. "You have me grossly outnumbered, gentlemen."

"Your sword, sir!" the leader shouted, raising his own weapon. The end of his blade quavered slightly, but the man's gaze never left Malik's. He was frightened but determined.

"I didn't realize that there was a law prohibiting weapons in the forest surrounding Thane. Things have much changed since last I passed through."

"Orders of the king. No one enters the gates armed or otherwise."

Malik glanced from one guard to the next, taking in every detail. Their only armor was a heavy leather chest plate that had been patched several times. The swords that were pointed at him were scratched and dull. They'd have better luck bashing at his head with them than they would trying to run him through. And judging by the way their hands trembled, he wasn't sure any of these men would have the presence of mind to defend themselves should he prove to be hostile. They were rather small, and their faces had a ruddy, malnour-ished pallor. These were not knights, but indentured peasants forced into service by his brother. As Malik looked around at his opponents, he realized most of them were either too old to raise a beard or too young. A tree branch crunched somewhere in the distance behind them, and Malik was certain that there were also archers in the trees surrounding the area. If they were anything like this rag-tag bunch of farmers, he wouldn't have trouble eluding their arrows. "What would you know about orders of the king, my friend?"

"I'm warning you…"

"Because unless I miss my guess, you lot aren't exactly knights of the royal regiment. You nor your friends up there with their arrows pointed at my head." He decided to humor them and drew his sword, placing it at his feet carefully, his eyes fixed on the guards. "I can assure you that I mean you no harm."

"State your business, outlander."

"I'm just passing through Thane," Malik lied. "My business is my own."

"Dragonmail is not something seen often in these parts," the leader said, gesturing at the black scales that peeked from beneath Malik's cloak. "In fact, the only people who have that sort of armor are gypsies or thieves. So which one are you?"

"Neither," Malik replied with a smirk reminiscent of his dragon form. "I'm afraid if I revealed my identity that you would not believe me."

The guards were silent, looking back and forth at one another as if trying to figure out what to do next. "Keiran! Search him!" the leader barked, gesturing at a small figure at the end of the line. As he drew near, Malik could see that he was just a boy. Malik raised his arms, allowing the boy to search the folds of his cloak and the medicine bag at his side.

"What's this?" Keiran said. He pulled Thalia's dagger from a sheath under Malik's arm and brandished it for his superior.

"You'll want to give that back, boy," Malik growled. That was Thalia's property, and he intended to defend it.

"No weapons beyond this point, sir," the boy said, looking to the other guards for reassurance. "By order of the king." Malik took a step forward, and the boy cowered, looking back at the old leader. "Silas…"

"If'n you're intending to pass through the capital, I'm afraid we'll be keeping your steel." The leader closed the distance between them in two long strides. Malik had to bite the inside of his cheek to keep from smiling. Obviously the man had underestimated the size of his opponent. His oily scalp barely came to Malik's shoulder, but he tried to look intimidating just the same. "Think of it as a toll," he said, reaching for the sword Malik had laid at his side.

"You'll get none of my steel today. In fact, I predict that you'll be most useful in taking me to King Tristan himself."

The guard cackled and looked around at the others, seeming to test the blade of the sword before tossing it to one of the others. Malik watched as the sword was tucked into a saddlebag, gone and of no use anymore. "Your arrogance is almost amusing." With a synchronized scream of their blades against the leather, the guards drew their weapons and took an attack stance. "But it will hardly save you."

"Planning to murder an innocent adventurer?" Malik said, backing away as they advanced.

"Innocent? Not in that armor." The leader lunged forward with his sword, but Malik was too fast, dodging the blow easily. The blade grazed the edge of the armor, and the guard fell forward. Malik grabbed his arm and pulled the man forward, bashing his forehead against the opponent and throwing him backward. The man was dazed, scrambling to his knees and sitting down hard on the underbrush. Two of the others rushed Malik, connecting with his midsection and throwing his body against the tree behind. Malik felt the breath forced from his chest, and he gasped. It was enough of a distraction for another guard to punch him, closed fisted across the bridge of his nose. His eyes glazed for a moment, and he could taste his own blood, but his recovery was quick. He shook off the blow and turned just in time for another to swing at him clumsily with his broadsword. The weapon was obviously too much for the guard, and as Malik dodged, the counterbalance threw him down and drove the blade into the soft ground. Malik grabbed the hilt and used it for leverage, leaping to kick the guard in the face and pulling the sword from the ground. A graceful turn and Malik's sword clanged against another. The leader of the guard was up again, and this time he was angry. He hacked and slashed against Malik's sword with a vengeance. Malik was proficient but unpracticed, and his movements were sloppy. He began to realize that he was tiring and soon he'd be bested. Obviously, he'd underestimated the farmer. With a deafening crack, the guard disarmed him sending the broadsword flying. Out of the corner of his eye, he saw the others regrouping and ready to attack.

"There's only two choices, outlander," the leader snarled, bringing his blade to Malik's throat. "State your business in Thane and perhaps we'll just throw you to the dungeons. Or resist and we'll just kill you." Malik's breath was heavy from the fight, and he could feel blood dripping down his face. This sensation of losing was most unpleasant. The irony of his situation got the better of him, and soon he was laughing. "What's so funny?"

"You," Malik stuttered. "Thinking that you could kill me." He pulled at the clasp at his throat and let the ruined cloak fall from his shoulders. "You, a shabby... sloppy... slow-witted farmer!" he spat, crawling to his knees. "Do you even know where the dungeons of Thane castle are?" The guard, sensing the madness lurking in Malik's eyes, began to back up. He kept the blade pointed at him, but Malik could see it tremble. "You have neither the strength nor the stature to best the likes of me!"

Malik stood, feeling a burning beneath his skin. He thought it must be the fire of his anger, for now he was enraged. These men were blocking his path to Thalia and, in turn, daring to challenge him! He stretched, feeling that his skin was stretched too taut over his body. "My blood runs through the veins of this city! My power is great, and my kingdom is unfathomable!" He felt himself growing: his neck lengthening and his limbs stretching further. His voice became a rasping growl, and his jaw cracked and shifted. "You will bow before me or be crushed beneath my feet!" And with that, his dragon form burst forth from his skin, knocking the guards backward with the force of his magic. The transformation was complete in a matter of seconds, and the guards could only stare up at him in shock and awe. As his head broke through the canopy of trees overhead, he let out a terrifying roar that shook the ground on which they stood. His wings unfurled behind him as he crouched down on his haunches, hissing and spitting fire over their heads. "I am the Dragon Lord of Osghast, and all shall bow before me!"

One by one the guards fell to their knees, dropping their swords to genuflect before him. The archers began to fall from the trees, fleeing the fight. "Sire... we did not know," the leader blubbered. "Please... spare us."

"Don't be stupid," Malik snarled. "As if such a meager mouthful would satisfy me."

"No, sire..."

Malik sniffed the air around them. "She is here," he hissed. "Somewhere near. I can smell her scent on the breeze." Gazing over the tops of the trees, he could see the castle rising out of the mist. The highest tower rose above all the rest, looking down on the surrounding city, keeping watch. Her soul was like a beacon. She was there.

"The bride of *Sheakhol*. Is that the woman you seek?" The young boy rose from where he knelt and approached the dragon. He still held the silvery steel dagger, clutching it tightly in his fist as if he were afraid Malik might turn on him.

"You know of her?"

"Aye, sire," Silas said. "King Tristan had her thrown in the Screaming Tower. She killed King Christophe!"

"Lies!" Malik hissed, making the boy cower.

"She's to be killed on the morrow, my lord. Impaled at the palace gates as all who betray the kingdom are."

Malik roared again in rage. "If you value your lives, you'll help me make sure that doesn't happen."

Chapter Twenty-Five

Thalia stared out at the courtyard below. The sounds of hammering bounced off the stone walls. They were erecting a large, wooden catapult in the center of the courtyard. It was meant to fire large, iron arrows. She had seen them before. Towns in the borderlands where dragons were still known to invade kept them in towers atop hills. There was also some sort of staging area at the gates. She was pretty sure that she knew what it was for. She was no stranger to local justice. Often when towns called for dragonslayers, they had already exhausted all the usual remedies for curses. Many times, those curses involved sacrifices and scapegoats. She'd seen women burned at the stake, men locked in cages atop the tower to starve to death and the meat picked from their bones by vultures. But the most severe crime that one could commit was treason. The people of Osghast were thirsty for blood after the murder of their king, and Tristan would be sure that their thirst was sated. Thalia would be impaled on a stake in front of the palace gates, a gruesome display that would serve as a warning to anyone who might dare to defy the new king. Nobles, commoners, and the chieftains of border realms like Tarkin—anyone who might seek to take advantage of the turmoil. Her death would give Tristan a double advantage. Not only would he incite a fearful respect in the hearts of his subjects, but his plot would surely draw in Malik, his only rival for the throne. Thalia was the bait for the trap, and she knew it.

She leaned against the window frame and stared into the night sky. Was he out there somewhere? Closing her eyes, she fell into the memory of her night with him. Every caress, whispered words of love, every kiss: they were her only comfort. Her heart ached for him, and though she wanted him so badly, she said a silent prayer that he would stay away from Thane. Tristan was ruthless and would stop at nothing to kill him. Thalia couldn't bear the thought of her own death if she didn't know that he would live on. Now that he had been given back his human face, he could start over. Find someone to love him. A single silvery tear ran down her cheek as she thought about how it might have been her. She remembered her vision in the gardens at Ellythin. Those children should have been hers, but it did not matter. As long as Malik lived, her sacrifice would not be in vain.

"I've brought you food, my lady." Thalia turned to see Balan entering the chamber with a large tray. She almost didn't recognize him. He looked so old. So unlike the man she'd met just over a month previous. His stance had once been proud and straight, but now he hobbled like a hunched over old man. His hair hung loose around his face, and skin had a waxy, wan look.

"Balan," she said, rushing to him to take the heavy-laden tray. "Are you all right?"

"Of course," he said. "I am just tired is all."

She set the tray aside and took his hand, pulling him over to the single, stone bench that sat in the center of the room. "Come, sit down. You don't look well."

He nodded and allowed her to help him. "I am... so sorry, my lady." As he said this, he began to cry, taking Thalia's hands and pressing them to his lips. He kissed them over and over, his tears wetting the back of her hand. "Please believe that I never wanted this to happen. If I had freed you, King Christophe would still be alive."

"Ssshhh..." she whispered. "Do not grieve so. None of this was your doing."

"The night of *Sheakhol...* I wanted to let you go. I would have let you go that night, but there were so many who were watching. And this... this is an evil business. Since King Christophe's death, things have been horrible. Tristan is paranoid and spies on all the servants, every citizen it seems. One poor lass was lashed because she didn't bow to Tristan in the corridor. People are scared, miss."

He wept against Thalia's shoulder, and she wanted to offer some comfort. He had only ever been kind. "What is Tristan planning to do, Balan?"

"He knows. He knows that the dragon will come for you. But this time, he has readied every knight in the kingdom to slay the beast and you as well. I heard him talking to that gypsy traitor, Grafton. Once the dragon, and I'm supposing you, are destroyed, he plans to wage war on the barbarian hordes that have been attacking along the borders."

"To what end?"

"He wants an all-out war, my lady! The barbarians are only the beginning."

"And he knows that as long as Malik is alive, his position will be threatened," Thalia murmured.

"Pardon?"

"Never mind." She grasped Balan's shoulders and forced him to look at her. "Look, I need your help."

"*My* help?"

"You have to believe me! I did not kill King Christophe. It was Tristan!"

"My lady! You can't mean that His Highness would murder his own father!" He tried to pull away, as if breaking contact with Thalia might help him elude the truth. "Innocent you may be, but..."

"Listen to me!" she shouted. "Tristan told me himself."

Balan shook his head. "No. I'm not getting involved in this." He pushed away from her with a violent shove and stumbled toward the door. "If I go against Tristan, I'll be executed!"

Thalia ran after him, grabbing his arm and falling on her knees, pleading. "Please, Balan. You're the only one I have a prayer of convincing. Please! I know I have nothing to offer you and you have no reason to help me..."

"Right!"

"Except your honor! When we met just a month ago, you were a proud man. Now, what I see before me is someone who has been broken. Who believes he has nothing left to fight for." Thalia closed her eyes and said a silent prayer that Balan would believe her story. "But Malik—the dragon. He is a Dragon Lord. He has foreseen Tristan's treachery and seeks to thwart it!"

"You *are* in league with the dragon," Balan whispered, his eyes wide.

"Yes! And so should you be! He is the only hope for Osghast. Malik is a Dragon Lord, yes, but he was made one..." She hesitated. The story sounded so unbelievable. And Thalia could tell that Balan was already so frightened that he wasn't willing to take a risk. "He is Christophe's son and heir to the throne of Osghast!"

Balan gave a snort of disbelief, shaking his head and turning to leave.

"Please! I'm telling you the truth!"

"The Wyrm of Gwynfir is the crown prince of Osghast? You're mad!"

"I wish I was," Thalia spat. "But it's true. Queen Katrin was cursed by the queen of the fairies! She gave birth to twins: one perfect on the inside but black as night in his heart. The other was distorted. A horrible monster yes, but believe me... his heart is true."

"So true that he was responsible for the deaths of so many!"

Thalia nodded sadly. "Yes. He was angry, so full of vengeance for his father and the entire kingdom for casting him out. But Balan, he is changed! The curse is broken and... he is our only hope. Osghast will fall if we allow Tristan to wage war." She grabbed Balan's hand and held it tight, forcing him to look into her face. "You already know this to be true."

Balan sighed, hanging his head in defeat. "Tristan is young and foolish. He believes he knows how to rule simply by being born, but in the short time he's been in power... The people are starving. The market towns are derelict. There is nothing to sell! Merchant ships are washing up, completely stripped. Pirates from neighboring kingdoms are starving us to death. Tristan says they're rogue thieves, but there have been too many of late to be random. Some say that they're being sanctioned by the governments. Tristan was right about that.

Christophe's enemies were aligning against him, but he ignored their threat. Now I fear it may be too late."

"And Tristan would mistake cruelty for strength. His foolish means will result in the loss of so many lives." Thalia looked upward into Balan's eyes. His resolve was crumbling. "Please, Balan. We don't have much time." Suddenly, as if to emphasize her words, there was screaming coming from the courtyard below. Both rushed to the window. Just over the tree line, a dragon soared against the dusky clouds. Thalia gasped as it circled the city, breathing fire into the air. "Malik," she whispered.

The siren bell began to ring from the battlements, alerting the townspeople of an attack. Any second, guards would begin pouring from the keep and surrounding the gates. The initial confusion would serve them well. She turned to Balan, holding her breath.

"Come on. We don't have much time."

Balan led Thalia to the door, a fingertip poised over his lips. There was a guard outside the door that they would have to get past first. This would require a weapon: one luxury no one had afforded her. She looked around for something, anything she might use to fight. The tray of food Balan had brought was still sitting by the door. She reached down and picked it up, turning it over and throwing the bowl of stew aside. "What are you going to do with that?" Balan whispered.

"Just trust me." She nodded, and he knocked at the heavy wooden door.

"Open the door!" Balan shouted. "I'm done." As soon as he said it, they both stepped back as the guard opened the door. For a split second, he was confused, not seeing anyone there. It was enough opportunity for Thalia to dart around the door and swing the silver tray with all her might. It connected with the guard's forehead with a resounding thud. It didn't knock him out at first, and he stumbled backward.

"What the fuck..." the guard groaned.

Balan was nothing if not brave and delivered a knee to the guard's groin as he tried to go for his sword. When he fell forward with a shriek of pain, it gave Thalia the opportunity to smash the tray over his head once more, knocking him cold.

Balan stared at her in disbelief. Thalia shrugged and threw the tray aside. "The element of surprise. Get his sword." Balan did as he was told and pulled the heavy sword from the guard's belt. It was almost bigger than he was, and he stumbled clumsily.

"Hurry. The others will have heard that!" she hissed, reaching for the sword.

"You'll never carry this. Get behind me, lass."

Thalia looked at him as if he'd taken leave of his senses. "Give it to me." His eyebrows shot up in amazement as she swung the sword a few times, testing its weight. Thalia might well be the bride of a Dragon Lord, but she was no princess. She would always be the Huntress. A slayer of Tarkin. "Let's go."

They were surprised to find no one as they slowly made their way down the long, winding staircase. They could hear commotion below, and evidently the entire castle guard was rushing to the gates to defend against the dragon attack. Their escape was almost too easy, but Thalia knew it wouldn't last. As soon as they emerged into a main corridor, they'd be spotted. Her tattered dress and hair flying about in a messy halo would give them away. Not to mention that Balan just looked suspicious: eyes darting everywhere, jumping at every sound. "Is there a back way to the gates?" she hissed, pressing their bodies against the stone wall as a couple of servants rushed past.

"There is a secret door in the library that leads into the servant stairs."

Thalia thought about how she'd helped Enke escape. It seemed like a lifetime ago. "How far do the servant stairs go?"

"All the way into the dungeons," Balan replied. "But that will only trap us there!"

Thalia shook her head. "No. It will take us to the river." She grabbed his arm and tugged him toward the main corridor. She peeked from around the corner and saw scores of people running amok. Every now and then there would be a dragon roar and more screaming. As they passed through one conduit after another, Thalia caught glimpses of the chaos outside. Guards had already begun to surround the castle. Which posed a problem for them as the idea was an impenetrable shield around the perimeter. No one would be able to get in or out. "We have to move quickly. Soon there'll be no getting out of here."

They sprinted along, keeping their heads down and praying that no one would notice them. Thalia kept her sword carefully hidden in the folds of her skirt, but it was growing heavy with her awkward grip. "This way," Balan said. They turned down a seemingly endless hall that was, thankfully, completely deserted. "The doors are at the end of the hallway. As soon as we get inside, I'll bolt them, and you find the rolling ladder. It will take us to the second floor of shelves. There's a portrait of Queen Katrin there, and the door to the secret stairs is behind it. Of course, we'll have to find the lever to open it."

"The lever?"

"Yes, a switch that will unlock the door."

"All right, what is it?"

Balan shrugged. "I have no idea. No one's used that passage in a hundred years."

"What?" Thalia shrieked. "You might have shared that little kernel of knowledge before now!"

Balan started to reply when they heard a clatter behind them.

"Oy!"

"Oh shit," Thalia whispered. They stopped dead in their tracks, not wanting to turn around. "What do we do?"

"Get to the stairs," Balan muttered. His gaze met hers, and his hand closed over the hilt of the sword she still carried. "Don't look back."

"Balan!" she cried. But it was already too late. With a bellowing howl, Balan ran at the two guards that were coming toward them, wielding the oversized sword. He swung it at the guards clumsily, the blade making a resonating clang as it bounced off their armor. It shocked her into action, and she ran off down the hall, trying not to hear her friend's cries of pain.

Chapter Twenty-Six

Grafton ran through the corridors in a blind panic as the dragon flew over the city. His stubby legs carried him clumsily up the stairs that led to the Great Hall. He'd been all over the castle searching for Tristan and come up short. Chaos was taking over in Thane, and the guards were overwhelmed. Grafton had tried to warn as many people as possible to get away, but it was as if no one could make a move without Tristan's direction. And the king was noticeably absent. The sound of the bolt tower collapsing as it burst into flames had drawn Grafton into action. He realized that the fortress was ridiculously unprepared for a dragon attack. Everyone knew that dragons would defend their treasure viciously and violently, and this girl Thalia was obviously the dragon's treasure. For the first time, Grafton was beginning to regret his alliance with Tristan. The boy was reckless, and though Grafton hadn't particularly liked Christophe, he hadn't wished him any ill will. Servants were already murmuring rumors that Tristan had killed his own father and was pinning it on this innocent girl.

"Grafton!" He stopped short, nearly bowling over a serving girl who was rounding the corner to run, screaming down the stairs. He turned to see Tristan and three guards coming toward him. The king was dressed for battle, having already donned his father's armor. He looked more serene than Grafton had seen him in ages. As if he were feeding on the chaos like a vampire sucking virgin blood. "Why are you running about?"

Grafton panted, bowing to the king as he tried catching his breath. "Sire... I've been looking all over for you."

"Obviously not. Otherwise you'd have found me in my chambers."

"Sire, the dragon has come to Thane! He's burned a perimeter around the castle grounds, and the men are overrun!"

"You say this like I'm blind and stupid, Grafton. That was the plan all along..."

"But sire, the people are running amok! Including our own knights!" Tristan looked stricken. Clearly he hadn't expected his own army to run and hide like frightened rabbits. "The dragon has destroyed the bolt tower already! And it appears that some kind of skirmish has broken out between the castle guard and some of the militiamen."

Before Tristan could respond, a servant intercepted them. She bowed low, her head kerchief falling at the king's feet. It was obvious she'd been running. Sweat poured from her brow and collected between her meaty breasts. "Sire... the girl. The one who killed King Christophe..."

Tristan looked down on the woman, a look of contempt and disgust on his face. "What of her?"

"She's gone! Escaped!"

He grabbed the woman roughly by the arms as if he might shake the information from her. "Gone where?"

"One of the guards saw her heading for the ruined battlements!"

Tristan threw the woman aside. If that little wench escaped, then all his leverage would be gone. "Find the captain! Send whatever guards we have left to find her! She mustn't escape!"

"But sire," Grafton sniveled, practically running to keep up with him. "We don't have the resources! In case you haven't noticed, there's a dragon out there!" As if to emphasize his words, a roar shook the castle. Grafton ran to the window and stared out at the burnished landscape. His eyes widened as the dragon blocked out the horizon, coming in close. He was playing with them. Challenging them. "By the gods..."

"Relax, Grafton. We don't have to. Those men down there are just a diversion. No one is to touch the dragon. He's mine."

"But sire...women and children... We need to get them to safety!"

"He's mine!"

Belladonna should have warned him that with his true form came emotions like fear, foreboding, and caution. Malik soared along the ridge line, watching the citizens of Thane scatter like roaches in the light beneath him. As he spit impotent fire into the sky, he could feel the fire burning in his chest and throat. He didn't remember it being quite so unpleasant before. Not to mention that his normal aerial acrobatics made his heart rush in a way it hadn't before. The fear of dying was there now. Not his own death, but Thalia's. He had to put her face out of his mind as he swooped low, burning a path through the trees along the avenue.

If Tristan wanted to lure him in, then Malik would not disappoint. A scaffold had been constructed in the center of the courtyard and already a large catapult was being heaved up the side of it. He almost laughed. They meant to shoot him down with arrows of iron. He'd seen such clumsy instruments before, and he could easily outrun them. No, he fully intended to meet Tristan face to face as a man. His dragon form was only a distraction to that end. As soon as Silas and his men from the forest were in place, he would walk right through the castle gates. Once more he dove, swiping at the guards who carried the catapult up the scaffold. His talons grazed the makeshift tower, shattering the planks in a shower of splintered wood. With another spout of fire, the scaffold was devoured in a column of flame.

Flying low, he took pleasure in watching the guards duck and run from him. Cowards! All but one. He was tall and lean with greasy hair and a rusted crossbow. His uniform was like the others, but instead of the royal purple of the knights, a heavy chain mail covered him, and Malik's superior vision could just make out the royal crest etched into his chest plate. This man was of importance. The captain of the royal guard. The man raised his weapon and took aim, but Malik was too quick. He swooped in and grabbed the guard in his talons. As soon as they touched, he saw Thalia screaming. This man had been the one who took her, beating her and throwing her into a prison of stone and mortar.

Malik shot into the sky, spiraling toward the clouds. The guard squirmed and tried to stab at the dragon's flesh, but Malik's scales were far too thick for such a thing. "Foul beastie!" he shouted. The harder the man fought, the tighter Malik's grip. Faster and faster Malik streaked into the sky, through the clouds and toward the moon itself.

"Do you want to fly, sir?" Malik growled.

"Let me go!" the captain shouted back.

"A very poor choice of words."

As the captain of the guard plummeted toward the earth, Malik followed in a graceful dive. Just before they hit the ground, Malik pulled up fast and jerked the captain from the clutches of his demise. He threw the man aside like a discarded child's toy as he landed in the center of the courtyard. With a roar of flame, Malik's body twisted and shrank. His scales split along his back, rearranging themselves back to the form fitting armor as his human form pushed through. In a matter of seconds, he stood before the remaining guardsmen between him and the gates. All of them, including the dazed captain, stared at the Dragon Lord awestruck. Malik stepped on the hilt of the captain's discarded sword, flipping it into his hand with a grace that could only be accomplished by the Fae. The knights gripped their weapons but made no move to engage. Malik was amused as they looked from one to the other, wondering if they should attack. Only one of them was brave enough to step forward, sword raised.

"Throw down your weapon in the name of the king!"

"Careful, boy." The old captain, Silas, stepped to Malik's side. "You don't want to be biting off more than you can chew."

The knight smirked. "Well, there seem to be more of us than of you," he said, gesturing to the other knights that were walking toward them, looking apprehensive. Out of the corner of his eye, Malik saw the other woodsmen close rank behind the knights. "Throw down now, and we won't have to run you through."

Malik chuckled low. "That would be tremendously ambitious of you." He nodded to the others, and they closed in behind the guards, making quick work of disarming them.

"Silas!" Malik shouted. "Bind these men so that they might think on their allegiances."

"Aye, sire!" He began barking orders to the others. Before long, the woodsmen had bound the castle guards. When it was done, Silas looked to his king. "What now?"

"Keep them here for now. They can either choose to follow their true sovereign, or rot in the dungeons beneath the castle." Malik turned, hearing a weak and watery chortle. The captain crawled across the mucky ground toward where Malik stood. His legs were broken, and it was obvious that every breath was more painful than the last.

"Sire? He calls you sire. What use is that? The allegiance of a simple, grubby farmer only fit to patrol the roads? King Tristan will make short work of you and your ragtag gang of simpletons, and then your precious bride will burn in your own fires!"

Malik could feel the fire of his rage flaring deep in his belly. He grabbed the captain by the neck, pulling him off his feet. "I spared you once, but I'm not likely to make the same mistake again."

The captain chuckled again, trailing off into gasping coughs. "I'm already dead, beastie. My body is broken..."

"There's still time to hurt you," Malik snarled. "Tell me where she is!"

"Do you know how they execute prisoners for treason, beastie? They're impaled. A wooden pole shoved through the most intimate orifice."

"Shut up!"

The captain gurgled and laughed, dangling in Malik's grip. "It must be like getting fucked by a dragon!" Malik's strength betrayed him, and a slight squeeze crushed the man's throat, quieting his taunts.

"Tristan!" he shouted to the skies. His voice resonated off the walls of the castle, rumbling and rolling like thunder. The windows rattled in their frames, some of them shattering and raining glass down on the courtyard below. "Come forth and face me, brother!" He dragged the body of the ruined captain of the guard toward the portcullis. Once reaching it, he searched the inside of the captain's cloak and pulled out the gate key before throwing the carcass aside.

Chapter Twenty-Seven

There is an ancient legend that the castles of Osghast were constructed according to plans designed by Queen Mab herself. The bowels of the fortress were a twisted, turning labyrinth from which no prisoner would escape and no intruder could hope to penetrate. During times of war, the people could hide in the dungeons safely for weeks of siege. As Thalia tried to navigate the hidden stairs, she was becoming increasingly convinced of the legend's truth. Dank with mold and sparkling with condensation, the close walls of the corridor were like crawling through a tomb. In places, the stairs were so narrow that Thalia had to turn sideways to move. In others they would end at a long passageway that stretched into darkness.

As she stepped carefully, still wearing silk slippers, she could hear the sounds of shouting and commotion coming from the outside. She thought she was getting close, but no matter which way she turned, she couldn't seem to get to their voices. She could feel herself moving downward, farther into the bowels of the castle, but she hadn't come to any more stairs. Or even the dungeons. Once she made it to the dungeons, she could follow the sewers to the river, but so far there was no sign that she was getting close. Only nothingness. Thalia began to wonder if she would die here, wandering in circles until her skin began to slough away and her eyes were blind.

Finally, she rounded a corner and saw more stairs ahead. "Thank heavens," she sighed. She only hoped that she could reach Malik before he did something irrational. She began to run, trying to block out the throb in her head and the burning ache in her ankle. As she reached the stairs, she stumbled and fell forward, scraping her knees on the edge of the step. "Damn," she groaned, trying not to weep. She'd been strong this long and now was not the time for sobbing like a child. She brushed herself off, ignoring the blood running down her leg, and started up the stone stairs. It only took a few steps to realize that this was the same staircase she'd been on before. As she looked around, it became frighteningly obvious that she'd been walking in circles. The dam broke, and Thalia sat down on the stairs and began to weep copiously into her hands. The tears of fear and longing—everything she'd been holding inside came rushing to the surface until she was shaking with ugly, wrenching sobs. Suddenly she was certain that never again would she see Malik or Ellythin. The whole thing, every single step of it, had been for nothing. It was all some cruel joke that had been played by the Fates.

After she'd been there for some time, Thalia began to hear an odd, squeaking sound. Looking up from her hands, she noticed a small mouse sitting on the step beside her. She gasped and tried shooing it away, but the little gray creature just stared up at her, completely unafraid. "Go away!" she shrieked tearfully. Finally it skittered down the steps and stood on the floor as if waiting. "What do you want? I don't have any food. And I'm probably more lost than you!" It walked a few more steps and stopped, looking back. Feeling like the world's greatest fool, Thalia stood and began to follow it down the corridor. "I'm following a mouse. I must be out of my mind." As they emerged into the passage once more, the mouse slowed and seemed to grow. Before her eyes, the mouse shifted and changed, growing into the tall, thin form of Bella dressed in fur from head to toe.

"You're so stubborn, mistress," she remarked, brushing herself off.

"What... Bella? How did you get here?"

"I told you having a friend like me could prove useful. The Fae go where they like."

Thalia couldn't help throwing herself against the girl and embracing her tightly. "Oh, Bella! I'm so glad to see you. I'm utterly, hopelessly lost, and I have to get back to Ellythin! I have to tell Malik to stay away from here!"

"Too late."

"What?"

"Too late. He's already here, love."

Thalia gasped and shook her head. "No! No, Bella... Esa... whatever you call yourself! We have to find him and get him away! Tristan means to kill him! And I can't let him die for me!" She grabbed the girl's arm and began pulling her down the corridor.

"Silly thing," she chuckled, staying rooted to the spot and nearly pulling Thalia off her feet. "Do you really think that a weakling like Tristan could best a dragon?"

"But...Malik gave up his dragon form. How?"

Bella said no more and put her finger to Thalia's lips then turned to the wall. She cocked her head to one side as if thinking very hard about something. Thalia began to pace impatiently. She wondered what the fairy could possibly be waiting for, and then she watched as the pixie drew lines of starlight in the air, making a door appear in the wall. She turned to Thalia. "Well... come on then. I have to get you out of here."

What could she do but follow?

⚜

When Thalia emerged into the light, Bella was gone, and she found herself on the eastern battlement, headed toward the burned tower. It was still smoldering from Malik's last visit, and the bricks were crumbling, but she was certain she would find him there. "Bella!" she hissed, spinning around and looking for the girl. Damned fairies! Fickle and unpredictable little beasties. Luckily the only people around were too busy running for their lives to notice her. She scanned her surroundings looking for any sign of Tristan. For a moment, she considered that perhaps her escape had been too easy. Perhaps this was what Tristan had wanted all along.

Gathering her skirts, she began to run toward the tower. She said a silent prayer that along the way she might find another weapon. She didn't know what she would find when she got there, but one thing was certain: Tristan was a coward, and he wouldn't be facing his brother alone.

"Thalia!"

The voice grabbed Thalia by the heart, and she nearly stepped off the edge of the battlement. She whipped around to see Malik sprinting toward her. He was wearing armor fashioned from his own scales, and he moved with a newfound grace. Suddenly, every ounce of strength she had drained away, and as he reached her, she fell into his arms. "Can it be? Is it really you?" she breathed, kissing him over and over.

"Of course it's me, Mouse," he said, embracing her tightly. "You didn't think I'd leave you, did you?"

"You idiot!" she snapped, pushing against his chest with both hands. "You shouldn't risk yourself for me!"

"Don't be stupid, Thalia. Tristan would have to bring more than a couple of hundred inept castle guards and a stone fortress to keep me away from you." She laughed and embraced him once more. Their lips met in a desperate kiss that stole Thalia's breath with its ferocity. "Thank you," she repeated against his mouth, reveling in his bittersweet taste.

He pulled away from her roughly. "What about you? How did you get here? I thought Tristan had locked you away in the tower."

"What?" she whimpered.

"I was supposed to rescue you! But you've already escaped!"

"So?"

"So... you're supposed to be the damsel in distress."

"Sorry to disappoint," she chuckled.

"No, you aren't." He growled and licked her mouth. "Let's get out of here. We'll go away... far away from Osghast where no one will ever find us."

"But Bella... the curse... you're the rightful king, Malik."

Malik shook his head. "I don't care. It has nothing to do with us."

He pulled her into his arms once more and silenced her protests with another kiss. She felt it in her center, and it radiated out through the rest of her body. Suddenly she didn't care about Tristan or Osghast or any of the rest of it. All that mattered was here and now.

Then pain. Stabbing, searing pain in the center of her back. It took her breath, and she bowed backward, unable to move. "Thalia?" Malik held her as her body went limp. "Thalia, what's wrong?" Her mouth worked, but no sound would come. In her head, she was screaming, *I'm dying*, but the words died in the blood already collecting her throat. The pain dulled to a throb that burned with every heartbeat. Slowly Malik lowered her to the floor as she stared up at him. Thalia could feel herself slipping away, fleeing the agony, but she wanted to be sure that the last thing she saw in this life were his eyes of fire and ice.

◈

"Well. The prodigal son returns to Thane at last." Tristan's eyes were cold and calculating as he stared down at his brother. The blade still lodged in Thalia's back acted as a stopper, keeping the blood from pouring onto the floor, making it seep slowly from the wound. Malik was fascinated by the sticky warmth running down his wrist. Looking down, he could see her blood soaking into the sleeve of his tunic. It was a reminder of the life that was slipping away like a curling plume of incense. The king had done his job well, throwing the dagger with fatal precision. "It's a shame really, brother. She would have made an exquisite corpse hanging from my battlements." Tristan stalked to where Malik knelt over her, cradling her dying body to his chest. He brandished his sword as he paced around Malik.

"Thalia... please," he whispered, pressing his lips to her temple. "Don't leave me." He drew her into his embrace, holding her tight to him as if he might will her wounds to heal.

"Cold... Malik," she whispered. "I'm... so sorry..."

"Shush," he said, brushing her hair back from her brow. "I'm going to get you out of here, Thalia. You're going to be..." He choked on the lie, feeling the tears stinging his eyes. "You're going to be fine."

Thalia forced a breathy laugh. "Liar."

Before Malik could respond, Thalia shuddered violently. "No, Thalia... No! You stay with me!" he commanded.

Her breath came in watery, heaving gasps. "Always," she whispered. "I always loved you... Malik. And... always will." Her heart gave one last flutter before she fell against him, lifeless. Malik held her tight, sitting down hard on the stone floor. Tristan, Osghast, being king... it all seemed so far away. Nothing mattered now. He could feel his heart breaking, his true human heart. The one he had so long kept buried and still in his chest. It was too much for him to bear, and he let out a cry of agony more frightening than the roar of any dragon, rocking Thalia's body as if to send her to sleep.

Tristan struck the stone floor with his sword, throwing sparks around them. "Get up. Let us finish this. Women are like flowers. When one is used up, there are so many others in the garden."

"She was nothing to you," Malik snarled. "Just a tool and nothing more."

"On the contrary, brother. She brought us together."

His brother's words brought forth all the rage Malik had been holding inside for all his life. It exploded like Greek fire, fueled by the arrogance of Tristan's grin. The only thing he'd ever loved in this world had been destroyed. Bella had been right. One of the brothers *was* a monster. "You are not my brother!" Malik roared. He leapt to his feet, his dragon form bursting forth from his skin in a rain of fire.

Tristan gasped, watching as the dragon grew, stretching its limbs and wings. Malik shook his head, the horned protrusions breaking stone and mortar until he towered over this meager king. With a hiss, he breathed a wide spume of flame. Tristan rolled away, barely dodging the embers. Drawing his sword, he charged at the beast, but Malik waved him away with a slight flinch of his wing. The force sent Tristan sprawling across the floor, crashing into a pillar that shattered with the impact. Tristan managed to regain his footing and ran toward the dragon. Despite Malik's size, he was quick, and he turned, catching Tristan with a swipe of his tail.

"Hardly a fair fight, brother!" Tristan shouted. Malik swiped again, but this time, Tristan was faster, grabbing the tail and swinging himself onto the dragon's back. Immediately, he began raining blows across the scaled flanks as he made his way higher. Malik twisted, trying to reach him with his teeth to no avail. The blade of Tristan's sword bounced off his scales, and he cursed. Finally, he jabbed, the blade slipping between the scales to slash at his brother's skin. Malik roared again, breathing another column of fire in his frustration. Just as Tristan reached the base of his skull, Malik threw his wings back, stretching his body then contracting. The shift was fast, throwing Tristan to the side. Malik screamed as his bones and skin reconfigured, but the pain only fueled his rage. He rolled to his feet and grabbed the sword that lay discarded where Thalia had fallen.

"Clearly you have me at a disadvantage, brother."

Both men froze as the doors leading to the battlements burst open. Knights began pouring into the narrow passage, rushing to defend their king. Malik took a deep breath, praying that he would have the strength to shift again. But as he watched, he realized that the men were rallying to him, not Tristan. Knights, guards, and even towns-people created a barrier, blocking the royal guards from coming close. It was a mess of confusion with swords clanging and fists flying. Despite his best efforts, Tristan would be facing him alone.

"Perhaps your subjects aren't so loyal as you'd like," Malik said.

Tristan responded with a swing of his sword that whizzed past Malik's ear so close he could hear the blade singing. He dodged with an awkward jerk, stumbling backward. Tristan took full advantage, bearing down upon him with enraged blows. Again and again their swords clanged together. Malik could only block as Tristan slashed at him over and over. Finally, he tackled Malik to the floor, using the weight of his body and the awkward length of his sword to disarm him. "They'll bow to me when I have your head!" Tristan bellowed, nudging the tip of his blade under Malik's chin.

Malik smiled, "Good luck." He managed to get his knee under Tristan's chest and pushed him back with all his might. It was enough to fend off Tristan's blade but that was all he needed. Once more he shifted, using the force of the magic as another weapon against his brother.

"The dragon!" some of the guards behind them shouted, throwing down their weapons to run.

Tristan was thrown back against the stones, sliding across the floor and losing his sword. The dragon stalked toward him, dragging the horned tips of his wings along the floor. Slowly he slithered, head down and shoulders hunched, closing in on his prey. And Tristan understood that he was the prey this time. "Enough games, sire!" Malik spat. "If you wish to have my head, come and get it."

Tristan crawled backward, dragging himself across the stones. He eyed the discarded sword, trying to work out how he might grab it. He looked to the guards who stood there speechless. The silence was deafening as all the fighting ceased. Out of the corner of his eye, he spied Grafton, cowering behind the line of woodsmen. "Grafton! Help me!" he shouted. The old gypsy's eyes were wide and full of fear. He shook his head. "You... treasonous coward!" The guards stood silent. He shouted to the young boy, Kiernan, from the militia. "You there! Boy! My sword!"

"You are not my king," the boy choked. He held up the dagger he'd taken from Malik in the forest. "Malik, Dragon Lord of Ellythin carries this and by rights is the heir of Christophe."

"You fool! That dagger means nothing! I have the other..." Tristan whipped his head around. He was looking for Thalia's body where the twin blade still lay. But she was gone. "I am the king!"

Malik laughed and hissed black steam. "Betrayal has many faces... brother." He spat this last word with venom and malice, tasting the sweet revenge of it on his tongue. Before Tristan could reply, he charged him, grabbing his body with his razor-sharp talons and streaking into the sky. Higher and higher they climbed until Malik's form was a mere speck of cloud across the setting moon.

"Please..." Tristan begged, gulping for air. "Spare me, brother! I was only trying to save our people!"

"And so am I." And with that, Malik let him go, watching as his body plummeted toward the earth and crashed on the rocky crags below.

Chapter Twenty-Eight

Bella held Thalia's body close, shielding her from the heavy rain that had begun to fall on Thane. It was a cleansing rain that would hopefully wash any trace of Tristan and his evil away from this place. But for now, there were more important matters to attend. In all the commotion, Bella had managed to pull Thalia away from the fight and into the burned-out tower. She'd watched from above as Malik defeated Tristan and the people of Thane bowed to him. He would be king, and this world would be safe. But as she looked down at the ruined body of poor Thalia, she wondered if the price had been too high. She stroked Thalia's hair back from her brow and kissed it lightly. She'd tried to pull her back from the clutches of death, but the girl was beyond Bella's powers to heal. The Fae were only able to heal if the soul was still intact, but Thalia's spirit was already gone. Her body was a mere empty vessel. She'd saved Malik, her son, only to destroy him again. Holding the girl against her, she wept, her impotent tears silver and cold.

"Bella." She looked up to see Malik land on the edge of the tower, shifting back to his human form in an instant.

"Oh, Malik," she cried. "I am so sorry... so sorry."

He went to her and knelt at her side. The anger that he expected never came, only an emptiness that settled in his chest. He put an arm around Bella's shoulders and kissed her hair. "For what? You didn't kill Thalia."

"Yes, I did! I killed her just as much as Tristan. I should never have let her go back. I should have forced her to leave with me!"

Malik shook his head, embracing the fairy. "Everything happens for a reason."

She scoffed, laying Thalia on the ground between them. "No. What possible reason could there be for the death of this innocent?"

"Restoring honor. Faith." He tipped Belladonna's chin higher. "You saved my life in so many ways, Bella."

"But not hers!" she spat. "I couldn't save her!"

"No. But I can." This new voice broke the stillness of the room, and both turned to see Queen Mab herself standing in the moonlight, staring down at them. Her silver hair and pale skin made her appear to glow in the dimness of the secluded tower. She wandered the tower, pausing to stare down at Thalia's limp body.

Belladonna bowed low. "My queen."

"Get up, banished brat servant," Mab said, a teasing smile playing on her lips. Then she turned her eyes to Malik. "Well, it would appear you've grown, my lord."

Malik stood and started toward Mab. "Arrogant, scheming pixie!" he snarled. Bella could feel the heat radiating off him. Any second he was going to shift and burn the Faerie Queen to ash. "This is all your fault!"

"You might want to pipe down, my lord. While I admire your passion, if you smite me, then there'll be no saving your queen." She brushed her fingertips through his hair and laughed as he ducked away. "I must admit, the two of you managed to outsmart me. When I told Bella here to destroy the dragon, I meant drowning it in the river, not making it a man."

"Perhaps there are some forces over which you have no control," Malik said.

"So it would appear. But it's all been so fascinating to watch." She knelt and dipped her fingers into the puddle of blood that surrounded Thalia. She brought them to her lips and tasted. "Are you certain that you love her, Dragon Lord? She would make such a delicious servant. After all, your brother's tribute is just wandering around Faerie like little destructors. But you know what they say, children need a mother. And you could keep clumsy Bella here with you."

"Of course I love her!" Malik roared. "Since the first time I laid eyes on her."

Mab giggled. "Oh, how very dramatic. But I suppose you've played your part well." She turned to Bella and smiled, beckoning her forward. "Come closer, Bella. Embrace me as you once did."

Belladonna cast a sideways glance at Malik. His fists were tense at his side, and he looked ready to defend her. "My queen," she whispered, allowing Mab to embrace her lovingly.

"You've done very well. So well that I'm obliged to allow you back to Faerie."

"Oh, thank you, my lady!" Bella cried, kissing Mab's hands and kneeling at her feet.

"But first things first," she said. "We must bring Malik's prize back from The Veil. If she wanders too far, she'll be trapped there forever."

⚜

*L*ost *in shadow, Thalia wandered. Where she was, she couldn't say, and she could feel the awareness of herself slipping through her fingers. The place seemed familiar. She could feel that she had been here so many times before, yet she could not even see the ground beneath her feet. Only sensation was there to guide her: the dewy grass between her toes, the cool breeze on her face and then her body. She was weightless and floated high above the world. Like she was pure energy oozing through this forest of night like will o' wisp.*

Up ahead she could see something glimmering in the moonlight. As she drew closer, the light grew until she was staring across a vast lake, its surface like unspoiled glass.

"Thalia!"

She looked up, hearing her name carried on the wind. The voice was so far away. Was it even still her name? She turned as it whispered again, this time pushing through her chest like an arrow. It took her breath, and she fell to her knees. "Who's there?" she called. "Is it you, prince?"

Prince. She remembered dreaming of him. The dark prince with the fiery eyes and cheeks of ash and roses. He whispered against her ear. A strange tongue that she couldn't understand, but it comforted her.

"You must come to me, Thalia."

She turned away from the lake, toward the dark trees at her side. The lake frightened her, and her mind screamed to run away. She could sense a strange magic rippling over the water, calling. "I'm afraid," she whispered.

"Do not fear." When she opened her eyes, she saw him, his body a phantom that merged with the mist on the water. "Come. Come back to yourself. Your soul has wandered too far this time, little one." And then he was near, reaching out. "Take my hand. Trust me."

҂

Thalia screamed awake, sitting up and gasping for air. The pain in her chest and back was excruciating, doubling her over. She couldn't see. It was all too bright. "Just a little more, child." Esa. The voice of her old guardian spoke to her, soothing her panic. As her eyes cleared, she could just make out her shape in the shadows. The woman was made of light as she knelt behind her. "Hold her, Malik! Don't let go." Once more that suckling agony deep in her chest and then a white-hot burning. She struggled, screaming again and begging to run. To die. But he held her. The dark prince. She could smell him, feel him. It was the only thing holding her to this world as the poisonous death borne of Tristan's dagger was drawn from her body.

Then it was over.

Thalia lay there for what seemed like ages, cradled in the arms of her lover. Malik. The Dragon Lord. Dragon king. Yes, she remembered him now. The dark prince of her dreams. "Malik," she whispered, finding the strength to raise her head. "Is it really you?"

He nodded, his eyes glistening with the tears he kept at bay. "Of course it's me, silly mouse. You didn't think I was going to go through all this only to lose you to The Veil?" He pushed her hair back from her brow, kissing her forehead and cheeks over and over until both were laughing.

Chapter Twenty-Nine

The day of the coronation of King Malik of Osghast was perhaps the most beautiful day that anyone could remember. The skies were a clear blue without a single cloud to obscure the golden light of the sun smiling down. The air was warm with a slight breeze to barely rustle the colors and bunting over the heads of the onlookers gathered in the courtyards at Ellythin. It seemed that Mother Nature herself was laying down her blessing on the kingdom of Osghast. The trees that lined the avenue all the way to Thane had burst into full bloom, seemingly overnight. The hills and mountains surrounding were almost unusually green. The birds, once frightened and kept away by the Wyrm of Gwynfir, had finally returned and gifted the world with their song once more. It was an absolutely perfect morning. The only possible rival to such a day would have been the one before when Malik and his queen, Thalia Baignard of Tarkin, had been joined in matrimony.

The ministers of every town in Osghast were in attendance as a symbol of their allegiance to the new king. Even Grafton and his minions from Isling had come. Royal courts from every realm on the continent were there as an offering of peace between the nations. And of course the Fae Queen herself, her servant Belladonna, and all of her consorts were there to pass their blessing and heal ancient wounds. It was to be the dawn of a new age of prosperity and rebirth.

Belladonna stood with the fairy court to one side and Balan at her other, wringing his hands. "But my lady, they should have been here by now! Should we not go up and find them?"

"I'll wager the honeymooning is still underway," Silas, the new captain of the royal guard, chuckled, pointing toward the tower over-head. "Perhaps the coronation ceremony should have come first."

"Well, this is completely unacceptable," Balan fretted. "Someone will have to educate the king in the ways of royal etiquette."

Bella shook her head, a thin-lipped smile betraying her annoyance. "I can assure you, sir. Malik will arrive in his own time. No one's going to take the crown away before he gets here."

"As the head of the royal household, I am charged..."

"Hush, Balan! Before I scar your other cheek!" she snapped. "You worry entirely too much."

❦

Thalia stood naked, save for a thin chemise, and stared down at the courtyard from the royal bedchamber. "I think the entire continent is down there," she said, peering through the curtain.

"Careful, Mouse. Someone might see you."

"And what if they do?" Thalia replied haughtily. "They should count themselves blessed to look upon the unblemished and very satisfied flesh of their queen."

Malik sidled up behind her, wrapping his arms around her waist and drawing her into his chest. "But then I'd have to pull their eyes out, one by one," he growled, pulling the cuff of her ear between his teeth and nibbling.

She giggled. "You mustn't be so violent, my lord. In an hour's time, you shall be King Malik, the mild and just sovereign of Osghast. Not the fearsome Wyrm of Gwynfir."

His hands slid over her belly, feeling its gentle curve before straying to her bosom. "I don't think I'll ever be mild, Thalia." She turned to face him, arching her neck until his mouth was against hers. His tongue swept along the seam between her lips until she granted him entrance. He pulled her tightly against him, deepening their kiss with obvious intent.

"And I'd never want you to be," she said, breaking their kiss. "Come on, then. Balan looks as if he's about to burst something." She pointed toward the tall man that paced back and forth shaking his head.

"He always looks like that," Malik grumbled, crossing to the wardrobe.

Thalia sat down at the vanity, brushing her hair until it shone like summer cornsilk. She watched as Malik pulled his boots on, fascinated by the way his muscles moved beneath the skin. Such magic his body could perform. Just the thought of it made her head light and her mouth water. She looked away quickly, remembering that everyone waited for them.

"Malik?"

"Hmm?" he hummed, pulling a tunic over his head.

"It's been three months... since the battle. And you haven't changed."

"No. I haven't," he replied.

Her eyes lit on the large trunk under the wardrobe. He'd put away his dragon armor and locked it away tight. "Do you think... I mean... can you?"

"Mab says that if ever the peace in Osghast is threatened, that I will feel the burning under my skin, and I'll become the Dragon Lord once more." He said this all with a dramatic lilt to his voice that made Thalia giggle. "But I wouldn't hold out much hope."

"Oh."

"Why? Do you miss him?"

"Well... I don't know if *miss* is the right word," she stammered, rising from her stool and going to him. "Perhaps I enjoy his... aggressive nature."

Malik growled and wrapped his arms around her waist, boldly squeezing her buttocks as he pressed her body to his. "Perhaps he's still there, lurking beneath the skin. Just waiting for the perfect opportunity to devour you completely."

She stretched up into his kiss, tasting the ash and spice on his lips. "I hope so, my lord. I certainly hope so."

THE END

About the Author

Alexandra Christian is an author of mostly romance with a speculative slant. Her love of Stephen King and sweet tea has flavored her fiction with a Southern Gothic sensibility that reeks of Spanish moss and deep-fried eccentricity. Her guiding principle as a romance novelist has always been to write romantic adventures for people who think they hate romances. After all, love itself is life's greatest adventure.

A self-proclaimed "Southern Belle from Hell," Lexx is a native South Carolinian who lives with an epileptic wiener dog and her husband, author Tally Johnson. Her long-term aspirations are to one day be a best-selling authoress and part-time pinup girl. She's also a member of Romance Writers of America. Questions, comments and complaints are most welcome at her website:

http://lexxxchristian.wixsite.com/alexandrachristian

Also by Alexandra Christian

Naked (Phoenix Rising 1)

Neo-Geisha (Phoenix Rising 2)

The Ghost & Dr. Watson (A Shadow Council Archives Novella)

Chasing the Dragon

Falstaff Books

**Want to know what's new
And coming soon from
Falstaff Books?**

Try This Free Ebook Sampler

https://www.instafreebie.com/free/bsZnl

**Follow the link.
Download the file.
Transfer to your e-reader, phone, tablet, watch, computer,
whatever.
Enjoy.**

www.ingramcontent.com/pod-product-compliance
Lightning Source LLC
Chambersburg PA
CBHW060546190726
48283CB00003B/890